PURPLE LOTUS

PURPLE LOTUS

A Novel

VEENA RAO

SHE WRITES PRESS

Published 2020
Printed in the United States of America
Print ISBN: 978-1-63152-761-6
E-ISBN: 978-1-63152-762-3
Library of Congress Control Number: 2020906103

Interior design by Tabitha Lahr

For information, address:
She Writes Press
1569 Solano Ave #546
Berkeley, CA 94707

She Writes Press is a division of SparkPoint Studio, LLC.

In memory of my father
and
For my family, both Indian and American

"*Nothing that grieves us can be called little:
by the eternal laws of proportion, a child's loss of a doll
and a king's loss of a crown are events of the same size.*"
—MARK TWAIN, *Which Was the Dream?*

Chapter 1

The sleeper class compartment was dirty. The noisy family of four that had occupied the berths opposite had alighted sometime in the middle of the night. But they had left their presence behind, in the peanut shells and crumpled newspaper strewn over the floor. The alley was wet with rainwater. Each time the train slowed down or pulled into a station, the stink of urine emanated from the toilets three compartments down the corridor, overpowering Tara's senses.

The West Coast Express spewed black columns of smoke that trailed over the coaches. The soot had settled over Tara, darkening her face, lodging under her fingernails. The wind mangled her short hair as she peered into a vast canvas from the window-side seat. Her happy thoughts splashed everything she saw in bright watercolors. The rain gods had worked furiously all night. The rice fields were waterlogged along the way, shimmering emeralds. There were dark clouds too, smudges of dense black ink that threatened to let their wrath loose again, but she only saw how an orange sun reached out, dousing everything he embraced in his glow.

Beside Tara sat Amma, her beautiful face still clean, hair coiled into a neat bun—like Belle in *Beauty and the Beast*. But her eyes, like the ink clouds on the horizon, were mist laden. Her blue-and-yellow sari with the geometric patterns fluttered every once in a while, revealing her taut, bloated belly. Amma's belly reminded Tara of a birthday balloon every time she looked in her direction, but she didn't smile, because Amma looked sad.

Every now and then, when her happy thoughts permitted her, Tara wondered about it: Why was Amma sad? A few times, Tara put her dirty little hand on Amma's swollen, hard belly and gently stroked it. Amma said little; she only looked at Tara with those large, melancholic Belle eyes that threatened to brim over. But Tara's thoughts were whimsical; they strayed and inevitably wandered back to Pinky, her new doll, and a gush of joy erupted in her chest.

Daddy was still asleep on the top berth, as if he were the one under the sleeping spell. He had slept almost all the way—during the first leg of their train journey from their town by the Great River off National Highway 5 to Madras Central—and now, from Madras to Mangalore. He had come down once last night, though, to order railway meals for the three of them, his usually slickly brushed, lush hair unruly, and his handsome face a bit frog-like from all that sleeping. He had ordered two plates, and the three of them had eaten in bland silence, amid the cacophony of their travel companions across the berth.

Amma and Tara had shared a plate. Tara had hard, flaky *puris* dipped in *sambhar*. Amma had the rice with the rest of the sambhar, yogurt, and lime pickle. The mother from the opposite berth had offered Tara a ripe, black-spotted plantain after their meal. Aunty from the opposite berth looked kindly, but Tara had declined, with an uncertain shake of her head, because she had received no cues whatsoever from Amma—no nod or subtle nudge on her elbow to indicate that she should accept the plantain. Amma was busy staring at the palms of her interlocked hands that guarded her belly, as if there were so much to decipher in them.

And Daddy had already reclaimed his spot on the top berth. Soon, his snores had wafted down, rhythmic over other human sounds and the steady clanging of the moving train.

Tara had slept well and dreamed long dreams of lovely Pinky. She remembered only snatches of her dream, but every shard of what came back to her was imprinted with pink skin, luminous golden hair, and violet-blue eyes that closed and opened and closed and opened.

Pinky was like a real person, not a doll. She even wore a real blue-and-white-striped frock, and her soft feet were encased in white rubber shoes. If only Amma had thought of giving her the doll before her best friends Pippi, Leenika, and Runa had left for the summer. What a smashing hit Pinky would have been! She could imagine the wonders that came with owning the prettiest doll in their neighborhood, the clamor of her friends to play with Pinky at her house. She had never had that standing before.

The day Amma gifted Pinky to her, Tara had spent all afternoon in the square shoe room next to the verandah, the only calm spot in a chaotic house. Seated among empty shoe racks, she had brushed Pinky's golden hair, fed her make-believe tea and biscuits, run her forefinger over her long curled up lashes, stood her up and laid her down again and again to make her open and shut her beautiful eyes.

The packers had come in. Twelve sturdy wooden boxes were being filled with household items. Daddy and Amma were busy packing the two metal trunks, a green canvas holdall, and the large, brown, leather-trimmed suitcase they would be traveling with. Tempers were frayed, and Tara knew better than to be in her parents' way. In the evening, Daddy had peeped into the shoe room, a frown on his sweaty brow.

"You can play with it at your grandparents' house in Mangalore," he had pointed toward Pinky. "It needs to go into the trunk now."

She knew better than to displease Daddy when he was tired and irritable. She had handed Pinky over to him, and then followed him to the bedroom and watched as he laid her down in one of the two identical trunks, over Amma's peacock-blue-green-yellow sari, the one with the whirlwind-like swirls.

One afternoon in a shoe room; brief enough to seem like a dream. Almost. But Pinky was real, even if she was not of flesh and blood. She felt more real than their long train journey.

Tara turned toward Amma, tapping her arm. "Amma, how much longer?"

"Soon." Amma had turned monosyllabic as soon as they had left home.

"Soon," repeated Tara, then in a whisper, "Don't worry, we'll get you out of the trunk soon, okay?"

Pinky didn't get out of the trunk soon. The day they arrived at Shanti Nilaya, Amma only opened their brown, leather-trimmed suitcase to draw out essentials—home clothes and toiletries. The next morning, Amma had just unlocked the trunks when Grandfather Madhava, Daddy's father, called out, rather loudly, his older son's name. The urgency in his gravelly voice made Amma stop her job at hand and follow Daddy downstairs to the verandah. Tara had no choice but to do as Amma did. The prime minister had declared internal emergency in the country, Grandfather Madhava said. The Philips radio that sat on the blue-linen-clad round table in the verandah was crackling, and over the shortwaves, a child-like voice filled the room. It drew Grandmother Indira and Daddy's younger brother Uncle Anand out to the verandah as well. They huddled around the radio as the prime minister used big words in her speech—*widespread conspiracy, inciting our armed forces to mutiny, country's stability to be*

imperiled, deliberate political attempts to denigrate, and she used the word *democracy* many times, even though, Daddy said, Madam Prime Minister had just suspended the democratic rights of six hundred million people when the country was under no threat of war.

When the speech ended, the prime minister's subjects, those circled around the Philips radio, found themselves in uncharted territory.

"Emergency may not be such a bad thing. We need discipline to progress," Grandfather Madhava said in his gruff voice.

"Such a bold woman," whispered Grandmother Indira, of her namesake.

Uncle Anand only shook his head, the slightest hint of a smile on his face, as if he had secret insight into the matter.

Amma, seated at a distance on a wicker chair, muttered to herself with a big heave of her chest, *Emergency in the country and emergency in my life!*

Tara knew what the emergency in Amma's life was. It was the poop that was accumulating in her balloon belly. Also, perhaps this gloomy antiquated house was growing more real to Amma, as it was to Tara.

From down the dirt road leading up to Morgan Hill, Shanti Nilaya had looked like an imposing castle—the kind that fairytale princes and princesses lived in. But now it was just a large old home with a moss-ridden compound wall and narrow blue front gates. Its ample front yard was thick with coconut palms, mangos, and jackfruit trees that formed a thick canopy and kept the sun out. The semicircular verandah was large, but the many inner rooms were small and dark. The kitchen was dungeon-like, and the flames from the wood stoves danced and leaped like dragon's tongues. At night, the incandescent bulbs threw strange shadows upon the walls, and biscuit-colored lizards with bulbous eyes lurked on the wooden beams of the ceiling.

All of yesterday, Tara had latched on to Amma, clutching a fistful of her sari like a handkerchief. At night, the family had slept in an ornate teak bed in Daddy's childhood room upstairs, and the wooden floorboards had creaked like in a haunted mansion when Tara stepped on them.

Daddy said he had happy memories of his room, which smelled of dusty old books, because bookshelves filled with hardcovers and paperbacks lined almost the entire far-end wall. But Tara couldn't help but focus on the rickety fan that rotated slowly, as if burdened with age and secrets, and wonder if it would come unhinged and crash over them. Back at home, they had large air-conditioned bedrooms. Their living room was flush with sunlight and furnished with beautiful colonial-style furniture, and their garden was a profusion of colors. If only she had Pinky in her arms, she could make her new surroundings fade away from her mind.

After the unnecessary, endless flutter created by the voice on the radio had died down, Amma finally swayed up the stairs, her breath a series of whistles, to unpack the trunks. In their room, Tara hopped from foot to foot and clasped and unclasped her hands.

"Amma, Pinky!" she cried every now and then, lest her mother forget the most important thing in the trunks.

"Stop whining. You are not three years old, Tara."

"I'm only six."

"I am trying to find her, no?"

Soon, both the trunks and the suitcase were empty, Amma's peacock-blue-green-yellow sari—the one with the whirls—was in the pile on the bed, and Pinky still had not been found.

Amma's eyebrows furrowed. She turned to Daddy, who was lolling in bed with the Hindu newspaper.

"I don't understand it. Are you sure you put the doll in one of the trunks?"

"Positive," Daddy replied.

"Strange. I don't understand it," Amma repeated, pulling Tara to her bosom. She sounded too anxious to be reassuring. Daddy must have made a mistake, she said. Instead of packing the doll in the suitcase, he had dropped her in one of the boxes that were being shipped into Mangalore. The boxes would arrive by ship next month. "That's not very long, is it? That's less than thirty days."

What? How was it possible? How?

For a moment Tara was bewildered. Then she was shaking like a boat in a sea storm. When her wails, loud and piercing, drew Grandmother Indira and Uncle Anand into the room, Tara buried her face deep in Amma's sari and continued her howling.

"What happened?" asked Grandmother. "Did she hurt herself?"

"I cannot find her doll," said Amma, stroking Tara's hair.

"Make her stop crying," Daddy said to Amma. "You'd think she hurt herself or something."

"She hardly got to play with the doll, poor thing." Amma turned to Tara. "Shhh, now. Good girls don't cry."

Tara stopped sobbing and cleaned her running nose on Amma's sari. She didn't feel like a good girl, but she was afraid of upsetting Daddy.

Uncle Anand stooped down and wiped the tears from Tara's cheeks with the pad of his fingers. "It's only a doll. Come, let's go to the barn. I'll show you a real baby. Amba delivered her new calf only last week."

Uncle Anand was tall and lean like Daddy, but his face was younger and kinder. Also, his voice wasn't commanding like Daddy's voice usually became when she cried. Tara let go of Amma's sari and allowed Uncle Anand to lead her to the barn.

They watched from the barn door—and it was fascinating—Amba fawning over her newborn, Appi, and Appi, her soft black coat twitching, trying over and over again to stand, as if her legs were on slippery ground.

That night, Tara dreamed that she had morphed into a calf. She struggled to stand, bounced about in the barn, then dropped on her fours, palm-hooves deep in dung, searching, desperately searching for Pinky.

Chapter 2

The calf emerged before her eyes now, a quarter century later, as she gripped the handrail and steadied her feet on the escalator. It was easy to feel lost in this enormous gleaming airport, even for an adult. The sudden burst of people who emerged into view at the top of the escalator crowded her mind. She blinked a couple of times. She had finally made it to the arrivals lounge after walking through a labyrinth and riding a train. She scanned the crowd—past people holding placards and others waiting for their loved ones—for the brown face among the different shades of humanity.

She was relieved when she spotted him finally, but her chest heaved involuntarily at the sighting. He stood—as broad shouldered as she remembered him—one hand in his pocket, a flip-top cell phone in his other, looking dapper without trying. He wore faded jeans, a blue-and-white-plaid cotton shirt that was open down to the second button, and a faraway expression on his face.

Tara knew him as an enigma, the stranger she had married three years ago. She felt lightheaded with apprehension as she waved to catch his attention, to see a glimmer of recognition in his lost eyes. He pursed his lips into a straight thin line when his eyes fell on her. She tried to read his smile—if it was a smile at

all, because it fell short of reaching his eyes—but a fresh bout of
nervousness impeded her deduction abilities. He motioned her to
walk toward baggage claim, then caught up with her in a few giant
strides. She was tall, but he was many inches taller.

She wondered if she should give him a hug. She didn't.

"Hi," he said. "You had a good flight?"

"Hi, Sanjay," she said self-consciously. "Yes, it was comfortable."

"Was it smooth sailing at immigration?"

"Yes. They even welcomed me to America."

"Good."

"This is a huge airport."

"Hartsfield–Jackson airport is the busiest in the world," he
said. "I hope you took the train?"

She nodded. "I followed the others." She left out the silly
details, like feeling weak-kneed as she stepped out of the aircraft
into the looming unknown, or her anxiety at the immigration
line, or her fear of not being able to get into the right train to get
to baggage claim.

His American twang seemed even more pronounced now,
after three years. It made her acutely aware of her own convent
school English accent. He said her baggage would arrive at Aisle
5, so they walked up to it and waited. The bags were slowly being
loaded on to the conveyor belt; the early ones traveled in an elon-
gated circle, waiting to be picked up. She wondered who the bags
belonged to. Were they people like her, on the cusp of a new life?
Not one person seemed nervous—tired and sullen maybe, but
not nervous. They looked like they were eager to get home—to
love and warmth, to comfort and cheer. She didn't know what
awaited her.

He said little; his eyes were fixed on the conveyor belt. She
filled the silence with senseless non-thoughts that weighed her
heart down. She wished her bags would arrive quickly. It seemed
like an eternity since she had left home. She was hungry and

tired. She looked around again. Her mind swam as it absorbed the picture—the deeper picture. It cast her under the spotlight because she looked so different from everybody around her; so different even from the man next to her. A deep yearning arose in her chest for the comfort of the familiar.

She had waited three years to get here. Now, she was being ridiculous. That is what Daddy would say; perhaps Amma would concur. *Stop being ridiculous*, she said to her mind, to her heart, to the tight knot in her belly. *Tara, you are finally where you belong.*

Marriages are made in heaven, but theirs had been made through a matchmaker. Their families were both from Mangalore but weren't known to each other, although a distant common family connection had been discovered during the bride-viewing three years ago.

Sanjay's family's visit had been brief, the party small. Only his father and mother had accompanied him and the matchmaker to Tara's home. Amma had insisted on an Indian-English high tea—triangle-shaped mint chutney sandwiches, vegetable cutlets, and her homemade fruit cake with tea, all set out in their fine old china—because she didn't want to appear clueless about Western ways before the groom. Small talk was made. Daddy had been extra courteous. Amma had talked too much, as usual. Then Tara's parents had suggested that she and Sanjay take a stroll outside to learn more about each other.

It was a humid summer evening. She had felt overdressed and sweaty in her yellow chiffon *salwar* suit, her short curls tamed with hairspray, as they walked down a by-lane in the quiet but ostentatious Mangalore neighborhood. He had been a dashing figure in his pressed black dress pants and starched white shirt, hands in his pockets.

The stroll was a short one. He had been polite but brooding. She had been anxious to get back home, to not be overwhelmed by the onus placed on her to be liked by this suitor. Her throat was parched, her tongue dry. But she had liked the aquatic notes of his cologne, the way he rolled his R's, the Americanness that exuded from him.

"So, you are a journalist at the *Morning Herald*." His first question had sounded like a statement.

"I am a backroom journalist, not a reporter," she had replied. "I mostly edit news reports and give headlines."

She had not cared to mention that she sometimes wrote features for the magazine section of the newspaper. That a feature she had cowritten with a senior colleague, a deathbed interview with a victim of domestic violence, had won several national media awards. He had asked her no further questions about her job.

"What are your other interests?"

"I like to read," she had said.

"Do you watch movies?"

"Oh, yes, I like movies, too. I watch them all, Hollywood and Bollywood."

He said he hated soppy Bollywood trash, but watched Hollywood movies that had good reviews. His great love was for American football and, as an Atlantan, he felt compelled to root for the Atlanta Falcons, although he was a New England Patriots fan.

She didn't tell him she had never heard of the Atlanta Falcons or the New England Patriots. "What about cricket?" she had asked.

"What's to watch? The matches are fixed. I'd watch if I were in the betting game," he had said with a dry laugh.

She had forced a smile to her lips. His Americanness had become a bit too much for her. Did they have nothing at all in common?

When they returned, she had slipped into the kitchen and whispered her doubts into Amma's ear.

"It takes years to know a person, build common interests," Amma had whispered back in a dismissive tone. "Besides, there will be plenty to talk about once the children come along. Don't you worry about that."

She understood Amma's desperation. Tara was desperate too, because at twenty-eight, everybody else in her age group was married. It embarrassed her, the questions from the community that seemed like thinly veiled barbs directed at her and her parents. They made her feel like a defective piece of merchandise.

Sanjay's proposal had come as a relief. When his dad turned in a positive verdict the day after the bride-seeing high tea, her doubts had seemed suddenly flimsy, even to herself. She had looked at Amma and Daddy's shining, happy faces, and felt only relief that they had finally been relieved of their burden, and she, of hers.

And three years later, here she was, at Aisle 5 of Hartsfield–Jackson International Airport's baggage claim lounge, finally spotting her two suitcases. He helped her yank them off the conveyor belt. She wished Daddy hadn't insisted on binding them with fluorescent green plastic rope. The straps looked so absurd here. She glanced at Sanjay, almost expecting to see scorn between his dark brows, but his face was a wall.

He loaded her bags into his silver BMW sedan.

"Nice car," she said, once they were in it.

"I've always wanted a Beemer. Finally bought this baby last year."

She got a whiff of his cologne, of his masculinity over the smell of new leather, and the newness of it all hit her senses with acuity.

"You've got to wear your seat belt. It's the state law," he reminded her. She struggled to get it on and felt stupid when he showed her how it was done. Daddy had a showroom full of cars.

They had two at home. Why had she not practiced buckling up when it was still a trifling thing to learn?

He pulled the BMW out expertly into the night. The interstate was a revelation to Tara. Not one honk. The cars moved quietly, smoothly, within their lanes, at speeds that seemed inconceivable in Mangalore. Such discipline! Soon, the BMW was passing through downtown Atlanta. He pointed to the Georgia State Capitol, CNN Center, the Bank of America Plaza, and some other tall, impressive buildings the names of which did not register in her mind.

Soon, downtown Atlanta was past them, and the buildings and shimmering lights made way for smaller, less impressive buildings that lay in semi-darkness.

"I'm sure you are hungry," he said, as he pulled into an exit. "There's a Chinese and a Mexican restaurant close to my apartment. Or are you craving Indian?"

He had said "my apartment." And yes, she craved rice, dal, and fried mackerel.

"Chinese or Mexican is fine," she said.

But he didn't take her to the Chinese or Mexican restaurant. They pulled into the driveway of a Wendy's. He ordered a chicken sandwich for her and a cheeseburger for himself.

"This is faster," he explained. She nodded.

The apartment was on the second floor of a three-storied structure in a sprawling community of silhouetted sloping roofs. He had furnished it well. The living room was populated with deep leather—a three-seater sofa, a loveseat, and a reclining chair. A large TV console occupied one corner. A couple of tall floor lamps lit the room. An array of magazines lay, neatly arranged, on the glass coffee table. Glass balcony doors covered one section of the

wall, partially hidden behind venetian blinds. The carpet felt soft
to her bare feet.

The far end of the living room contained a small dining table
of dark wood and four chairs. Tara peeped into the open semicircular kitchen. The four-burner stove was clean. The counters
sparkled. A white fridge stood in one corner. The kitchen was
lined with white cabinets.

The living room led to a short hallway that lay in darkness,
beyond which were the two bedrooms. Tara walked back to the
living room and flopped on the sofa. She had stressed about traveling alone for so long, and she was glad the journey was over.
And yet . . . She took her light jacket off and dropped it on the
sofa beside her. It felt good to get all that weight off her.

"There's a coat closet to hang coats. Do you mind hanging
your jacket?" He pointed toward a white door near the entrance
to the apartment.

"Yes, of course." She pulled herself up, feeling her cheeks burn.

The closet was neatly lined with his coats. It smelled mildly of
leather, of the unfamiliar. She found a spare hanger for her jacket.

They ate in the living room, the rustle of the wrappers filling
the silence. He had occupied the loveseat adjacent to her. Tara
cast sideward glances at him, thinking of something to say. Such
distant eyes on such a handsome face, she thought. In the end,
she said nothing, but was careful about disposing of the wrapper
immediately, and not embarrassing herself again. After they had
eaten, he showed her the bedrooms. The master bedroom was
furnished with a queen-sized bed that was dressed in a russet-
and-sand-brown duvet and matching pillow covers. The bedside
tables, of dark wood, each supported a lamp and other assorted
items. A dresser stood at one end of the room. On the other side
was a walk-in closet, next to which was the door to a beige tiled
bathroom. She noticed that a blue, green, and white-striped plastic shower curtain covered the beige bathtub.

So this was her new home, the space she would be sharing with the man next to her. A mild shiver emanated in her chest. She had tried very hard, every single moment of the past two months, to bury the resentment she felt toward him for abandoning her, then resurrecting her on a whim, as if she were mere clay in his hands.

She walked into the guest bedroom. He said he used the room as his study. It had a desk with a computer, a swivel chair, and a large bookshelf.

"You can use the closet in the study for your stuff," he said. "That way, you can have the whole closet to yourself." He had already parked her two suitcases there.

"Oh, I have some food stuff in the luggage," she said. "I'd better take them out and leave them in the fridge. Amma sent some *laddoos* for you."

"Laddoos?" Was that irritation in his voice? "Okay, I'll have them tomorrow. Listen, why don't you relax now? Take a shower if you wish. Go to bed. I have some work to finish. I'll join you later."

Tara nodded. She made her way to the guest bedroom closet. She sat on her haunches and opened the smaller suitcase. She got her nightclothes and toiletries out. She found the laddoos, felt them through their plastic cover. She could tell that they had retained their ball shape, despite the long journey. They had fared better than her spirits. The sharp, spicy aroma of the *masala* packets that Amma insisted she take hit her nose. They made her violently homesick. She pulled them out too and held a packet to her cheek.

"I have some work to finish," he had said. Did he work this late every night? The truth was that she knew nothing more about his life in America than she did when they got married three years ago in an elaborate four-day Hindu ceremony. He was a handsome but stoic groom; she was a nervous bride bedecked in silk, gold, and flowers. After the initial bride-seeing visit, they had met only once before the wedding, at a restaurant, where the din of chatter around them and his complaints of the noise had made their silence acceptable. Her heart didn't leap and flutter like a burning candle, a feeling she knew she was capable of, not even when they consummated their relationship the night of their wedding, in Sanjay's childhood room at his parents' terraced home. She didn't see romance, even in the bed that was sprinkled with soft fragrant flower petals, like in the movies.

"It is a bit awkward being with him," Tara had confessed to Yvonne, her best friend from high school, when she and Sanjay returned to her mother's house for the night, as tradition demanded, after *Sathyanarayana Puja* the next day. "We don't seem to have anything to talk about."

Yvonne had tittered like it was a joke. Her own two-month-old marriage to her boyfriend made her a pundit on the matter.

"You did it without saying a word to each other first?"

"Does small talk count?"

"Did you bleed?"

"Yeah, it was so painful."

"At least he knows you were a virgin."

"I am not sure he cares."

"Of course he cares. You can take an Indian out of India, but you cannot take Victorian values out of an Indian."

It would get better, Yvonne promised. Once Tara got comfortable with her husband, she would get addicted to him.

Yvonne was right. Like a waxing moon, Tara had felt a new need for her new husband warming her body on the fourth night, probably because he was leaving for Atlanta the next day, and that made it a suddenly emotional experience for her. His two-month vacation had come to an end. He had to get back to work. She had felt a rush of regret at not having had enough alone time to know him better. She wished her in-laws' middle-class house was not filled to the seams with relatives, that the marriage rituals and lunch and dinner invitations hadn't consumed all four of the five days that Sanjay had left of his vacation.

He would apply for Tara's dependent visa and send for her soon, he had promised before leaving. At the departure lounge of Bajpe Airport, with her in-laws flanking her, she was given no opportunity for an intimate farewell. She had stood with clasped hands as he said his good-byes, quelling a desperate need to rest her head on his shoulder, to claim his attention only for herself. On her way back from the airport, her eyes had misted. She was missing him already.

His first call had come after Tara had returned to her parents' home so she could resume work at the *Morning Herald*. She had taken the call in the living room, a little breathless, her heart racing. Daddy left the room, but Amma hovered, making Tara self-conscious and inhibited.

The conversation had been formal, polite. He asked her how *things* were, and she asked him about the Atlanta weather, his work. When he was ready to end the call, she had stalled, looked around the room furtively and, spying Amma's back at the far end of the room, whispered a quick, "I miss you."

He hadn't heard her; she should have been louder.

"Bye now. I'll call again soon," he had said in response.

After Tara put the handset back in its cradle, she had hurled an angry verbal missile at Amma for being so clueless about privacy and personal space.

She tried again the next time he called, a week later. This time she knew he had heard her, because Amma had cleared out of the living room in a hurry, and Tara had said it boldly, clearly into the receiver. His response had been inappropriate this time, too.

"All right. I'll call next week," he had said blandly.

Tara had felt letdown but learned soon—after four weeks and four calls from Sanjay—that disappointment is an easier emotion to bear than despair. Sanjay stopped calling. Tara had tried to reach him, out of her own volition in the beginning and because of pressure from her parents later, but he didn't ever take her calls, not even accidentally.

It must have been something she said or didn't say. A very inappropriate response to something he said, perhaps? Maybe he hated how she sounded over the phone. Or hadn't he found her desirable in bed?

He has an American girlfriend, Yvonne suggested. That was the simplest explanation. Amma vehemently disagreed. Sanjay had asked his parents to find a bride for him. No one had forced him to get married.

Tara's mind was in a whirl, always in a whirl. She now had a stamp on her forehead that said *Abandoned Wife*. She imagined a dark veil over her head, woven of shame. She would spend the rest of her life in his house trying to figure out which was worse—the whispers and taunts of all around them, the exaggerated sympathy of relatives, the tears of her mother, or the silent despondency of her father.

Now she looked at her watch. She had remembered to set it to Eastern Time at the immigration line. It was past nine at night. She wondered if Amma and Daddy were up. It was after six thirty in the morning where she came from. She would have to call and tell them she had arrived.

She deposited the laddoos and masalas in the fridge and walked out into the living room. He sat on the recliner, leaning far back, his legs up. The TV was on CNN, but he wasn't watching, and certainly not working. His eyes were closed. The back of his right hand rested on his forehead, fingers curled in.

She wasn't sure whether he was asleep and if she should wake him up.

"Sanjay?" she said softly. He opened his eyes with a start. "Sorry!"

"Oh, uhm, I was relaxing a bit before getting back to work."

He squinted and looked a little sheepish, she thought, as he shifted position on the recliner.

"Can I call Amma? They . . . Amma and Daddy will worry if they don't hear from me."

Sanjay helped her dial the number to her maternal home. It was odd, thinking of home as *her maternal home*. As if she didn't belong there anymore. As if she were suspended midway between the past and her family's hopes for her future.

Chapter 3

Tara slipped under the bulky covers of the master bed and rested her head on a soft pillow. She felt better after her warm shower. She had changed into her nightclothes, floral pajamas and a pink T-shirt. It felt good to get out of her jeans and tunic and scrub herself clean. She left the lights on, not knowing when he would come in. Her heart raced in anxiety and anticipation at the thought of him joining her in bed.

She waited a long time until her eyes began to feel heavy. Somewhere in the apartment, a clock ticked, and it was mildly comforting that its mechanical *tick-tock* sounded the same in this part of the world. She could still hear the faint hum of the TV, although he had turned the volume down low. Her thoughts drifted. At the other end of this vast country was her brother, Vijay, making a mark in a new job. She wondered how far San Jose was. She wondered what Amma was fixing for breakfast. Had Daddy set out on his morning walk? They had both been relieved when she finally boarded her flight to America. She was, too. Three years was a long time to be married and not set eyes on the groom after the wedding month. Why the sudden change of heart? What had prompted the email out of the blue two months ago—a very brief and formal one asking her to scan and send the necessary documents to file for her dependent visa? She and Amma had wondered, with no answers.

"What's gone is gone. Look ahead and make it work," was Amma's advice to her.

Tara's mind flitted between sleep and wakefulness. *How does one make it work*, she wondered drowsily. *What was required of her?* At thirty-one, she was still so utterly clueless about marriage.

She opened her eyes, took a moment to clear the fog inside her head, and was wide awake. The blinds were closed but aglow with the sun outside. The room looked unfamiliar. Of course. She was almost nine thousand miles away from home.

The spot next to her did not look slept in. So, he never had come in. She wondered if he had gone off to sleep on the recliner. He was in the bathroom now. She could hear the shower. She turned her attention to the sound of spattering water. She tried to imagine what he looked like under its stream, naked, with lather on his chest. But the water stopped, and she got up hurriedly to make the bed.

He came out of the bathroom, a towel wrapped around his torso, before she could finish. He was a strapping, strong-armed man with fine chest hair.

"Good morning," she said softly.

"Good morning," he said, ruffling his wet hair, not looking at her.

"You did not come in to sleep."

He ignored her last statement. "Got to rush. I have a meeting at eight."

"How far is your office?"

"Not too far, but it takes me longer in rush hour traffic. About twenty minutes."

"What about breakfast? I can make an omelet if you have eggs."

"Don't worry. I had oatmeal." He disappeared into his closet, then stuck his head out.

"Listen, see what you can fix yourself for lunch. There's some instant noodles, or you can make yourself a sandwich."

"Oh, don't worry. I'll find something," she said.

"I'll try to be back a little early in the evening. I'll take you grocery shopping."

"Okay." Tara sat on the bed she had just made. And waited.

He came out of the closet fully dressed. He looked smart in a powder-blue shirt and khaki pants. She had heard so much about software professionals going to work in shorts and T-shirts. Apparently, this software professional was not one among them. She caught the notes of his cologne; they whipped up in her an alchemy of desire, fear, resentment.

When he left, Tara loosened up, relieved to have her space. She opened the glass French door in the living room that led to the balcony and stepped out barefooted. The sun had warmed the wooden floorboards, but the air was still cool and felt good on her skin. She inhaled deeply. How peaceful it was out there. The balcony overlooked a clean, empty road, on the other side of which was a serene red brick structure with a sparkling white steeple tipped with a cross. It was a church, no doubt. A sign near the entrance confirmed this. It read:

West Hill Baptist Church
Sunday Worship: 11 a.m.
Bible Class: 9:30 a.m.
All are Welcome

Past the church, on the other side of the road, were red, brick-fronted homes with green manicured front yards and tall pine trees. One little house looked like a cottage straight out of Enid Blyton's books. It had a white, wood-paneled exterior and a white picket fence that enclosed a green, grassy yard lined with red flower bushes. She absorbed the newness, the expansiveness of the panoramic view, and tried not to feel alone. Or trapped.

She spent the morning unpacking and arranging her clothes in the guest closet. It felt good to have something to do. She had left most of her Indian dresses behind. Not that she had too many of them. She had never been very interested in dressing up. Yvonne had said she would have no need for Indian clothes, so she had brought only pants, blouses, and tunics. Amma had tried to shove a couple of chiffon saris into her suitcase, but Tara could not be persuaded to leave them there.

When she was done with the arranging, and the closet looked a little fuller, she had exhausted her options for keeping busy. She peered at the stack of books in Sanjay's study. They were technical manuals, every one of them. *Does he not read at all?* The manuals, of course, might as well have been in Greek. She was grateful for the copies of *Time* and *Newsweek* on the coffee table in the living room. She curled up on the sofa and began to read. The phone rang, its shrillness shattering the silence. It made her jump. She wondered if it was her brother, Vijay, and if she ought to pick up.

What if it was Sanjay? She picked up the third time the phone rang, around mid-morning. It wasn't Vijay or Sanjay. She didn't understand much of what the guy at the other end said. Only that he asked for Sanjay Kumar, although it sounded more like *Saanjay Koomar.*

"He is not at home," she said. "I beg your pardon?" Did the American voice just ask her when he could call back? She wasn't sure. She never had trouble following the American accent in the movies, but it sounded so foreign over the phone.

"After six o'clock," she said anyway, and disconnected.

She made herself a frugal bowl of microwaved instant noodles for lunch and felt her eyes getting heavy thereafter. She shuffled into the bedroom and crawled under the sheets. She was out
in seconds. The phone rang a couple of times, but she was lost in
a deep stupor.

Somewhere, a phone rang. She was back in Mangalore, and back
in her bed, asleep but awake. She was trying desperately to open
her eyes. "Tara, phone!" she heard Amma call out. She tried to
wriggle out of bed. But her body was immobile, it weighed a ton.

"Tara, that was Sanjay," Amma's voice sailed through her
head. "You lost your chance."

She tried to move her head side to side, but every bit of her
was paralyzed.

"Still sleeping?" That wasn't Amma's voice.

She snapped her eyes open. He was in the room, at the foot
of the bed, looming large before her. She got up with a start, but
her head collapsed in her hands. She felt woozy.

"Sorry. I think I am jet-lagged," she slurred, rubbing her face.

"Why didn't you take my calls? Did you sleep all day?" He
made no effort to hide his annoyance. "I tried a couple of times
in the morning, too."

"I didn't know." Even her embarrassment wasn't waking her
up fully.

"Didn't know what?"

"I—I didn't think you'd call."

"Seriously?" He shook his head, and disappeared into the
bathroom, leaving her to stare stupidly at the footboard. When
he came out, the scowl on his face was even deeper.

"So, who did you think it was?"

"What?"

"Who did you think called you?"

"I took a call in the morning. It wasn't you." Her embarrassment was growing. She looked down at her hands.

"Who was it?"

"I don't know. I could not follow the accent. Somebody asked for you, I think."

"You think? Are you from the bush country? From some tiny, godforsaken hamlet? Aren't you supposed to have a master's in English literature?"

She fled to the bathroom, knocking about on unbalanced feet, locked the door, and sat on the rich blue cover of the toilet seat, blinking. She couldn't let him see the tears. She felt so stupid. She had already rubbed him the wrong way. The tears flowed, hot and earnest.

"All right," he knocked on the bathroom door. "Get dressed. Don't you want to go to the market?" His voice had mellowed.

She splashed water on her face, trying to fix the ugly puffiness of her eyes. She felt a little more composed after she had scrubbed her face clean of emotional residue with bar soap. He was out of the bedroom by the time she came out. She could hear the TV blaring in the living room. She had changed into khaki cargo pants and a midnight blue T-shirt, brushing her short, curly hair until it was reasonably tame. She always sought the help of strong hair spray to keep her hair in place. She sprayed some now, all over her curls, and applied a light coat of plum lipstick to her dry lips.

The farmers' market in Decatur was a surprise. She had never seen so many varieties of fresh fish or colorful vegetables and fruit in her life. Row after row of produce, some with names and forms and colors she had never even heard of. She looked for the familiar ones, running her fingers over shiny red apples, picking a large head of crinkly cabbage, and scanning the orderly line of jumbo-sized kingfish in their bed of ice, before pointing to the one she thought was the freshest one of the lot. Sanjay was happy to let her pick and choose, silently pushing the cart behind her.

They stopped at an Indian store on their way back, where she bought a sack of rice, a five-pound bag of split lentils, small packs of turmeric and chili powder, and whatever else she could think of that was essential to Mangalorean cooking.

Back in the apartment, she got busy in the kitchen. She put a cupful each of lentils and rice to cook in two identical containers, which she inserted into the small stainless Hawkins pressure cooker that Amma had insisted she carry. She marinated kingfish fillets for a while in Amma's spice blend, and then fried them with a little vegetable oil on a hot griddle. She shredded one half of a cabbage head, and made *upkari*, a dry side dish, which she garnished lightly with grated coconut.

"The fish is stinking up the place," he complained from the living room. She had the fan on; what else was she to do? She covered the griddle with a large lid and was relieved when the fish looked brown enough to cut the flame.

She thought the plates looked pretty. It was not as if she had much experience with cooking. If she weren't so anxious about his approval, she would probably have been proud of her culinary creations. The red-brown, spiced kingfish was a stark, inviting contrast to the white rice, yellow lentils, and the mild green of the cabbage. But he ate silently, scantly, setting his fork down again and again. Sweat beads formed on his dark brows. The fish lay largely untouched.

"You don't like fish?" she asked, surprised. She couldn't imagine somebody from the coast not liking fried fish.

He shrugged like an American. "Not much of a seafood lover. Besides, I can't handle too much spice anymore."

"Oh! Is it too spicy?" What was she going to cook tomorrow? It was a worrisome thought that she crumpled and stuffed into the back of her head for now.

They ate silently. After dinner, he accepted one laddoo that Amma had specifically sent for her son-in-law, and she ate three before stashing the box back in the fridge. She cleared the plates and loaded the dishwasher. He showed her how to run it. She set about cleaning the kitchen. When she was done, she took a shower and changed into her pajamas.

When she joined him in the living room, he was on the recliner, his back propped far back, in a gray T-shirt and khaki shorts, which were probably what he slept in. He had his laptop, but his attention was on the sitcom that was playing on TV. He was grinning from ear to ear. She had never seen him smile this wide before. His face was less granite-like and more handsome. But the smile waned a bit and turned plastic when he saw her. She sat on the sofa and tried to follow the antics of the TV family. It was much easier to follow the American accent on TV than it was over the phone.

"What show is this?" she asked.

"*Everybody Loves Raymond.* It's quite funny," he said.

She attempted to watch what he watched for the next hour, but she didn't see much because her thoughts kept scattering here and there. She missed watching *Kyun Ki Saas Bhi Kabhi Bahu Thi* (Because mother-in-law was once a daughter-in-law, too). She missed arguing with Amma that the soap saga was such a lowbrow, pedestrian insult to Indian sensibilities. She wondered whether they'd have had some conversation, if not for the TV. There hadn't been much talking on their way to the farmers' market or back. The guy on the TV show had an amiable nature, and his wife was pretty and dominating. But they talked and talked, like normal families—except when they paused for canned laughter.

Sanjay did not come in that night either. Sleep did not come to her aid quickly. She wished she hadn't slept all afternoon. She lay still on her back, her focus on her breathing, on the small heave and fall of her chest. Many a time, this technique had helped relax her mind and put her to sleep. Not tonight. She wondered if she should get up and warm a cup of milk in the microwave. She was so used to the hot milk and banana routine every night. She decided against it. She didn't want to wake him up, in case he had gone off to sleep in the living room.

No stray dog barked. If the moon was up, she did not see it, because it was eclipsed by the streetlight, thin strips of which slipped into the room through the blinds. The light was just enough to keep the room from darkness. Occasionally, she heard a car pass by. The TV was still on; it was his companion, she had learned.

Again, for the millionth time in three years, she wondered why he had married her if he didn't like her. And he most certainly didn't like her. She waited in darkness for the void of sleep. In the meantime, she wallowed in the larger void she felt suspended in. She put her hand over her chest, felt the rhythm of her heart. It was a beat she had known for thirty-one years, and yet, she felt, it was yet to assume meaning.

Tara had almost been engaged once, when she was twenty-four, to a doctor from Bombay, but the alliance had fallen through, because, after rounds of discussions over tea and snacks, and after the elders had planned out the nitty-gritty of a summer wedding, the groom-to-be's father had demanded a fat dowry. Shaken though he was at being ambushed with the uncouth demand, Daddy had refused to give in.

Amma had cried herself silly, even threatening to go on a hunger strike if Daddy did not change his mind. But Daddy was not one to bow down.

"If the educated amongst us do not take a stand against this evil practice, what hope is there for this society?" he had said.

Amma, mortified at the thought of her innocent daughter being offered as a sacrificial lamb at the altar of social reform, had tried to touch Daddy's emotional nerve.

"I don't know of any boy who has refused dowry. Why do we have to be martyrs? Do we love our daughter any less?" She had wept.

"The right man will come. And he will marry my daughter for the right reasons."

Daddy had his way, as always.

At twenty-four, with fresh-out-of-college idealism running strong in her veins, Tara had shared Daddy's views. But the years wore on, and no match seemed to click. She had endured humiliating bride-seeing trips, a couple of them out of town—once in Bangalore and the second time in Hyderabad. Most families found her too tall for their boys, others found her too plain. For most young men though, or at least for their parents, Daddy's no-dowry clause was a deal breaker.

"No dowry. Our son is very progressive," Sanjay's father had confirmed to Daddy over the phone the day after the bride-seeing high tea.

"Too progressive to even like his wife," Tara whispered to the shadows. She turned to look at the digital clock on the bedside table. It was almost three in the morning.

When the birds started to chirp outside—she had no idea what birds, they were not crows or sparrows, but they were just as vocal—and the first signs of dawn filtered into the room,

Tara was still awake. She heard the light rustle of footsteps on the carpet; then a light came on. The hallway outside the bedroom was faintly aglow, so she knew he had turned the kitchen light on. She lay still, her mind drained of its nighttime rush of thoughts. When the smell of freshly brewed coffee wafted into the room, rich and strong, it jarred her senses and caused a furor in her mind, a whirl of disjointed feelings. She shivered for no reason, so she pulled the duvet up to her chin. She wondered if she should get up and help. She did not. She kept her eyes closed as the footsteps made their way to the bedroom and then on to the bathroom. Melancholy, darker than black coffee, jabbed at her heart.

Silly me, silly me, she repeated to herself. *Everything will be okay.* She took deep, deep breaths.

"You don't have to cook for me," he said before leaving for work. "I am not much into Indian food anyway. I usually eat an early dinner right after work, with my coworkers."

Tara's face fell, even as a small part of her brain registered relief. Now, she didn't have to worry about toning down spices or stressing over what to cook. But he was her husband. Wasn't he supposed to eat with her?

"Oh! What did you take me to market for, then?" she asked.

"Because I don't want to deprive you of the foods you are used to."

"How thoughtful!" Did she just say it out loud? Was her voice laced with sarcasm?

"Are you mocking?" she heard him say.

She bit her lower lip. "No, no. That really was thoughtful of you."

She was relieved when he let it pass.

"Oh, and you can use the internet on the home computer if you wish. The password is LizSan, L-I-Z-S-A-N," he spelled it out.

"L-I-Z-S-A-N. Thanks."

"And that was what I was calling you about yesterday," he added.

Chapter 4

"Have you settled down? Are you over your jet lag?" Amma asked, on Tara's sixth day in Atlanta.

Tara had finally learned to make long distance calls to India using a calling card that had eight numbers listed as Atlanta access numbers and a ten-digit PIN; a pretty Asian girl smiled against a red background on the other side.

"Time moves slowly," Tara replied. "I have trouble sleeping at night, so I end up sleeping all afternoon."

"Try to stay awake one afternoon. Your body will adjust quickly," Amma suggested. "Is he okay with you?"

What was she going to tell Amma? "He is very quiet. Like me."

"Everything is still very new for both, no? It takes time to get to know each other. Did he like the laddoos?"

"Yes," she lied. He had eaten one laddoo, and she had polished off twenty-four of them, until only three remained. Each laddoo had made her feel good for a few minutes.

"How much of Atlanta have you seen?"

"He took me to the market one day, to the social security office two days later."

"That's all?"

"Yes."

"Where is he now? Does he work on Saturday also?"

"I think so. He left a while ago."

"What did you cook for him? Did you use my masala?"

"He said not to cook for him. He doesn't like Indian food."

"What?" Amma sounded shocked. "So, what do you do all day? How do you spend your time?"

"I don't know."

"You don't know? What do you do, darling?"

"I don't know, Amma. I don't know. Let me go now. I don't want to use up the calling card. I'll call again soon."

There was a sniff at the other end. "Keep talking to him, engage him in conversation. Everything will be okay, child. It might take a little time, but all will be well."

"I know." Tara had a sudden urge to take a jab at Amma, as if putting her in misery would magically make her feel better; as if happiness were a seesaw of inverse proportions.

"You are all the same, though—Sanjay, Daddy, and you." She slammed the phone down before Amma had the chance to react.

The guilt came soon enough. It always did. It made her feel like vermin, a mean, little, black-hearted vermin. She called Amma back.

"Amma, I'm sorry."

Amma's hello was thick and nasal. She had been crying.

"It's not so bad. It really isn't. I spend time vacuuming or cleaning the bathrooms. We have a computer, so I spend a couple of hours surfing the net and writing emails. I am learning to watch some of the daytime TV shows too."

Amma continued to weep into the phone. "I want you to be happy," she said. "That's all a mother ever wants."

That was Amma's favorite line, repeated every so often, as if she had a constant need to be absolved of guilt. But if the past could be wiped clean at will, who would atone for the deep etches of memory that felt like scars?

Tara often wondered if her childhood memories would have been shaped differently if Pinky had been found in the boxes that arrived at New Mangalore Port by cargo ship four weeks after Tara and Amma moved to Shanti Nilaya. Would her transition to a new life have been easier?

Amma had spent an entire morning searching, emptying the boxes. But Pinky wasn't there. Tara did not cry this time, because the four weeks of her new life in Mangalore had scattered her pain among new challenges. But the skies cried heavy sheets, flooding several low-lying areas on the west coast.

Tara stayed huddled inside their upstairs room with Amma after school, revisiting again and again the one afternoon she had spent with Pinky. Daddy had left to establish a new fairy tale for his family in Dubai. He would send for them after he had settled down, but it would take time. Until then, Shanti Nilaya was home to Amma and Tara, whether they liked it or not.

Amma had cried for a couple of days because she missed Daddy and her beautiful colonial home, her chauffeured station wagon, her kitty party friends. Then she had grown sullen. She came alive only at night, to help Tara with her homework. Her belly grew bigger by the day, like a ripe jackfruit. Tara knew now that it was not poop in her mother's belly, but a baby that kicked her hard. The knowledge meant nothing to her, because the baby was only a ball inside Amma's belly.

Six days a week, Tara trudged to St. Margaret's Convent School, bundled up in a blue, red, and white flower-patterned raincoat with a massive hood. The first few days, Uncle Anand had walked with her. Then she walked alone, black rubber rain shoes on her feet, and a blue canvas school bag on her back, under the raincoat. The stretch from Shanti Nilaya up to the T-junction was the toughest to cross. The mud road was pitted with gaping craters that filled with water when it rained. Tara's foot would invariably slip into a pool, filling her rubber shoe with muddied water. The first few times she had shuddered with revulsion—there was no telling what the water had touched. The lane was littered with cockleshells, and on the occasional day when it did not rain, she saw fresh goat droppings as well.

Walking to school was bad enough, but school was worse. There were fifty-three girls in her class, and she talked to none because her hair was too short—too short to plait or tie into pigtails; too short to look like her classmates. Each morning, before she left for school, Amma spent several minutes brushing her hair with a neat side parting. But by the time she reached school, wiry curls were springing up and sticking up in all directions, like an unkempt shrub.

"Your mummy doesn't comb your hair?" Zainaba, the girl who sat next to Tara in class asked one day.

"She combs." Tara felt her face growing hot.

"You must ask her to apply coconut oil. Your hair will grow long and thick like mine."

Zainaba's hair was always neatly braided into two plaits that were folded up and secured behind her ears with black ribbons. Sometimes, Tara saw black lice crawling up the side of Zainaba's neck or on the top of her white shirt collar. Nobody pointed this out to Zainaba, so although Tara was repulsed by the lice the first few days, she changed her opinion quickly and wanted to cultivate some in her hair.

Every morning, after Zainaba's advice, Tara insisted that her hair be drenched in oil before she set out to school. This pleased Grandmother Indira, who believed that coconut was essential to their lives—in their food, for prayers and as nourishment for hair.

Grandmother Indira was kind, but she stayed in the kitchen and cooked four meals, brewed tea and boiled milk, or she gave all of herself to her barn chores, retiring only after dinner with a long sigh, and the sigh was the only luxury she allowed herself. Grandfather Madhava was a postmaster in his post office, and a reader of news at home. He left home precisely at eight thirty each morning and returned an hour before daylight faded. But before he left home and after he returned, Tara rarely stepped out to the verandah, where grandfather spent much time on an easy chair, feverishly rustling newspapers and gleaning the same news on All India Radio, as if some glitch in censorship during the emergency would allow real news to trickle into his day. Grandfather did not see little Tara, and when he did, his gruff manner sent her scurrying inside.

Uncle Anand held a clerical position at the Department of Central Excise in Attavar. He was the opposite of his father, Madhava. He allowed Tara to trail him like Mary's little lamb. Often, when the rain gave respite in the evening, he took her to the Beary store past the T-junction and bought her peanut *chikkis* or coconut-jaggery candy.

Some evenings, when the mood struck him, Uncle Anand ambled to the verandah of an old vacant house down Morgan Hill, Tara in tow, an enormous, prickly, brown-green jackfruit wrapped in sheets of newspaper in one hand, and a sickle in the other. Tara sat beside him on the steps leading to the house and watched in fascination as he spread newspaper sheets on the dusty red verandah and placed the fruit at the center. He expertly sliced the fruit in half, wiped the oozing white gum away with several sheets of newspaper, cut the halves lengthwise again, and carefully removed the fleshy yellow bulbs. He piled Tara's side of the newspaper high with the sweet, pungent bulbs, and showed her how to pull the seed out before plopping one into her mouth. Tara did not remember eating jackfruit before. Once she got used to its rich odor, she enjoyed its full, sweet taste.

When Amma got to know about the jackfruit events, she

forbade Uncle Anand from giving Tara any. Not from a piece of paper, not sitting in a dirty verandah, she said. That was asking for a stomach upset. But Uncle Anand cast aside Amma's concerns with a laugh. Tara believed him when he said Amma was being overly fussy, that jackfruit was the healthiest fruit on earth. Besides, somehow, jackfruit tasted better after Amma forbade her from eating it. So she indulged in the only sweet moments of her day, and listened to Uncle Anand narrate stories of Tulu Nadu, their land encompassing the southwestern coast of India.

Each time, he drew out a different fable from memory. The first time, it was the story of Koti and Chennaya, the legendary twin heroes from a Tulu epic who were raised by King Perumala Ballala of Padumale and fought valiantly against caste discrimination.

By the time Koti fell to a treacherous arrow from Perumala Ballala, whose very hands had fed him as a child, and Chennaya, unable to bear the grief over the loss of his twin brother, had killed himself, Tara had wet, brimming eyes.

The next time, it was the story of Abbakka, the warrior queen of Ullal who put up a spirited resistance against the Portuguese army. Then it was the story of Punyakoti, the noble cow, for whom keeping promises mattered more than life itself.

Uncle Anand's stories made Tara forget the day spent among fifty-three other girls she did not talk to, the fat black widow spiders in the bathroom, the lizards that watched without blinking from the ceiling beams. They made her forget the day she had spent in a quiet square shoe room with a doll whose golden hair and violet eyes had made happiness seem so real, yet so fleeting.

"It was only a doll. Plastic shell and empty inside," Uncle Anand told her, every now and then. "Did you put your ear to her plastic chest? If you had, you would have known. Dolls have no heart; they cannot love you back. Only living things can."

In August, when Tara's little brother arrived, she made sure he had a heart. She put her ear to the baby's chest and concentrated until she felt the faint human *thump-thump*. He looked like a fragile doll, swaddled in soft, white voile, asleep in the hospital crib next to Amma's green metal bed. Round, red face. Eyes tightly closed. Tara looked at him in wonderment. She couldn't imagine this little creature had been in her mother's stomach so many months, and she wasn't fully aware of his existence, at least not as a human of flesh and blood—with a heart that could love back.

"Amma, did he really come out of your stomach?" she asked.

Amma laughed. "Of course, Tara, I carried him in my belly for nine months, just like I carried you."

Tara couldn't imagine living in a dark belly for nine long months, curled up, constricted, unable to move around, alone. She certainly wouldn't want to go back in there. She looked at the baby again. She was glad he was out in the world, out of darkness, out of solitude.

Tara stroked the baby's soft cheek. He was magical. She felt a surge of love. Uncle Anand didn't tell her this, but this love was a new feeling, quite different from what she had felt for Pinky. This was a love with no sense of ownership, no neediness. "You are my brother," she declared to him proudly.

The resentment had come later—little bouts of dark emotion that Tara had tried all her life to shake off, get over, bury.

Last night Vijay had called again, his second call since her arrival in Atlanta. Sanjay had picked up. Tara's ears had perked up when he said, "Hey, Vijay. What's up, man?" She had taken the receiver from Sanjay eagerly.

"How are you? Do you like Atlanta? Is he treating you well?"

She had held on to Vijay's familiar voice, savoring the known in an unfamiliar world. "I am fine," she had said in a low voice, hoping Sanjay hadn't heard Vijay's last question.

Vijay said he would pay her a visit at the first opportunity.

"Come soon," she had implored.

California was at the other end of the US, he had reminded her. They even had a three-hour time difference between them. "I'll have to wait for the next long weekend."

"I'll be waiting for the next long weekend."

"I'll call often," he had promised.

Chapter 5

Tara double-checked to make sure the front door was locked. She made her way down the flight of steps, walked on the sidewalk past the soft cream siding and red brick apartment buildings with sloping black shingled roofs. The sidewalk took her, in wavelike fashion, to the tall, wrought iron, main gates. She took the little pedestrian gate beside it, and found herself outside, on a side street of Atlanta.

She stood by the gate, contemplating which way to turn. One side led to the main road just a short distance away, where the traffic was heavy. The other side seemed to stretch on as far as the eye could see.

West Hill Baptist Church loomed right opposite the road, its red bricks radiating warmth, but it was still a very foreign-looking structure. She turned to the right and walked down the road, passing the little red-brick-fronted homes she had seen from her balcony. They were just as interesting up close: the green lawns, the flower bushes, the closed doors and glass windows. She slowed down when she passed the picture book white house with the neat little garden. A squirrel scampered across the grass and disappeared into a bush; a dog barked from the backyard, shrill and excited, but no human was in sight. Not here, nor outside any other home, or on the sidewalk.

So, this is America, she thought. *Not a soul in sight. Where are all the people?*

The only people she passed by were those she did not see, or barely caught a glimpse of, because they were in the cars that whizzed past on the two-lane street.

She had walked about ten minutes when she came to a major intersection. Crossing the busy road seemed too scary a task. She turned around and started to walk back, sweat beads glistening on her forehead. She had not imagined America as being hot in summer. She would have to start earlier tomorrow.

The walk back home involved an uphill segment. Tara panted a little from the heat and wiped her brow on her sleeve. Sensing the hum of a motor close to her, instinctively, she looked over her shoulder. A car had slowed down, a yellow taxi with a white hood. The driver had a broad grin on his face, his teeth exposed, stark white against his chocolate skin.

He held a card in his hand, which he had stretched out in Tara's direction through the open window.

"Miss, if you ever need me," he said in a foreign accent.

She looked away and increased her pace. Did she hear him jeer? Her heart raced. Was he following her? She looked back after a while. He was gone.

Tara half ran until she was back in the safety of the apartment. The pounding in her chest took a while to subside. She was so thirsty, she thought she would choke. The clock on the microwave said ten thirty in the morning. Countries north of the hemisphere could get hot too, she had learned. She gulped a tall glass of chilled water, then another, and finally it dawned upon her. The taxi driver was only trying to score a customer, and she had been a stupid scaredy-cat.

"Are you from the bush country? From some tiny, godforsaken hamlet?" she mimicked Sanjay, and then in her regular voice said, "Yes, yes, I am from the same godforsaken hamlet that you come from, you fake American."

She slipped behind the computer in the study. "Open sesame," she murmured as she typed in "lizsan" on the keyboard. *Lizsan, what did it even mean?* she wondered. *Why not something that made sense, like lizard, or lizclaiborne?* The desktop appeared. She surfed the Internet for the next two hours. She checked out the Indian news websites, played some Hindi songs on a live streaming website, checked her Hotmail twice. She had no new emails. She looked to see if any of her contacts were on MSN messenger. Only Sharat, her colleague at the *Morning Herald* appeared online, and she wasn't going to chat with him. She allowed her mind to wander. She wondered how prison inmates in isolation must feel, the walls eating into their mind each day. She typed in "prisoners in isolation" on Yahoo. The search took her to an article on solitary confinement and the effects of this cruel, inhuman punishment on the human mind. She shuddered.

She was beginning to feel a little hungry, but she decided that a shower was in order first. Water always had a calming effect on her. Besides, the walk had been sweat inducing; she felt dirty and smelly. She stood under the shower for the longest time possible, allowing the warm water to percolate into her body and permeate her being. She turned her face up and allowed the water stream to douse her face. She hummed softly, a Hindi song from the biggest Bollywood hit of the year so far:

Kaho na pyar hai
Kaho na pyar hai
Haan tumse pyar hai
Ke tumse pyar hai

Say you love me,
Say you love me,
Yes, I love you
Yes, I love you

She mutilated the song, going from verse to chorus to verse, over and over again, her mind a tangle of thoughts. Did she love her husband at all? She would, if only he'd make it easier. Love wasn't a shower head; it didn't just automatically pour out of your heart because your parents decided you would be together for life. Why did Sanjay make himself so unlovable? To what end?

She turned off the water stream and stepped out of the shower. Low, muffled voices reached her ears. She listened keenly, her stomach in knots, ear against the door. She heard faint drawls, but then she heard music. It was the TV. She did not remember turning on the TV at all. Was Sanjay back? She quickly dried herself and dressed in her sweaty clothes; she regretted not taking fresh ones into the bathroom. She opened the bathroom door an inch and peeped out cautiously.

"Sanjay? Are you back?" she called out.

"Yup, it's me." That was most certainly Sanjay's deep voice.

She tiptoed into her closet and changed into fresh clothes—floral culottes and a gray top.

"So, you are a bathroom singer," he said, when she came out to the living room, her damp hair brushed into place. She blushed.

"I had no idea you'd be back so early."

"I thought we could talk."

"Talk? About what?" Talk? Sanjay never talked. Did he mean a chitchat kind of talk or a serious discussion? Why was his face so grave?

"Never mind. It can wait."

It can wait? So it wasn't chitchat? She knotted the end of her top with nervous fingers. She sat on the loveseat, because he had taken the three-seater. She could hold back no more.

"You don't like me." She had meant that to be a question, but it sounded like an indictment.

He looked taken aback but recovered quickly.

"I have nothing against you. I barely even know you." At

least his voice was passive, even gentle, she thought. "It's just the whole arranged marriage thing. I've never really believed in it."

"So why did you get married?"

"It was part impulse, part giving in to my parents' wish."

"Oh!" Tara looked down at her hands, her heart sinking.

"I am not a cruel person, but I don't see how this can work. We are so different from each other."

"But we are married now." She hoped her angst had not reached her voice, that she had not sounded imploring.

"I know, and I am deeply sorry about that. I didn't set out to ruin somebody's life. I wish I had thought through it better." He closed his eyes, rubbing his temples with the tips of his long fingers.

A weird thought crossed her mind before she lost it to her sinking heart. He was being the kindest she had known him to be, when he was saying the cruelest things.

But he wasn't done yet. "I am sorry. But you are free to leave. It might be the best thing to do."

She stared at him. "I am not leaving." Her voice was throaty. "Please, I cannot go back."

He sighed, looked away, and studied the carpet. The silence gnawed into her, so she chewed on her lower lip until she tasted blood.

"All right," he said finally. "You will get your green card in less than two years. Perhaps you can hang in until then. A green card will open up possibilities for you, and you don't even have to go back to India."

How nice he sounded, spouting dispassionate, practical ideas for her future—a future that he did not see himself in.

"Why did you apply for my green card? Why did you send me a visa?" she asked.

"I was giving it a try."

"But you haven't tried."

His lips moved; he started to say something but stopped. "I can't," he said instead.

She got up and lumbered into the kitchen. She opened the fridge and stuffed her mouth with two laddoos from the box, then shuffled with purpose to the bedroom. She flopped on her back, rested her forearm over her forehead. She noticed that the vent puffed icy air directly onto her face; that the ceiling had a sprinkler to subdue flames. Insignificant things to notice when her life was falling apart.

"Useless observations of a useless person," she muttered. She put a hand to her chest and moaned. It felt like a nail was lodged in her heart. The hurt was not new to her. She was a magnet to nails. The first one had been driven into her soul a long time ago—after only twenty-one months at Shanti Nilaya.

Life had established a set pattern. She went to school, had Parle-G biscuits dunked in tea that Grandmother Indira served her when she got back home, and when it didn't rain, Uncle Anand took her and her baby brother, Vijay, up the hilltop for an outing.

They sat on granite rocks in a grassy clearing near the banyan tree and watched Vijay, who ran around in glee, picking pebbles and plucking grass. Tara was in awe of the tree, of its massive arms, its hanging ropelike roots. The banyan tree was the *kalpavriksh*, Amma had told her once; the divine, wish-fulfilling tree. Tara was too afraid to sit under it, but from a distance, she closed her eyes and wished fervently for Daddy to send for her, Amma, and Vijay to Dubai.

Beautiful Amma now looked more thin than statuesque; her collarbones jutted out above the hemline of her blouse, making an unsightly hollow between them. Her face, once a lovely portrait of class, was now a contrast of dark shadows and ashen skin. Daddy had still not sent for them. She fretted, became depressed, and no longer slept soundly, tossing and turning and sighing for most part each night.

Because Amma no longer painted her toenails, Tara painted them for her, applying scarlet vertical strokes. It bothered Tara that Amma was sad. She wished she had a magic wand that would make Daddy send their tickets to Dubai, so Amma could go back to being happy.

Each night, after sunset, Grandfather Madhava led the devotional before the numerous frames of gods and goddesses in the inner hall of Shanti Nilaya. Everyone joined in, singing Kannada *bhajans*, as Grandfather Madhava did *aarti* to the gods with a brass lamp lit with five cotton wicks soaked in ghee. At the end of the ritual, they prostrated themselves before the deities, praying for good health and the wellbeing of their clan. Tara bowed before the gods, kneeling and bent over, head touching the floor, hoping to please the gods with her earnestness.

"Oh God, please make Daddy send us tickets to Dubai soon. Please make Amma happy again."

Several afternoons at school, after their lunch break, she went to the school chapel. She knelt before the figure of Jesus on the cross, locked her fingers in front of her chest like she had seen the nuns do, and repeated her prayer to the Christian gods.

"Oh Jesus, oh Mother Mary, please take us to Dubai."

Amma did not leave the gods alone either; she even attempted to bribe them, as grown-ups often did. She and Grandfather Madhava made trips to the temple towns in the district. They went to the Kateel temple of Sri Durga Parameshwari and prayed to the feminine creative form in the inner sanctum. They visited the Subramanya temple of the Lord of Serpents, beseeching the celestial being, through a *puja* performed by the temple priest, to rid her family of any *sarpa dosha*, curse of the serpents. Every temple they went to, Amma promised puja sponsorships or special offerings to the gods if her prayers came true.

Tara imagined a group of gods, blue-skinned, shiny gold crowns on their heads, seated on majestic thrones in a regal court nestled among cottony clouds, laughing at Amma's plight.

"Amma, don't be sad," she said. "You have me and Vijay."

Amma sighed. "Yes, Tara. You two are the only reasons I am still alive."

In March 1977, the cosmic balance finally shifted, and a blue-skinned god smiled a condescending smile, held his radiant hand up, and said, of the innumerable prayers offered to him: *tathastu*, so be it. Or so it seemed.

The prime minister finally lifted emergency rule. Amma's personal emergency also ended. Daddy's letter arrived. The shadows that Tara had come to accept on Amma's face disappeared, banished by good news. Daddy would send for them soon, Amma said. His letter had promised her that.

"When Amma? When are we going?" she asked.

"Very soon, Tara."

"Will I have friends there?"

"Yes, you will have friends there. Maybe it will be like back home."

"Will the bathroom have a bathtub? Will there be ACs in the bedrooms? Will there be a clubhouse?"

Amma laughed.

"You will have to ask Daddy all those questions," she said. "I have not been to Dubai yet."

"Will I have to go to a Dubai school?"

"Yes, Tara."

Tara wasn't happy with the idea of changing schools again. But she wasn't going to worry about that now. She snuggled up to Amma at night, the comfort of her sari against her skin, thinking about Dubai and the little characters she made up in her mind that populated the desert city. She saw soaring buildings, gleaming foreign cars on wide roads, and sparkling homes with abundant date palms in the yard. When she imagined friends, they were usually her old friends Pippi, Leenika, and Runa. And even though she thought she was too old to play with dolls, they appeared on their own, on neat little shelves in her room. They had shiny golden hair and violet-blue eyes; they were the sisters, friends, and twins of Pinky.

It made her feel a little guilty that she rarely saw Daddy in her imaginary world. She saw other men—a white-uniformed chauffeur, a gardener dressed nicely in pants and shirt, and lots of Arab men in flowing robes and headgear in the open markets— but Daddy, he was always away at the office. But it was just as well, she found out when Daddy's next letter arrived, because Daddy did not think about her. He thought about Amma and the son he had never seen. But he did not think about Tara.

When Amma, teary-eyed, gently broke the news to her, all Tara could do was bury her face in Amma's sari and lay very stunned and very still and wonder if there was a way to go back into her mother's womb, or to hide in her suitcase when she left. There was little use in pleading, begging, or crying. Tara wasn't six anymore. She knew Amma did as Daddy commanded. But she had to know, so she asked, stifling the urge to scream out the hurt and fear from her lungs.

"For your own good, Tara," Amma replied tearfully, drawing Tara close to her bosom. "The schools in Dubai are not up to Indian standards. Someday, when you are a doctor or engineer, you will thank Daddy for this decision."

"Why does Vijay get to go with you?"

"Because he is still a baby. He is not in school yet, no?"

Amma wept all night before their departure. She would miss her sweet daughter every single minute, but Daddy needed her as he found his feet in a new country, she said. It would be a tough life in a desert country, where the heat was oppressive, and they did not know many people. Of course, Tara would visit during the holidays. Amma and Daddy would come home to visit their little angel often.

It was curtain call for Tara's pretend Dubai world. The sharp edifices of her imaginings crumbled like Parle-G biscuits dropped in hot tea, until there was nothing left but desert sand; miles of it stretched ahead of her. Weren't families meant to be together? *We two, ours two*, like in the family planning advertisements? Why did Amma and Vijay get to fly to the happy world, while she had to stay back? How could God do this to his little children? What was the use of prayers?

Chapter 6

She suddenly understood when the taxi driver whispered in her ear, "It's the same story. Always the same story. Don't you get it?"

Tara opened her eyes in panic. She tried to move, but her body felt like a ton of bricks. She tried to scream, but no voice emerged. The taxi driver's voice grew louder as she struggled to move her fingers. "Your parents had your brother. Your husband has another woman. Don't you get it?"

She felt breathless from her efforts. She struggled to open her mouth to let in more air, but her airways felt constricted. She could see the ceiling, the vent, the sprinkler, but she sensed that she was in prison, under solitary confinement.

He whispered something else, this time from the foot of the bed. She couldn't hear him; she had all her focus on trying to open her mouth. She finally managed guttural sounds.

"Aaah, aaah, aaah."

"Tara? Tara, what happened?" He was bent over her, shaking her arm. It wasn't the taxi driver. It was Sanjay. She sat bolt upright, gulping in air.

"You were making strange noises," he said.

She wiped her forehead with the back of her hand.

"Did you have a nightmare?" He sat on the edge of the bed. "Are you okay?"

She blinked and stared at her hands, her breath rugged and wheezy. "Is there another woman?"

"What?"

"Is there another woman in your life?" she rasped.

"No."

She looked at him, and she was neither shy nor afraid. He kept his gaze on her as she probed his eyes. Did she see honesty in them?

"Then why won't you try?" she asked.

He stretched his arms out. She blinked and looked away.

"Come," he said, leaning forward, gathering her in his arms, leaving her stupefied through the haze of her mind.

He felt so masculine and tender, and she felt so confused and heartbroken, that the tears started to pour. They rolled down her eyes in torrents, racked her slender frame, and wet his linen shirt. He rubbed her back gently, patiently, until she had exhausted her tears.

His arms felt warm and secure, as if their conversation of a couple of hours ago had not happened, and she didn't want to ever move away. She wiped the tears away from her face with the pads of her fingers. He hooked a forefinger under her chin, and lifted her face up, until they were face to face.

"Hush now." His voice was gentle. He kissed her forehead softly. She closed her eyes. He stroked her cheek with a thumb. Warmth arose in her, and her skin burned. He outlined her moist lips with his forefinger; she felt his lips pressing into them. She parted them, allowed him to claim her mouth. She kissed him fiercely, hungrily, not conscious of the soft moaning sounds that were erupting in her throat. He was burning, too. He had never kissed her before, not once during the four nights they had spent together in Mangalore.

He slid his hand under her top and rubbed the concave small of her back. She unbuttoned his shirt and caressed the fine hairs of his chest.

"Take that thing off," he whispered. She pulled her blouse over the top of her head and yanked it free, while he took his shirt off. She was suddenly conscious of being exposed in a bra. But he quickly closed the gap between them. He was on top of her, kissing the hollow of her neck, the valley between her small perky breasts, her taut belly. For once, she let go of all abandon, unleashing her deep longings. She led him on with her recklessness. They made love with the ardor of lovers.

He rolled away and lay on his back next to her. She propped herself on her elbow and looked at his flushed face, his heaving chest, his manliness, now spent and flaccid.

"That was something," he said, running his fingers through her hair.

"What about me?" she said.

"Tell me how."

She closed her fingers around his forefinger. "This is how."

He obliged, until she convulsed with pleasure. The release was intense, and suddenly the world turned balmy—the afternoon, her thoughts, the beat of her heart. The vent blew cool air over her moist body.

Her eyes had started to close again, when she heard him laugh. She raised her head to look at him.

"Who would have known?" he said.

"Hmmm?"

"Who would have known that a shy girl like you can be such a bitch in bed."

Did he just call her a bitch? She blushed happily.

They made love again that night, this time with protection he had bought at CVS Pharmacy, after he had taken her out to dinner at Olive Garden. For the first time, they had talked, over gnocchi soup and chicken parmigiana. He talked fall in Atlanta, baseball, sushi. He opened up about work, about the effing main office in DC that didn't understand the value of his innovative suggestions, about his ambition of securing a management position, about his dreams of one day heading a Fortune 500 company. She absorbed everything he said with keen-eyed interest, nodding, asking questions, engaging him in conversation, like Amma had advised.

On Sunday, he took her to see Richard Gere's *An Autumn in New York* at Regal Cinemas, after they had made love in the afternoon. She cried for the dying Charlotte; he complained about the soppy storyline.

On Monday, he came home from work and declared, "You gave me blue balls today."

"What's that?"

"It's an affliction that tortures men when they are at work thinking about the wild weekend they've had." He guffawed.

Her heart did a little jig, as if she were drunk.

That night, he lay sprawled on the sofa, nursing vodka over ice, glued to his laptop. She sat on the loveseat, absorbed in that week's edition of *Time* magazine, educating herself on the Bush dynasty, especially presidential candidate George Bush.

"Hey, Tara." She looked up at him.

"You want a sip?" He stretched his arm out. She took the tinkling glass from his hand and took a sip of the clear liquid, twirled the glass, sniffed the sweet odor, gulped a big mouthful.

"Don't gulp it down. It's not Coke." He was mildly amused. "It'll hit you." She returned the glass to him.

On rare occasions, when he was in an exceptionally affable mood, Daddy had allowed Tara a few sips of his scotch and soda. But vodka was softer and smelled better than Daddy's scotch.

Tara turned her attention back to the magazine. After a couple of minutes, he offered her another sip, then another, and she was beginning to feel lightheaded.

"I think I'd better stop. I'm feeling tipsy."

"Come here. Let me show you something on my laptop."

She glided next to him, rested her floating head over his shoulder, crossed a leg over his. Her eyes were glazed, giddy from the smell of his cologne.

The laptop had moving images; it was a video, a voyeuristic recording of a well-endowed ripped white male and a buxom blonde in the act. Tara's eyes opened wide, and she clamped her hand to her mouth in shock. She giggled uncontrollably. She had never seen pornographic images before. There was nothing left to the imagination. It was all right there for the camera.

"Oh, my god!" she exclaimed. "Oh, my god! They're doing it all."

"Can you leave God out of it?" he said with a laugh. He snuggled closer, brushed her hair away from her face, and nibbled her ear. He slipped his hand inside her T-shirt and felt her softness. She warmed up immediately, her tips swelled. She had a sudden, alcohol-fueled idea. She kissed him passionately, then slithered to the floor, got up on her knees, and pulled his shorts down in one deft move, as if she were skilled at this. She did what she had just seen the woman on the screen do. Her hands, lips, and tongue took him to heaven.

Later, lying on her back next to a gently snoring husband, Tara laughed. She could only guess what had brought about the sea change in him. Perhaps he had discovered that he liked igniting her sexual side. Maybe it stoked his male ego. She had made her husband like her, even if it was just for one reason. It was a beginning.

Chapter 7

Tara had heard that the best way to a man's heart was through his stomach. Sanjay said he liked Italian and Mexican food. After spending a considerable amount of time on the Internet researching Italian and Mexican recipes, Tara finally took the plunge. She would draw up a list of ingredients she would need, and if he was in the mood, Sanjay would take her to Publix when he got home. Her first attempt at making veggie lasagna was a disaster, but her refried bean enchiladas turned out better—the cheese had melted sufficiently, the sauce was still bubbling when she pulled the dish out of the oven, and the chopped black olives and cilantro added aesthetic appeal to their plates.

"It's good," he said, after the first mouthful; she savored the compliment all evening. There were days when he still preferred to eat out with his coworkers, but she thought four days out of seven was still a small victory for her attempts at making her marriage work.

Sometimes, when the craving hit her, Tara grabbed a fistful of coins from a little glass jar in one of the kitchen cabinets that Sanjay deposited spare coins in, counted out a dollar and some more, walked a mile and a half to Bharat Bazaar Indian grocery store late in the afternoon, and bought herself a pack of peanut chikkis. The store owner, a graying grouch, always checked her out in complete silence, the only sounds coming from his greasy till.

"Hello, Uncle," she greeted him on her third visit.

"Hmm," he grunted, eyes on the till, fingers clanging the math.

"Mister, does it cost you money to smile?" she yelled—inside her head, of course.

She did not see the taxi driver after her first solo adventure outside. She almost wished she would, if only to prove to him that she wasn't that fresh off the boat anymore. Perhaps she would turn around and wave at him, or greet him with a casual, "How are you doing?"

She craved human interaction. Now, except when she was having sex, the silence that filled her emptiness was deafening. Then, one evening, on her way back from her evening walk, she saw a petite young woman from a distance as she approached her building. She stood in the parking lot, leaning against the back of a white Mini Cooper, feet crossed, keeping watch over her young boy who was on a razor scooter, pushing it up and down the paved, rectangular stretch. She was dressed in a short, paneled skirt and black tank top, but it was the pink streak in her short blond hair that called out for attention.

Tara wondered if she should greet her. But the woman beat her to it

"Hi! Are you my new neighbor?" she called out. Tara smiled, nodded. The girl was not beautiful—long, slightly hooked nose, deep-set blue eyes—but her smile was dazzling; it suggested a bubbly personality. She walked up to Tara and held out her hand.

"Hi! I am Alyona Patterson. And that is my son Viktor." She pointed toward the boy who continued to push his scooter, oblivious to his surroundings. Tara noticed that Alyona had an accent that was not American. She didn't say Victor like the Americans might.

"Hi. I am Tara," she said, shaking Alyona's hand.

"My God, you are so tall and beautiful. Are you from India? Indian girls are very beautiful. But they are not tall. How come you are tall?"

Tara smiled politely. "Thank you." She offered no explanation for being Indian and tall.

"I had a coworker who once brought *biryani* to work. So delicious! You cook biryani?"

"I've never cooked it so far, but my mother has a good recipe." Tara's smile broadened.

In the ten minutes that she spent in conversation with Alyona, Tara learned all the basic facts about her life. She was a Russian immigrant and worked as a hairdresser in the little salon called Eclips next to Bharat Bazaar. She had been married to an American, but they divorced last year. Viktor, who was seven years old, lived with her, but spent his vacations with his dad in Charlotte, North Carolina. Tara would see them more often, loitering in the breezeway and in the parking lot, now that Viktor was back from his summer vacation at his dad's.

Tara was suffused with cheer that evening. Alyona had an easy, warm nature. It was strangely comforting to Tara that Alyona was a foreigner like her and spoke English with an accent. She made a mental note to ask Amma for her biryani recipe.

Tara's apartment was often the setting for afternoon bonding sessions over hot cups of cardamom-flavored chai. Alyona talked. A lot. She had fair command over the English language, and words tumbled out of her mouth in accented glory. She talked about her former life in Russia, where she had been a lawyer; about her seven-year marriage to Andrew, whom she had met at the Ruby Tuesday in Charlotte where she was a waitress, and he the manager. Her marriage had fallen apart when Andrew left her for another girl he had met at the same restaurant. She spoke about her boss, a Russian woman named Lyudmila, who had taken Alyona under her wing after her divorce, providing her training and a job at her salon, and about the other girls, one an Indian Ismaili, who worked there.

Sanjay was obsessed with elections all fall, watching every presidential debate and every analysis on CNN, until even Tara, who didn't know much about American politics, was hooked. But Alyona had no interest in who became president. Ironically, Alyona could vote, Sanjay could not. Alyona could also laugh, at the silliest of things. Sanjay did not.

A few times, Tara offered to babysit Viktor after he got back from his after-school program while Alyona ran errands, for which she was rewarded with a hug and a kiss, both from mother and son. Viktor was easy to babysit. He watched the cartoons on PBS or did his homework, while Tara sat next to him reading a magazine. Sometimes Alyona allowed him to bring his Gameboy over, and that usually meant Viktor would be lost to the world, engrossed in his Pokémon games.

Tara loved to hear little Viktor talk, and immersed her curiosity in gleaning whatever tidbits she could from him about life in America. He said, at school, he had chicken nuggets or hot dogs or mac 'n' cheese with chocolate milk. Mommy also fixed the same kind of dinner every day. But Daddy cooked almost every evening. He baked chicken or fish, put together casseroles, cooked a pot roast or chili, and made fresh salads.

Viktor had a friend, Julian, at school, and sometimes Mommy planned with his mommy to have playdates and sleepovers. Julian lived in a home with a slide and swing in the backyard, and a playful German Shepherd called Max. Sometimes, Julian's parents had family barbeque nights. They grilled hot dogs and cheeseburgers on an outdoor grill in the backyard, but they didn't do that so much anymore because it was getting cold outside. Like a patchwork quilt, from Viktor's accounts, Tara stitched together a fair idea of American life. To this she added the TV show accounts, until an American family birthed in her mind—an amalgamation of the Barone family, the Cosby family, and Julian's family.

Thanksgiving brought colder climes to Atlanta. The clocks fell back, which meant the days got shorter, and darkness lingered. The trees shed their fall magnificence, and within no time, they became eerie contortions of bare arms that stretched out toward a bitter sky. The low temperatures made it increasingly difficult for Tara to step out. She didn't have a coat or warm clothes, save for her one light jacket, but she was too embarrassed to ask Sanjay to buy her anything.

"You are stupid!" said Alyona bluntly when she saw Tara shiver, back hunched, arms crossed against her chest, after a short walk to the mailbox one afternoon. "You cook, cook, cook, buy so much grocery. Why you can't ask for coat? You ask husband today, okay?"

Tara laughed to cover her embarrassment. She had hoped Sanjay would notice her need for a coat and offer to take her to the mall, but Alyona was right, she couldn't wait any longer.

"Alyona said coats are on sale now," she broached the subject after they had watched *Everybody Loves Raymond* that evening.

"What's with Alyona this and Alyona that?" He sounded irritated. "Do you have to be friends with a hairdresser?"

It was the way he said *hairdresser*, in the flagrant manner his prejudices showed up. "I thought America is a classless society." she said sharply.

"There is no such thing as a classless society, not even in communist countries."

Tara bristled but said nothing after that. It suddenly seemed to her that she had married a Jekyll and Hyde character—the sensitive Sanjay emerged only under the sheets. Outside of it, she still had a cold man to deal with.

"Did you ask Sanjay for coat?" Alyona was on her case again the next afternoon. There was no getting away from her friend's persistence.

"I didn't have the chance."

"You silly girl! Come, I will take you."

Tara's eyes widened in alarm. A few quarters, dimes and pennies sitting in a little glass jar were all she could lay her hands on.

"No, no. I will definitely ask him today," she said.

"I will pay you for babysitting Viktor. You can buy coat."

"Oh no, I can't accept money for babysitting Viktor."

"Yes, you will. Come on now."

Because Alyona would not take no for an answer, Tara followed her to her Mini Cooper and wrung her hands and chewed on her fingernails during their drive to the thrift store in Decatur. She didn't know what a thrift store was; she had never heard of one before. The price tags on the coats made her eyes bulge.

"Everything is so cheap!" she exclaimed.

"This is thrift store, silly. All used clothes here," Alyona giggled.

"Oh! A second-hand store?"

"Yes, dear. Buy a coat, and some sweaters also. You will need them if you want to survive winter."

The musty smell of mothballs and mildew seemed suddenly stronger, and the clothes on the hangers appeared very second-hand. Not that it mattered—not that she was in a position to let it matter.

Tara returned home with a bag stuffed with two turtleneck sweaters and a black cardigan. She wore her new black woolen coat, which was not a very good idea because it had made her hot and sweaty during their ride back home.

Sanjay was home early from work. She found him on the sofa, still in his office clothes, forearms resting on his thighs, hands clasped together, and something about his expression told her she had tested his patience.

"You got home early today," she remarked.

"I thought you said you wanted to buy a coat?"

"Oh! I . . . I didn't know you had heard me." She perched on the edge of the loveseat, trying to think of something to say. She was suddenly so hot, she felt sick. She took off her coat and laid it on her lap.

Sanjay looked at her coat, at the bag that she had just dropped by her feet.

"You went shopping?"

"Alyona took me to the thrift store. I really had no idea you'd be home early to take me shopping"

"Thrift store. Seriously? Thrift store?"

His voice was rising, driving jagged bits of alarm into her heart.

"What did I leave work early for? You couldn't wait one evening? And thrift store? You disgust me." He stormed out of the living room. She heard the water run in the bathroom after a while, and she imagined an angry steam thickly cloaking him— like attracting like. She sat on the loveseat feeling weepy.

When he returned to the living room, her voice was still shaky with guilt. "Can I serve dinner?" she asked. He looked fresh after a shower, but his face still had *grumpy* written over it. He ignored her question and settled on the recliner, a glass of red wine in his hand. He turned on the TV, switched channels.

Tara tried again. "Will you be having dinner? I made some minestrone soup to go with garlic bread."

He kept his eyes glued to the TV and acted like she didn't exist. She waited an hour for him to say something, anything, before she decided she had to eat before going to bed. She shrank into the kitchen where he couldn't see her, hunched over her bowl on the counter. Her appetite faded after four spoons of soup and a thin chunk of garlic bread. She was upset that she had upset him. But somewhere at the back of her head, in a little crevice, was a slim happy feeling too. He had made the effort to come early to buy her a coat. If only she hadn't listened to that foolish Alyona.

Sanjay did not speak to Tara the next day or the day after. Fear burgeoned in her heart. She hoped Sanjay would not ignore her forever. By the time they went to bed the third night after the incident, Tara could take his silence no more; it had left her too high-strung all day. She pulled his rigid arm out with all the strength she could muster, and snuggled into him. He didn't react.

"I am sorry. Please let it go, no?" she implored. He lay immobile, eyes closed. She slipped her hand under his T-shirt and gently played with his chest hair. He didn't react, but he didn't push her hand away either. Encouraged, she played more; her fingers explored, caressed, moved downward, until they disappeared into his shorts. He grabbed her by her shoulders and turned her over. His passion was back, and hers even stronger after the strains and fears of the past three days. She melted into him with all her being.

He did not offer to buy her a coat again. Tara spent the winter wearing the black woolen thrift store coat, which hung a little too loose on her lean frame.

"It is the thought that counts," Amma said during their next phone chat. "Don't encourage the Russian girl if he doesn't like it."

"But Amma, I don't have anybody else to talk to."

"Doesn't he have any friends?"

"He does, but they don't ever come home. He goes out with them sometimes."

"Are they bachelors?"

"I don't know who they are."

Tara had once met Sanjay's coworker. They were on their way home from Publix when Sanjay had made a quick stop at Target to buy a razor. She was sure she hadn't imagined it—Sanjay was taken aback when the friend called out his name in the parking lot. It was an Indian guy, a little older than Sanjay, with a friendly manner. His name was Avinash, she learned. He worked for the same company as Sanjay, but that was the extent of Sanjay's introduction.

"This is Tara. She is visiting from India," Sanjay had grudgingly introduced her to Avinash, who kept glancing in her direction, all smiles, questions bursting from his bespectacled eyes.

Tara had only said hello, when Sanjay had quickly mumbled an excuse about being late for an imaginary engagement and run into Target.

Sanjay was awkward, and it troubled Tara. Was he ashamed of her?

"Why didn't you say I am your wife?" she had asked him on their way back home.

He was dismissive. "Oh, didn't I? I thought I had."

"Why did you say I am visiting from India?"

"Are you nitpicking?"

"Are you ashamed of me?"

"Now you are making me mad."

She had bitten her lip and looked away.

When Christmas season arrived, little lights mushroomed everywhere. Elves, reindeers, snowmen, Santas—they all came alive each evening, in the front yards of West Hill Road. Pretty wreaths adorned the front doors and windows, and a twinkling, decorated

Christmas tree stood inside each home, visible from the road, through the frosted glass windows. The little white house had a nativity scene, much like the Christian homes in Mangalore.

Sanjay took her one evening to see the seventy-foot-tall pine Christmas tree that had been hoisted to the roof of the Lenox Mall in Buckhead. What a magnificent sight it was! Thousands of lights, ornaments, and mirror balls glistened in the night, merging into one glorious, luminous pine shape.

"People come from all over the Southeast to see this tree," said Sanjay. "The Rich's tree has been an annual tradition since 1947. Just this year, it was moved from Underground Atlanta to Lenox Mall."

Tara looked around her. Some of the hundreds of visitors who came every year were here tonight, looking at the tree with as much interest as she was. Inside the mall, little kids flocked around a rotund Santa who sat on his throne in a white fence enclosure, a kid on his lap, smiling benevolently for the cameras. Some of the Christmas spirit was rubbing on to her, even though she wondered what the festival actually meant for Americans, beyond the lights.

Alyona's wreath was old and slightly misshapen, and her tiny tree was fake and had built-in lights. Viktor had left for his dad's for the holidays, so Alyona had no plans to celebrate at home. Two days before Christmas, the owner of Eclips Salon hosted a party for all her employees, with fruit punch, *olivje* salad, salami sandwiches and *lymonnyk* pies.

That evening, Alyona arrived with Tara's share of the party goodies, and a Christmas gift—a small square box wrapped in shiny red paper with a gold bow stuck to the top. Tara smiled happily for Alyona's gleaming digital camera, holding her wrapped gift lovingly against her cheek. Her smile widened when she opened the box. She loved the tiny, shiny turquoise earrings set in white metal, more so because they were a gift. She picked up one earring, held it against her ear, and the stone and metal radiated the joy she felt across her face.

"Thank you!" she whispered with moist eyes. "I shall treasure these earrings forever. This is the first gift I have received in America."

She was rewarded for her gratitude with whoops of joy and a warm bear hug. Tara wondered what she would give Alyona in return. She had no money to buy her friend a gift, and she could not ask Sanjay. She pondered over it all evening. Then she had a brainwave.

On Christmas Eve, she took a large casserole filled with chicken biryani over to Alyona's. The culinary adventure had taken four calls to Amma for consultation and guidance, and two major crises of confidence. It was an elaborate dish that called for the chicken to be marinated and cooked in a gentle blend of spices, the rice undercooked just right and lightly folded into the curried chicken in layers, and the mixture baked in the oven until it came out fluffy, aromatic, and multicolored. In the end, the rice was a little too dry, the chicken a little overcooked, and she had added a little too much salt, but Alyona savored every morsel like it was the most delicious food she had ever eaten.

The holiday season had done wonders for Tara's spirits, but the rest of winter had been depressing. She hated how her black coat weighed on her shoulders every time she went out. The first three months of the New Year were dreary: the trees bare, their boughs melancholy, the sun setting at five o'clock.

So when spring arrived in a burst of vivid exuberance, it was a season of revival in her, all around her. Purple, pink, and white flowers bloomed in every yard, the grass turned green with new life, and even the trees that lined West Hill Road were a riot of colors.

It was a season of rejuvenation for Alyona also, who dropped in one afternoon, her eyes dancing more than usual, her voice dripping excitement.

"I have a date!" she announced. "Please, please, please help me go."

A handsome customer with thick wavy blonde hair, had asked for her business card last week. Alyona didn't make anything of it, didn't expect to hear from the guy. But he had called in the afternoon and asked her out, sending Alyona into a tizzy.

"How can I help?" asked Tara, smiling.

"Can you babysit Viktor on Friday night? Please say yes, please say yes!" Alyona had her hands clasped like in prayer, and the most imploring look on her face, but for Tara, it was hardly a straight, simple matter. She was in a quandary. She didn't know how Sanjay would react to having young Viktor at home while he was around. But then, she didn't know how to say no to Alyona, who had been so helpful to her.

"Sure," she said, trying way too hard to sound cheerful. She had three days to worry about what she was going to tell Sanjay.

"What happens on a first date?" she asked, as Alyona did a noisy chicken dance, and stomped the living room carpet.

"Nothing happens. I'll meet him at restaurant. We talk over dinner. If I like him, I will let him kiss me on my cheek. That is all. Then I come back home and wait for his call."

Tara's heart turned mellow with good wishes for Alyona. She told Sanjay, when she couldn't not tell him any longer. Alyona's big evening was less than twenty-four hours away, and within an hour they would go to bed. He reacted the way she thought he would. At first, he grunted, eyes glued to the laptop. Then he chewed his cud slowly, deliberately. When he finally looked up, a scowl on his face, she knew that to be a precursor to an hour of unpleasantness.

"So, each time the Russian bitch wants to get laid, you are going to babysit her son?"

"Alyona is not a bitch, and she is not getting laid." It always irked her, the way he spoke about her friend.

"Right. She is only going to church with the guy. On a Friday evening."

"She is only planning to have dinner with the guy."

He sniggered. "Grow up, honey."

Honey. An endearment uttered for the first time. But said in rancor. Which didn't make it an endearment at all. Yet, she found herself foolishly, helplessly searching for hidden interpretations.

Alyona returned late, very late. Viktor watched TV, played Pokémon on his Gameboy, played a word game with Tara, and, when he could not keep his eyes open anymore, curled up on the sofa and slept. Tara pulled a fleece throw over the boy and turned off the lights in the living room. Sliding into Sanjay's favorite spot, the recliner, she prepared to wait. Her many attempts at reaching Sanjay had been futile, until his recorded message—in his deep radio jockey voice—made her nauseous. He had never stayed out this late before. Doubts, suspicions, and anxieties multiplied with each passing hour. She tried to stay with the ebb and flow of air in her lungs, but her mind digressed to a frenzy of thoughts.

Every once in a while, she sat up because she imagined the sound of his key in the front door. When he finally walked in at ten minutes past midnight, she waited in the darkness with bated breath. A light came on in the hallway. She heard him shuffle straight to the bedroom, feet dragging on the carpet. Ghost-like, she followed him there. Sanjay was sprawled on the bed, his shoes still on, reeking of alcohol and stale cigarette smoke.

"Where were you?" she demanded.

He made an attempt to look at her with glazed eyes, and grinned from ear to ear like she had said something funny.

"You didn't want me at home," he slurred.

"Where did you go?"

"To the place men go to when they are not wanted at home."

"Where is that?"

He laughed, closed his eyes. She bent over him and shook him by his shoulders.

"Did you go to a strip club?"

He laughed again, the obtuse, silly laugh of a drunk. Jealousy jabbed at her. She grabbed the front of his shirt and shook him harder "Tell me. Did you go to a strip club?"

"Let go, woman! I went to the bar with a couple of friends."

Tara let go, relieved.

"Am I getting some love?" he slurred.

"No. There is a kid sleeping in the sitting room."

Sanjay was snoring before she even got back to the living room.

Tara was upset with Alyona. Upset because she had come back so late to pick up Viktor, and upset because Sanjay had stayed away so late because of her. Besides, she had looked disheveled; hair messy, smudges of eyeliner and mascara below her eyes, and was in her pajamas when she knocked on Tara's door at two in the morning. She offered no apology, no explanation, and Tara sought none, not when any conversation could wake Sanjay and stir up a hornet's nest. But the next afternoon, it was the same bright-faced Alyona who knocked on her door, bursting with news.

"Greg is the one," she announced. He was sweet, kind, considerate, and a wonderful conversationalist. They had hit it off instantly, and spent hours talking.

"You were at the restaurant till two in the morning?" Tara asked, unbelievingly.

Alyona stuck her lower lip out, threw her arms around Tara and buried her face on her shoulder.

"You took him to your apartment?"

"Yeah."

"And?"

Alyona giggled.

"Oh my God, you slept with him?"

"It's okay. He is perfect guy, and I am in love with him."

"You don't even know him."

"I feel like I know him all my life."

"Did he call today?"

"Yeah, twice." She held two fingers up, sunshine on her face. "I am seeing him again tonight."

Tara hoped Alyona wouldn't ask her to babysit Viktor again. She didn't, thankfully, because she wanted Greg to meet her son. Tara felt her annoyance dissipate. Alyona's excitement was infectious.

"So, did your friend get laid last night?" Sanjay wanted to know that evening. Tara was amused that he was curious enough to remember and ask.

"Alyona is in love with Greg. She is sure he is the one."

"Aha! See, I told you."

Tara went red. "It's not like that."

"So, what is it like? Ooh, is it love at first sight? When Harry met Sally?"

"It wasn't love at first sight for Harry and Sally," she reminded him.

"Okay, whatever. You get my point. When this guy has had enough of her, she is never going to hear from him again. You mark my words."

Sanjay was right. Greg broke up with Alyona even before spring had officially ended.

"I think we need to see other people," he had said, after their last time together. Alyona came to Tara's apartment the next afternoon, demanded hot chai flavored with ginger and cardamom, and sobbed until mascara and eyeliner streaked gray rivers down her cheeks, and the tip of her nose turned red and shiny.

Tara's heart went out to her friend. She didn't know what she could possibly say to make Alyona feel better. All she could do was sit beside her, gently stroke her hand, rub her back. Poor Alyona. Sanjay could never be so cruel to her, not anymore.

Alyona mourned for a week, then picked herself up and moved on.

Chapter 8

Tara learned about the September 11 attacks from Amma. It started out as just another day. She settled down with her cup of coffee in front of the computer after Sanjay's hurried exit—he was rushing for an eight o'clock meeting. None of her contacts were on MSN chat, and her inbox was old and clean. With nothing to focus on, she began to notice the little things. The computer had gathered a little dust, especially around the CD-ROM and floppy disk drives. The desk was accumulating a litter of unnecessary things—a planner, notepads, a red diary, sticky notes, two pen holders, a calculator, a candle in a jar. Sanjay liked an immaculate house. She made a mental note to dust and declutter the desk later in the day. She pulled up Indian news websites and scanned the headlines lazily, looking for something interesting to read. Nothing earthshaking had happened that day, so she clicked on the Bollywood news section. Gossip was always interesting.

Then, Amma called, urgency and distress in her voice.

"Tara, turn on the TV, quick!"

"Why? What happened?"

"Quick, watch CNN. I'll speak to you later." The line went dead.

Tara ran to the living room and turned on the TV. It took her a few moments to comprehend the scenes that filled the screen. Her hand flew to her mouth, and she watched with horror as the North Tower burned. What was happening? Did people die? Were there people in the airplane?

At 9:03 she watched, paralyzed, as another plane crashed into the World Trade Center's South Tower. When Amma called her again, the South Tower had collapsed, and Tara was shaking like a leaf, weeping into the phone.

Tara tried to reach Sanjay several times during the day, hoping he'd come back home. Amma had warned her not to step out of the apartment, to be safe, to not call attention to herself. A third hijacked plane had crashed into the Pentagon, a fourth in the fields of Pennsylvania. Alyona and Viktor came over that afternoon, and they huddled together on the sofa, watching CNN, grieving for the thousands who had died a senseless death. Tara was glad for her friend's company, for some respite from the churning in her gut, for somebody to allay her fears. Where was Sanjay? Was he stuck in traffic? Or in his office?

When Sanjay came home, later than usual, Tara almost broke down again, from relief and the aftershocks of the apprehensions of the day.

"Where were you? I was so worried."

If he had met her eye, he'd have seen the agitation on her face, in the gray puffs under her eyes. He focused instead on taking his shoes off. "Sorry, I meant to call you, but I got really busy at work."

"Work? Today? Weren't all offices closed?"

He ran his hand through his hair. "Terrible thing, the World Trade Center and Pentagon attacks." He shook his head.

"I worried about you all day."

"You shouldn't have. What was going to happen to me here in Atlanta?"

"You could have called me."

"I know. I am sorry." He settled on the recliner and turned on the TV, and that was the end of their conversation.

She tried to snuggle into him that night, seeking comfort in the warmth of his arms, in the familiarity of his chest, but he seemed rigid, aloof.

"What's wrong, Sanjay?" she asked.

"Go to sleep. I am tired. You must be tired, too."

"I wasn't trying to seduce you."

He grunted, eyes still shut, and stayed immobile until she moved away. What a complex man, she thought. After a year of living together, she still had trouble understanding his many moods. Perhaps, this was his way of grieving?

Six weeks after the day of unforgettable tragedies, Tara received a letter in the mail from the Immigration and Naturalization Service. In it was a red, blue, and white card—the ticket to the American dream. UNITED STATES OF AMERICA EMPLOYMENT AUTHORIZATION CARD it declared boldly. She stared at the card long and hard, trying to catch a happy feeling over the din of other thoughts. She was allowed to work. But where? How? She didn't have a car. She didn't drive.

Tara preferred words to coding. She had worked for seven years at the news desk of the *Morning Herald*. A few months before leaving for the US, at Vijay's insistence, she had trained in computer programming at the Athena Multimedia Institute in Mangalore, barely passing her certification course. Her master's degree in English literature and work experience with an Indian publication were of no value in America, Vijay had warned her. No media house would want to hire her. They had Americans for those types of jobs. It was the tech jobs that Americans sucked at and needed Indians to fill. But programming had never been her cup of tea. The thought of taking up coding as a real job terrified her.

"I got my work permit yesterday," she told Alyona the next afternoon. She had not yet told Sanjay, who, in any case, was increasingly busy at work. "It's a project that is about to go live," he had explained, of his late nights.

"Yay! Girl, I am so excited!" Alyona high-fived her. "Now you are free. You can buy clothes, makeup, shoes, bags, whatever your heart wants without asking that husband."

"I don't know." Tara studied her hands.

"What, you don't know?"

"Who will give me a job? I don't have a car. How will I get to work?"

"I will get you job. You clean houses with my friend Nadya. She has very good cleaning service. She will pay you."

Tara smiled. Alyona had made cleaning seem like the perfect job. She wondered how her parents might have reacted to Alyona's suggestion. She thought of her high school years in Falnir, after her family had returned to Mangalore from Dubai. How often had Daddy said in those days, in rage and disappointment each time Tara came home with a poor report card, her math grade circled in red, that she was only suited to wash dishes and clean homes? Amma had, at most such times, cushioned her from Daddy's ire, promising him that Tara would do better in college, when she didn't have to study math and science. Amma was right. Tara had done well in college, where she studied English literature, sociology, and psychology. Daddy's dressing-downs had stopped. Still, it was a lifelong disappointment to him that Tara had not become a doctor or an engineer.

"I have to ask Sanjay," she said now, not knowing how else to decline her friend's kind gesture. But Alyona would not take no for an answer. She bustled into Tara's apartment one afternoon and grabbed hold of her arm.

"Let's go."

"Where?"

"Nadya is visiting. She is in my apartment."

Tara's instincts told her what Nadya's visit meant.

"No, no, Alyona. I have not discussed the matter with Sanjay yet."

"We are only going to talk. If you don't like Nadya's offer, don't work." Alyona led a protesting Tara out of her apartment, down the breezeway, into her own kitchen.

Tara had seldom been to Alyona's one-bedroom apartment; nine out of ten times it was Alyona charging, gregariousness and all, into hers. The apartment was surprisingly neat for somebody so whimsical. The living room was a cozy interplay of lace and dark wood. A large woven tapestry—a detailed hunting scene with four men and a dog—hung over the beige sofa. Assorted memories and keepsakes populated a bookshelf—a dainty gold-rimmed tea set, a gift from her ex-mother-in-law; four Russian dolls dressed in national costume; a vintage bottle of Coca-Cola; and several framed photos of Viktor.

Nadya sat erect, her expression grave, at the round, glass-top dining table, sipping hot tea from a dainty cup. She was tall, and her profile bore a straight nose with pride. Her hair was short and sandy blond. She wore a knee-length blue dress belted at the waist, and tan mid-calf boots.

"Hello," she said, rising from the sofa, stretching her hand out to Tara. A faint smile touched her lips, and died before it reached her eyes.

"Hello." Tara smiled nervously.

Nadya pushed a chair out for Tara, and then set about piling a plate with *sushki* cookies and dried fruit, which she placed before her. Alyona took the third chair, after she had brought Tara a cup of tea from the kitchen.

Tara nibbled on a dried fig as the conversation turned furiously Russian. She waited, a little bewildered, wondering what negotiations were happening on her behalf.

"Nadya does not speak much English. So let me translate," Alyona said finally. "She can pay twenty-five dollars for two to three hours work per day, Monday, Wednesday, and Thursday. You help her clean offices near Lindbergh. She will pick you up and drop you."

Tara cleared her throat. "Alyona, I told you, I haven't discussed it with Sanjay yet."

Alyona ignored her. "You make seventy-five dollars a week, three hundred dollars a month, then you go to Macy's and buy nice clothes and new coat."

"You look more beautiful," added Nadya, patting Tara's hand. This time, her smile reached her gray-blue eyes.

Chapter 9

Tara tried to be as still as possible in bed that night, not wanting to wake Sanjay, who lay on his back, snoring gently. But it was hard to stifle her need to toss and turn when her thoughts were racing in different directions. She felt constricted and conflicted. She was annoyed with Alyona. So pushy, so overbearing, she thought. Why couldn't she just mind her own business. For some inexplicable reason, she was suddenly reminded of her first friend in Mangalore, a near illiterate Muslim girl, who rarely minded her business; who had also put anxious thoughts in Tara's head.

Zeenat, the *rickshawallah's* daughter lived in the Beary compound down the hill. She came every morning for a measure of cow's milk, as did three other boys from the neighborhood. Amba and Ammi in the barn were full-uddered and bountiful, so Grandmother Indira dispensed her milk to those in need, like babies and guests, at a few *paise* a measure.

The first time Tara saw her, which was two days after their arrival at Shanti Nilaya, Zeenat had looked like a fairy in her long printed green skirt that flowed up to her ankles, white long-sleeved cotton blouse, and a purple voile veil over her head. She was very light-skinned and pretty, with pink lips and a pinker tongue, which she kept sticking into the gap between her front teeth.

Tara had said nothing to Zeenat because she appeared older and a few inches taller. Besides, she was strange, staring unblinkingly, first at Tara, then at Amma, then back at Tara as if they were fascinating fairytale creatures.

After Amma left for Dubai, when Grandmother Indira got busy in the barn, and Uncle Anand went out into town, Tara retired behind the wooden clothes stand in her room, hidden behind a wall of clothes, playing with her marbles. She stayed there for hours, lying on her stomach. This was her chamber now. She wished the oxide, red-bordered wall had a hole that led to a tunnel full of wonders. She remembered watching *Tom and Jerry* cartoons on the green clubhouse lawns with her friends Pippi, Leenika, and Runa. Sadness passed through her like a wave at the memory of her past life. She wished Jerry, the mouse, lived in a hole here. She would visit with him, have high tea with him in a miniature teacup with saucer, and keep him safe from Tom, the cat.

One day, hours after she had made herself comfortable in her hidden chamber, a face framed the foot-long gap between the wall and the stand. It was Zeenat on all fours, so cat-like that Tara almost expected a meow from her.

"Here you are. Hidden like a mouse," Zeenat said in Kannada, the language Tara's family spoke. "Your grandmother has been searching all over the house for you. Come out now. Don't you want to have lunch?"

This was the first time the fairy had spoken. Her voice was too loud for a face so sweet, and her Kannada was accented because she spoke a different language, Beary Bashe, at home. Tara did not ask Zeenat how Grandmother Indira had allowed her in. She came out of hiding and ran toward the kitchen, leaving the fairy to stare at her back.

Zeenat didn't often cross the threshold into the house, but sometimes, over the weekend, Grandmother Indira allowed her to use their spare granite stone to wash her clothes. The community washing stones in the Beary compound were continually reserved by older women.

From the verandah, peeping between the silver-painted grilles, Tara watched the fairy wash clothes on the granite block beside a clump of colacasias. Zeenat hummed Beary songs as she worked through a large mound of clothes, beating each suds-soaked piece of clothing on the granite block with gusto, wringing the water out of them, and dropping them into a pail of fresh water for rinsing. She often rewarded Tara with broad, toothy smiles. One day, late in August, Zeenat motioned Tara to come out and stand by her as she toiled on a dull yellow sari.

"How sad you are. Why did your daddy and mummy leave you behind?" Zeenat asked, with no salutation nor small talk. Tara felt ambushed; she had never been posed this question before.

"Because I have to go to school," she said.

"They took your baby brother with them."

"He doesn't go to school yet."

"I think they took him because he is a boy and they love him more."

Tara kept her focus on a shiny black-and-yellow millipede that was creeping on the cemented area around the washing stones.

"You don't believe me?"

Tara said nothing.

"Parents always love boys more. Girls are a burden on their parents. Boys look after them in their old age."

"I will look after my parents in their old age," Tara said defiantly.

"You will not. Your parents will spend all their money on your dowry. You are not fair like your mummy, so your dowry will be fatter. Then they will be left with nothing. Your brother will have to take care of them."

Tara couldn't let Amma and Daddy love Vijay more simply because they had to pay for her dowry. "I am not getting married," she said.

"Yes, you are. All parents get their daughters married. It is their duty."

Tara couldn't argue, now that duty was involved, so she stared at the millipede instead, which was slowly working its way to where Zeenat stood, stopping a few inches away from her black rubber slipper-clad right foot. She was pretty sure she was not a burden on Amma and Daddy. Amma had never said that to her. Ever.

"Are you jealous of your brother?" asked Zeenat.

Tara wasn't sure of what was in her heart for her brother. She rushed toward Zeenat instead.

"There's a worm near your foot."

The millipede had just started to coil, realizing the danger it was in, when death came suddenly, between damp cement and Tara's Bata slipper.

Tara cried for the poor dead worm that night, under the safety of her handloom blanket. Her cruelty had been sudden, and shocking to her. And even though some lives seemed as senseless as death, Tara vowed never to harm another worm again.

Zeenat was a fascinating storyteller, even in her less than perfect Kannada, and Tara was drawn to her new friend even though she put disturbing thoughts in her head.

"Do you know why I only go to the *madrasa* in the evening and not to an English school?" Zeenat asked one day.

"Because you are a girl?" Tara suggested helpfully.

"No, no. Do you know that a bee entered my head through my right ear when I was small? The doctors could not get it out. It lives in my head, buzzing about, eating my brain. How can I study with half my brain gone?"

Tara was horrified. "Will it eat all your brain?"

Zeenat nodded gravely. "Yes, as I grow up it will eat more and more of my brain until there will be nothing left."

Tara could not sleep well that night. She wondered how poor Zeenat lived and looked so pretty with half her brain gone. But the next morning, Zeenat had another riveting story to tell, so the bee flew out of Tara's head.

"You know what my Kuwaiti uncle bought me for my birthday? A magic doll. You turn her left arm, and orange candy appears out of her left palm. You turn her right arm, and lemon candy appears out of her right palm."

"Really!" Tara cried. "Can I see her?"

"Sure. I will bring her tomorrow. You can turn her arms if you wish."

But tomorrow never came. Each morning Tara asked, and each morning Zeenat slapped her forehead and said, "Oh I forgot. The bee must have eaten the remembering part of my brain." By the seventh day, Zeenat had changed her mind about bringing the doll.

"It is a precious doll. I don't want to break or lose her," she said. "Why should I take chances for you? Your father is rich. Ask him to buy you a doll from Dubai."

Tara looked away to hide her disappointment. "I had a doll," she whispered. "She got lost."

No, Alyona was not like Zeenat. Alyona was generous and loving. She whispered a silent *sorry* to her Russian friend for making the unfair comparison. Perhaps she had a point. Nadya's proposition seemed like an easy way to earn some dollars to cover needs other than her daily bread. But she knew Sanjay would be horrified if she told him, and so would her parents. Could she pull it off without telling anybody?

Nadya had four girls to help her in her cleaning business, but only two could make it to clean a row of offices off Mountain Valley Way near Lindbergh, three miles away. A third pair of hands would make things easier for Nadya. Tara would be picked up at four thirty in the afternoon and dropped back home by seven thirty at the latest.

Tara knew she'd be back home much earlier than Sanjay, who got home really late these days. He would probably never find out, if she played it smart. But a wordless whisper at the back of her head put a damper on her devious plan. A marriage was built on honesty and trust. She couldn't possibly live a double life. But then, he would say no. Toward dawn, from her ceaseless circle of thoughts, her tired mind picked a solution. She would work with Nadya for a week without telling Sanjay or Amma. At the end of the week, if she liked the job, she would talk to Sanjay. Her dilemma resolved, Tara finally turned a few times and slept.

Nadya was an efficient cleaner and a good teacher, even with the language barrier between them. She gave Tara a pair of yellow latex gloves to put on, and showed her the tricks of the trade. Together they went from office to office, dusted and sanitized the office furniture and equipment, vacuumed the carpet and mopped the floors, cleaned the mirrors and glass surfaces until they shone, emptied and removed the trash. Then they cleaned and disinfected the restrooms.

Most of the offices were small tech firms, but there was also a tax firm and a law office in the building. The offices were mostly empty by the time they went in to clean. Sometimes they encountered a lone techie or two working away on the computer, who rarely even acknowledged the presence of Nadya, but looked curiously at Tara.

"An Indian cleaner?" a lanky Indian techie with a goatee commented once, a smirk on his face. Tara turned red. She wished she didn't have to encounter other Indians at her job. It embarrassed her no end. She stretched her lips into a thin smile and kept her gaze on the job at hand, moving the vacuum quickly around the room.

"Why don't you work in a motel instead?" he asked loudly, over the white noise of the vacuum. "You might end up buying one someday, ha-ha." Tara kept her head down and escaped to the next room as soon as she could.

Nadya was happy with her trainee's progress and diligence. By Thursday, she had enough confidence in Tara to allow her to take on some chores independently.

"Monday, you clean tax office," she said, as she handed over $75 in cash in a sealed envelope. Tara had finally earned her first dollars in the US. For a while, it made her feel like she had been rewarded for a secret mission of great importance. It was exhilarating, even more so than her first paycheck from the *Morning Herald*.

"Thank you, Nadya!" She was genuinely grateful to the grave-faced, kind Russian woman for giving her a sense of self-worth, of freedom, even if it was with a job she was ashamed of doing.

Nadya's approval felt like a badge of honor, but Tara still had to tell Sanjay. She thought and rethought of ways to broach the topic. She could wait for him to be in a good mood, but he was so rigid and vacant these days. She could wait until they had made love, but then, they had not made love in over two months. The new project at work was killing him, and Tara wondered why Sanjay's employers had to slave drive him. Was it even legal?

On Monday morning, she stood behind the doorway to Sanjay's closet where he was picking out his clothes after a shower. The booming of her heart, the dryness of her mouth made her feel stupid, as did the fact that she had spent an entire weekend fretting over this conversation.

"Sanjay?"

"Mmmm?"

"Sanjay, Alyona's friend has a cleaning agency, and she has kind of offered me a job, and I was wondering. . ."

He didn't let her finish.

"Yeah, it might be a good idea for you to get financially independent."

He had not looked in her direction once, as if finding the right pair of socks from the box he was rummaging through were more important. What in the world did he mean by good idea? Did he even pay full attention to what she had said? She felt relief, and a tiny feeling of dejection. Did he not care about what kind of job she took up? Didn't he care about anything at all anymore?

She tried again. "I am starting work this afternoon from four thirty to seven thirty in a cleaning agency. As a cleaner."

"Good." He came out into the bedroom and busied himself buttoning up his gray shirt. Tara said nothing more. The feeling of dejection expanded and gave way to anger. It was as if she didn't exist for this man.

That winter, from the money she earned, Tara bought herself a new tan coat, some new clothes, and a pair of black leather ankle boots that made her look taller than Sanjay. With Alyona, she indulged in shopping for deals at the after-Thanksgiving Day sales. The two women spent an entire morning store-hopping at the mall and shrieked at the bargain prices. Then, they had Chinese lunch at the food court. She had never shopped at a mall before, not in the one-and-a-half years that she had lived in Atlanta. She sat in the food court with her friend, her shopping bags by her feet, pricking her flimsy plastic fork into chunks of orange chicken and fried rice, and laughed with abandon, despite her aching feet. It was fun to do something for herself.

A week before the Christmas weekend, Alyona prevailed upon Tara to get a hair makeover. "I will make you look sexy," she promised, "Like Marilyn Monroe."

"Nobody can help my hair," Tara protested. "It's useless trying. My grandmother gave up trying to tame it."

Alyona would hear none of that. "You come to my salon. We'll see."

Tara was wrong. In Alyona's expert hands, her hair became shorter, more even, and her dense curls framed her face, giving her soft features a sassier look. Her hair was now surprisingly more manageable.

"See I told you. You look like different person," Alyona said. "Next time, we give you highlights."

Tara was glad she had listened to her friend. She felt smarter and prettier, and she was anxious to see Sanjay's reaction. He took the wind out of her sails. He didn't react.

"Sanjay, you like my new hairstyle?" she asked him finally, but only after they were in bed, in semi-darkness.

"Nice."

She rolled over to her side, facing him. "You noticed?"

"Yeah."

She tried to snuggle into him, but he remained rigid. "I am tired. Go to sleep. Nice hair, yeah."

It had been a long time, and Tara felt good about herself that night, and she was in no mood to let Sanjay have his way. She slid her hand inside his shorts and stroked him. He tried to push her hand away, but it was too late. He was breathing harder. She pulled his shorts down. Her mouth took over from her hand.

"You are seducing me," he protested, before surrendering meekly. It was good to have her way sometimes.

Alyona had reason to have a spring in her step that winter. She was going out with a suave American who opened doors for her, carried her bags, and made her feel like a princess. Derek Quinn was floor manager at Nordstrom in the Perimeter Mall, and he carried the polish of a sales executive outside of his job.

"Derek is the one," she had declared, after their third date. "He makes me feel very special."

"I am very happy for you." In her heart, Tara didn't trust Derek as much as Alyona did. By now, she was inclined to second Sanjay's thoughts about dating men, but she said nothing to discourage her friend. But then, perhaps Tara's reservations were unfounded, because by spring, Alyona was spending more of her spare time, little Viktor in tow, at Derek's home in Chamblee Dunwoody, and Tara saw less of her in the afternoons.

Tara continued cleaning every office room and restroom with zest, aiming for perfection each day. But she wished she could work all seven days of the week. Sanjay's late nights continued; it was as if they were man and wife only on the apartment lease. On her off days, Tara felt a vacuum build within her toward afternoon, when she often caught herself filling with gloom. Where was she going? Was there a rainbow at the end of this all? Was Sanjay really busy or was he staying away on purpose? He had not once made the first move in bed in the past six months. Was he dealing with issues that she was not aware of?

Chapter 10

The rap on the door was loud and urgent; Tara almost jumped out of her skin. It was a hot, late summer evening, and she had not ventured out on her walk even at eight thirty in the evening. She peered out of the peephole, her heart racing, and was relieved to see Alyona, her nose longer through the concave lens, face bobbing up and down.

Tara opened the door with a quick jerk. "Hi! Is something wrong?"

"Tara!" Alyona grabbed her by the arm and made a dash to the living room. She collapsed into the sofa, dragging Tara down with her.

"What is it?" Tara scanned her friend's restless face.

"I don't know how to say." Alyona fiddled with her fingers.

"Say what?" Tara frowned. Alyona was never short of words. "What happened?"

"Your Sanjay. He is having affair!" Alyona blurted.

Tara stared at her friend blankly, her mind registered nothing.

"I saw him with blonde girl at Nordstrom. He bought her boots. I checked same model after they left. It cost a hundred twenty dollars! He bought her boots for a hundred twenty dollars!"

A shiver emanated in Tara's chest; it clasped her heart and squeezed it, but her mind jumped into defensive mode. Surely, there had to be another explanation.

"But Sanjay is busy with his project. It must be somebody who looks like him."

"Not possible, I saw him from this much distance." Alyona held her arms out to indicate a few feet.

"Did he see you?"

"I don't think so. He was busy looking into her eyes and talking, laughing, talking, laughing, rubbing her back, touching her arm."

"It must be a colleague."

"Tara!" Alyona grabbed Tara's shoulders. "This girl is his lover, I tell you. Why he would buy boots for coworker? Derek saw him at checkout register. Sanjay used his credit card."

The ice in her chest spread rapidly, its hold on her intensifying until she felt breathless and bent over, coughing. She gladly accepted the glass of water Alyona brought her, but gagged on a little sip, suddenly sick. She ran to the bathroom and bent over the toilet, waiting in a daze. She retched, then again and again, with little output. Alyona had followed her to the bathroom and was rubbing her back, talking incessantly. Tara's mind blocked her out.

"Tara, come, lie down, dear," she heard her say, finally.

She lay in bed, Alyona rubbing her feet, a warm cup of chamomile tea by her on the bedside table. The sickness subsided after a while; only a sharp, shooting pain remained, now steadfast and unperturbed by its physical manifestations. She wondered how she was ever going to survive pain of this magnitude.

"He buys her brand name boots for a hundred twenty dollars. You buy twenty-dollar boots at Payless. He shops for her at

Nordstrom, you buy at thrift stores. Your man is an ass!" Alyona's diatribe continued, her voice pitched high and thin in anger. Tara closed her eyes and crossed her hands over her aching chest. She wished Alyona would leave her alone.

"Is she beautiful?" she asked her at last, not wanting to know, yet unable to resist asking.

"Blonde, big boobs, nice shape, nice clothes. But all fake. Not real beauty like you."

Alyona's words speared her heart; she felt hot blood rush to her face. Sweat beads emerged on her forehead.

"You think Sanjay sleeps with her?"

Alyona went quiet, then asked her if she would like more tea.

"Alyona. Answer me."

"Hush now. You need to get some sleep."

"You think he does, don't you?"

"She is all fake, all dolled-up. Some stupid men like that."

Tara closed her eyes again. It was vivid, her mental imagery of Sanjay naked, having sex with a pretty, buxom blonde. She gasped for breath; the wetness on her neck trickled into the sheet. Tara was not blonde or shapely or buxom—she was just a very average looking loser who had begged Sanjay to keep her.

The chamomile tea calmed her nerves a little, and she finally dozed off, temporarily escaping reality. She woke up with a start when the light came on in the bedroom. He stood at the door, perhaps surprised to find her bedraggled in damp sheets. He searched her face but said nothing. She looked away, unable to even bear the sight of him. He went to his closet to undress, then disappeared into the bathroom. She waited, her heart racing, until she heard the running water of the shower. She rushed wildly, on rickety feet, to his closet. She fumbled through the breast pocket of the cream shirt he had worn that day. The faint, lingering smell of his cologne hit her senses, making her pain come raw again. She searched his pants, and found the cell phone she was looking for.

Her fingers were clumsy as she flipped it open and pushed up the arrow with two clicks to select text messages. She clicked again, and a series of messages popped up. They were incriminating, most of them. The last message in the sent folder was to Liz and it had been sent at 10:32 pm, perhaps after he'd parked his car. "Nothing trumps making you smile. G'night. Love you."

She clicked Liz's message which had come in at 10:20. "Love my new boots. Kiss kiss."

Tara pushed the back button and opened another message from the list. It was from Liz. "Still in my birthday suit, missing you already . . . xo xo."

She flung the phone into the laundry heap and ran out toward the front door. She found her flip-flops in the shoe closet, slipped impatiently into them, threw the front door open, and dashed out into the night. Down the stairs she rushed on weightless legs, and kept running until she was out on the road. She crossed the road into the church compound, as if with purpose. She had not joined her hands together in prayer since school, but she tried to yank open the large double doors to the sanctuary, frenzied in her effort. Her upper lip curled in, her teeth gnashed; deep troubled sounds erupted from her throat. But the doors stayed shut. She gave up, defeated, panting, her fingers sore, and sank onto the uppermost step leading up to the sanctuary. She bent over and buried her wet, sweaty face in her thighs. The tears finally came. They emerged in fits and starts before they grew to a steady flow. They purged her, then fed her more sorrow. It was a clear, warm night. A quiet, luminous moon, the same one from her childhood, was the sole witness to her coming apart.

It was almost dawn. A bird started to call from the church roof, and Tara could see the outlines of her apartment buildings opposite the road. It seemed like the beginning of just another day, but she had crossed a bridge that had collapsed after her. She sat spent, her tears dried up. She had to go back home, to her broken life; she had nowhere else to go. She pulled herself up and walked slowly out of the church compound. Her head throbbed with dull pain; the events of the night had triggered a migraine attack.

The front door was locked. She remembered leaving it open when she took flight last night. She hesitated before knocking. If only she could flee, and not come back.

He ushered her in and quickly closed the door behind her. She could not bring herself to look at him. She walked into the living room, shook off her flip flops and lay down on the sofa, face up. She stared unseeingly at the ceiling.

"Where did you go?" He had followed her to the living room and stood near the loveseat, arms crossed over his chest. She ignored him.

"Woman, you had me worried, I almost called the cops. And what did you do with my cell phone?"

She turned her gaze toward him. His forehead was furrowed, his brow creased into a frown. His eyes looked heavy as if he had stayed awake all night.

She opened her mouth to speak, but no words came out. She cleared her throat and tried again.

"I suppose you've figured out that your dirty little secret is out?" Her voice sounded hoarse, raspy.

She heard him sigh as he lowered himself into the loveseat. He rubbed his face, ran his fingers through his hair.

"And why exactly did you go through my cell phone?" His voice was high-pitched, defensive.

Tara ignored his question. He sat staring at the edge of the coffee table, chewing his lower lip. The silence between them reached a crescendo.

"I am human too," she heard herself say at last.

He ruminated her statement for a while, eyes still on the edge of the coffee table. "You chose to stay. It was your choice."

"I am your wife."

"It was never my intention to hurt you."

"Why did you marry me?"

He raised his eyes to look at her. "We've been through this before. It was a mistake."

Tara felt a lump in her throat. "After two years, you still think of it as a mistake?"

He remained silent.

She slid her feet down and sat up straight on the sofa. She felt tears sting her eyes again.

"Sanjay," she whispered. Her voice trembled with anguish. "When you made love to me, didn't you feel anything, anything at all in your heart for me?"

He turned his face away.

"Please tell me you felt some love for me," she implored, tears streaming down her cheeks.

He slammed his fists on the hand rests of the loveseat, pulled himself up, and silently strode out the front door. In a fit, Tara grabbed the copy of *Time* magazine that lay within her reach on the coffee table, and flung it wildly at his retreating back. It missed him by several inches, hit the wall with a crack, and lay limp on the floor by the coat closet. She slithered down to the carpet and slumped over, weeping.

She lay on the carpet, face down on her forearms, drifting between blackness, dreams, and grief. Somewhere, bells jingled; they were on Amma's feet, and she appeared looking young and beautiful, with Vijay in her arms. She waved from the train that was pulling out of Mangalore Station. "Bye, Tara, my sweet angel. We will be back soon." Amma's sari puffed and billowed as the train moved away.

Tara ran after the train as fast as her little feet could carry her. "Amma, don't leave me," she pleaded. But Amma was gone; she had vanished into the countryside like a mirage.

She woke up from her nightmare with a start, but before long another childhood memory came calling.

"See how your daddy and mummy abandoned you," Zeenat's harsh words rang in her ears. "Your mummy eats mutton every day, wears new saris, and has lots and lots of new gold. What do you have? Nothing."

Zeenat wasn't washing clothes that day. It was a Sunday evening, and they were at the back of the house, playing hopscotch hidden behind a mango tree, because Grandfather Madhava didn't approve of Tara playing with a rickshawallah's daughter.

Tara wished her friend would go back to her wild stories. She loved listening to them. But she hated it when Zeenat talked about Amma and Daddy.

"When Amma and Daddy come to visit, they will bring me new frocks," she said defiantly.

"You have too much faith in your parents," Zeenat said, shaking her head, as she hopped from square to square, her long cinnamon brown skirt pulled up to reveal fair bare feet. "I feel sad for you. For all you know, they might never come back. Then you will have to live here forever. I am only giving you fair warning."

Tara fought back the tears, but they seeped through her resolve and stung her eyes. Her heart yearned for Amma's comforting arms, to be reassured of her love. But Amma, she had abandoned her little girl.

Amma and Daddy and Vijay and Sanjay—they were all cast of the same mold.

When Sanjay returned a couple of hours later, Tara still lay on the carpet. He came out dressed to go to work after a while.

"Tara," he tried again, his voice was now calmer, more subdued. "Can I get my cell phone back?"

She didn't budge. She felt footsteps on the carpet; he was beside her, bending over. She smelled his fresh cologne, felt the moist heaviness of his breath. "Come now, get hold of yourself." She felt a light touch on her arm. She jerked her head up, and pushed his hand away.

"You touch me one more time, mister, and I will call nine-one-one." The shrill pitch of her voice shocked them both. He stumbled back and raised his hands. "Okay, okay, take it easy." The sleeplessness of the previous night showed in the puffy little bags under his eyes.

She buried her face again in her forearms. She felt his footsteps move away, heard the front door open and close, the gentle click of the lock. She was alone again, at the mercy of her anguish.

The phone rang. She opened her eyes, confused. She felt catatonic, she didn't want to move. She let the call go to voicemail. She heard Alyona's chipper, accented voice leave a message. "Hi Tara, this is Alyona. Just checking on you. Hope you are feeling better. Give me a call. Love you."

Alyona's calls came at steady intervals. The voicemail got them all. But when she heard a knock on her door, Tara pulled herself up and dragged her aching body to the front door. She put an eye to the peephole before she opened the door. Alyona burst in, carrying a brown bag and two sodas.

"All right girl, it's lunch time." She pulled out two chicken panini sandwiches and a bag of chips and set them along with the sodas on the dining table. "Come, sweetie, you must be super hungry."

Tara sat at the table. Her head still felt woozy and hurt from the migraine. "Thank you for doing this, Alyona."

"Of course, my friend. I've been through this. I know how it feels."

Tara sipped on the ice-cold Coke. It felt good. She was probably thirsty and had not realized it.

Alyona bit into her sandwich, and talked with her mouth full. "Did he confess?"

"He didn't deny anything." Tara took a small bite of her sandwich, but it was as if her throat had closed in. She struggled to swallow, winced with the effort, gulped more Coke.

"What an ass. You tell him—break up with blondie, or you will leave."

Tara nodded. "Alyona, how did you react when you found out about your ex having an affair?"

"I threw all his things out on the street."

"Really?"

She sighed and shook her head. "Sadly, that made things easy for that creep. He moved in with that girl and sent me divorce notice. After three months, the court made me move out of the house. So here I am."

"You are a strong girl."

"Life teaches you to be strong. You be strong, too, when you talk to that husband."

"Yeah."

"I know it is difficult for you to think. But he is not only man in the world."

Tara smiled dryly. "In my family, a woman is allowed only one man in her lifetime."

"So you become more American, think like American. You will be happy."

Tara smiled, wondering how Amma and Daddy might react to Alyona's advice.

That evening, Tara was seated on the three-seater, imagining Sanjay French kissing a naked Marilyn Monroe look-alike, when he walked in.

"What? You kissed her good-bye early today?"

He ignored her sarcasm and sat on the other end of the sofa, a cushion's distance between them. "If you are feeling calmer, we need to talk."

"Are you going to end your fling?"

"It is not a fling," he said calmly, causing her heart to heave. She saw no guilt, no remorse on his face.

"I am your wife now. You have to end it."

"Tara, I want to be honest with you," he said.

Tara blinked, but kept her gaze away from his face. "Do you love her?"

Sanjay sighed. "I know this is going to hurt you, but I want to be honest. Yes, I love Elizabeth. More than life."

Tara sucked in air. She looked at him in astonishment, his audacity crippling her capacity to react. He had said, "More than life," with so much vigor, so much shine in his eyes.

"Tara, you don't know what it is like to be in love. To be madly, utterly, helplessly in love."

"I don't? You tell me, Sanjay."

"I will tell you. From the beginning. Maybe you will understand, maybe you won't. But this has gone too far, and I'd like to be honest with you."

Tara watched him keenly as he related his story—at the sentiments that charged his face, blazing emotions that she had never once seen in his eyes before. She listened, feeling more and more stupid and irrelevant by the minute. By the time he finished, Tara knew that Elizabeth Bianchi was the love of Sanjay's life; that his heart would never open to another. Tara was not part-Italian, part-Irish, with eyes that hinted violet and gold locks that swayed and softly framed her classically beautiful, oval face. She wasn't a project manager at DCS Tech. She didn't intimidate men with her brains, and there weren't idiots aplenty dying to ask her out. She didn't have a great sense of humor and a husky, sensual voice.

Tara now knew the secret behind Sanjay's mysterious decision to marry her. It was to spite the tempestuous Elizabeth who had taken a transfer to Washington DC and broken up with Sanjay in 1998, after three years together. Sanjay was heartbroken when she told him she had met somebody in DC. In his misery, he had called his parents and asked them to find a girl for him. Liz had him in shreds, and all he wanted to do was make her jealous. He had married the first girl his parents chose for him. It didn't matter to him what Tara was like; she could have been a donkey for all he cared.

When Liz learned of his wedding in India through the office grapevine, she broke up with the other guy, an American, and came scurrying back to Sanjay. She was apologetic, remorseful, and wanted Sanjay back. And thus, Tara became the wife Sanjay completely forgot about, because lovely Liz was back in his life.

The Sanjay–Liz love story continued for almost three years as a completely oblivious Tara and her parents wondered what had happened to the perfect groom who had wanted no dowry. But Liz had broken up with Sanjay once again. This time, she had married the guy she moved on with, an American gastroenterologist in DC, Dr. Spinks. Her breakup notice to Sanjay had been a single line text message. He was disconsolate, but eventually resolved to stay away from Liz. He made arrangements for Tara to join him in the States. His heart wasn't in the marriage, but he had made up his mind to trudge along, plunging into work and career. But fate wasn't through with its whimsical surprises; it brought Liz back into his life a third time. A little before the September 11 attacks, she had returned to the DCS Atlanta office, minus her wedding ring. She had avoided Sanjay initially, but on September 11, she had sought him out, distraught from the tragic events of the day. Her brother had been in the South Tower that morning, and his family had not heard from him all day. They had ended up going back to her apartment. By the time the day had ended, they had learned that the brother was well, but it was too late to come out unaffected. Their old romance, which had never really died, was reignited. Sanjay learned that Liz had separated from her doctor husband—they had similar temperaments and seldom got along. She had taken the transfer back to Atlanta to take time off to rethink things.

"What choice did I have?" Sanjay said, eyes shining with earnestness. "Who knows why some people have that effect on you—why you willingly give up all control over yourself, why the rest of the world fades away, and why rules seem irrelevant. You don't go seeking to be helpless in love. It just happens to you."

Tara felt Sanjay's probing eyes on her face, but she said nothing. There was nothing left to be said. *You don't go seeking to be helpless in love. It just happens to you.* Tara understood that. Her own heart had melted once before in a way it had never melted for Sanjay. Still, it was difficult to feel any shred of sympathy when she was the irrelevant part of the love triangle; when her own destiny with her husband was sealed; when her heart was pulling up old fears from the back recesses of her mind.

Sanjay cleared his throat. "Well, I know I have hurt you and I don't know how I can make it right. But if you want to go back to your dad's place, I will make arrangements for your travel."

"I am not leaving." Tara said simply. "Until you divorce me or throw me out, I am not leaving."

When she turned to look at him, her breath was sharp but her gaze steady. "You have no idea what you put me and my family through when you left me behind for three years. The aunts and uncles, the neighbors, the community people—they would not let us live in peace. You have no idea. The questions, taunts, and unsolicited advice; I am not going through that crap again."

Tara had stopped attending weddings and housewarming ceremonies when the whispers got louder and more obvious, but she still had to contend with Amma's own extended family, especially when they gathered at Raj Bungalow for a cousin's daughter's wedding.

"Is your husband sending for you soon?" Amma's younger sister, Aunty Nanda, had asked innocently enough one time, the moment Amma disappeared into the kitchen. The family was gathered in the cool marble-floored living room, lounging on Italian sofas, and Tara would have vanished into the kitchen with Amma except that Aunty Nanda had put her arm out and caught hold of her as she rose from her seat.

Tara simply nodded and looked down at her hands.

"But why is it taking so long?"

"I know getting a visa doesn't take this long," Aunty Nanda's husband, Uncle Satish, said, his voice grating. "My nephew in Boston married a Mangalorean girl last year. She was with him in weeks."

"But Satish, that girl is very beautiful you know; ditto Aishwarya Rai," Aunty Nanda turned to face Tara, rubbing her back. "Eat more fruit and nuts, darling, put some meat on those bones."

She had additional advice. "And don't be a shrinking violet lost behind books. Be more lively like your mummy. Men like women with personality." She shook her head with a sad face. "Your poor mummy. How hard all this must be on her, even though she puts up a good show. What parents of girls have to endure!"

Tara mumbled an excuse and escaped into her bedroom, where she spent the next half hour shredding paper into thin strips, trying her best to stop the tears from creating embarrassing red rims around her eyes.

Unsolicited advice was the hardest to endure, as it made her seem like she was at the center of a scandal, exposed to ridicule, with nowhere to go to nurse her lacerated sense of self. She had endured enough. Escaping it all to be with the man she resented for putting her in that hellish situation had seemed like the only choice she had.

She looked at Sanjay now as he cracked his knuckles and decided on her future.

"You think you can take it?" he asked, eventually.

"I don't know. But I am not going back."

Sanjay chewed his lower lip. "Tara, I am not giving up Liz."

"Are you throwing me out?"

"No."

"Why not?"

"I am not. Liz is not ready to take any step yet."

"Does your blonde bitch know you've been banging your wife?"

"Jeez, what kind of language is that? It is so unbecoming of you."

Tara laughed hysterically. "Does your blonde bitch go down on you?"

"Stop it."

Tara laughed until she bent forward with the effort, gasping for breath, tears dripping on the carpet.

"Tell me, I need to know. Does she?"

"Tara, calm down."

"She doesn't, does she? She doesn't. I know Miss Hoity Toity doesn't." Tara fell off the sofa rasping, laughing, crying. She pulled herself up, swaying like a leaf.

"You are so undeserving, dear husband."

She dragged herself to the shoe closet, found a pair of sandals, and ran out the door, banging it shut, unleashing her turmoil at it. She walked all evening, down the main road, into the by-lanes, on little mud paths, allowing her feet to take her wherever they pleased. She saw people jogging and walking their dogs. Some greeted her cheerfully; they were jaunty aliens from a happy planet. A family of three little kids played ball with their dad in a front yard—so happy, so normal. Nobody seemed to have stumbled upon secrets that tore their lives apart.

She ended up in a deserted little park in a clearing in the middle of a thickly wooded area. A seesaw and a couple of rudimentary swings were all the park had. A dirty, cold grill lay on one end of the grassy stretch with a wooden bench close by. Tara made her way to the bench and rested her tired feet. A couple of chipmunks scampered past her. She sat there, her mind bereft of thoughts, the ache in her heart unbuffered. A gentle breeze swayed the old swings, their melancholy creaking so in sync with her mood. She stayed by the creaking swings until the sun set, and she could hear the crickets in the emerging darkness. The tall pines that ringed the park had turned into dark silhouettes. Somewhere, a dog barked in a backyard. When she finally made her way back to the hollow nest that was her home, nothing had changed, except that the sad creaking of the swings was embedded in her brain.

Tara avoided Amma's calls. They got more frantic after the third day, with more than a dozen missed calls and five voicemails on day four. On the fifth day, she picked up. There was no escaping Amma.

"Tara, is everything all right? Why haven't you been taking my calls?" Amma's high-pitched rush of words irritated her.

"Your dear son-in-law decided to take me on a honeymoon."

"Really? Where did you go?"

"To hell. That's where I am now."

"Tara! What happened, darling?"

Tara ignored Amma's question. "Amma," she asked, instead, "What is it like to be loved?"

"Why that question, baby?"

"Because I wouldn't know, Amma. I wouldn't know. I was abandoned by my mother when I was just eight years old. My father couldn't live without his wife and son, but he could live without his daughter. Now, my husband says he can never love me. How would I know what it is like to be loved?"

Amma's voice trembled, as it did each time Tara upset her. "You know we love you immensely, Tara. Tell me what happened, darling. Did you fight? Don't take his words to heart."

Tara quickly disconnected, tossed the receiver down on the floor. She lowered herself into the leather swivel computer chair and waited in stillness. The guilt and remorse, they always came. When they did, some of her anguish dissipated. She called Amma back.

Chapter 11

On Sunday morning, Alyona's day off, Tara knocked on her door with a request and a computer printout of a map. She had hated that she had to log on to the computer using *LizSan* to get the directions. Now that she knew of Sanjay's Romeo to Liz's Juliet, it didn't require a great mind to deduce what *LizSan* stood for. He hadn't even bothered to change the login name when she moved to Atlanta.

"Alyona, will you take me to the Hindu temple in South Atlanta?" she asked. Alyona, agreed without hesitation. "Let's drop Viktor off at Derek's first," she suggested. "I've never been to Indian temple. This will be so much fun!"

Alyona drove twenty miles down interstates I-85 and I-75 with her usual spirit of adventure.

The temple loomed into view, sparkling and pristine, after Alyona made a sharp right turn off the highway, through the open gates, and into the almost empty parking lot. The white *rajagopuram*, the steeple of the temple, built in *Chola* architectural style, towered in its magnificent splendor in front of them. The forty-foot-tall rajagopuram rose up five tiers, each tier rich in exquisite detail. Tara noticed a sculpture of Lord Narasimha on the top tier, and Maha Vishnu in various poses at the lower levels.

The girls walked up the steps to the shoe room where they left their footwear, and made their way into the main shrine of

Lord Balaji. Tara was thankful there weren't many people yet at the shrine. Even the priest was missing. She rang the bell outside the sanctum sanctorum, felt it reverberate in the chambers of her heart. She paid obeisance to the main deity of Lord Balaji inside the inner chamber before settling down on the red-and-gold-carpeted floor of the hall, folding her legs in lotus position. Alyona followed suit. Tara kept her eyes closed, while Alyona looked around mesmerized.

The temple was serene and smelled of camphor and sandal-wood incense. Save for a couple who circumambulated around the *navagraha*, the nine planets, the main hall was empty. Tara had not been to a temple in years. She had no idea why she was here or what she was seeking, but for a while, she had left the turbulence of her life outside the temple door. She didn't ask; she didn't pray. She sat in the stillness, in the present, her thoughts at bay, and that seemed like a blessing. Her breath flowed easy, unhindered by the powerful emotions that had become the mainstay of her life in recent days. When they pulled away from the parking lot of the temple, a seed was sown, a purpose was born, a determination grew to make a new life.

Tara was thankful to the universe for putting Alyona in her corner. She often wondered where she would have been if she didn't have her pushy, opinionated, but big-hearted friend by her side. In the next few days, Alyona helped Tara in a multitude of ways—a shopping expedition to buy a thin foam mattress, a single duvet, and sheets; a visit to Brad's Driving School; and a stopover at AT&T for a new cell phone connection.

Since the night of Sanjay's disclosure, Tara had been sleeping on the sofa. She didn't belong with Sanjay; she couldn't bear to be near him. With the new foam mattress, the study became her bedroom. She pushed the computer desk and swivel chair to one end of the room and made space to lay out her bedding at night. During the day, she rolled the mattress over, bound it with a plastic rope and stuffed it in her closet. Sanjay had said nothing about her moving out. Tara had not once looked in his direction; not a word or gesture or sign had passed between them. And yet she wondered if it pleased him that she had moved out of his way.

"Good riddance to bad rubbish, Mr. Sanjay Kumar," she muttered indignantly, as she lay in her new bed, under the cheerful yellow floral duvet, near the computer desk which creaked occasionally. She couldn't think of one logical reason why the desk should creak. It was not broken or unhinged—like her. Someday, when her heart wasn't as burdened as it was now, she would get to the bottom of the mystery. Her thoughts took off at a tangent. She wondered how Amma might react to Sanjay's brazen infidelity.

"We had a fight, and I am upset," was all she had revealed to Amma. Her pain was hers to bear, the challenges hers to overcome. She couldn't let her parents see how utterly unworthy Sanjay thought she was.

"Try to win him back, Tara. Try your best, darling." That is what Amma would have said, if she had known. As if Tara even stood a chance against the enchantress of DCS Tech, with whom her husband had proudly proclaimed to be "madly, utterly, helplessly in love." Amma didn't know what it felt like to be rejected, to be called a mistake, to be made to feel small, ugly, and unwanted.

Invariably, Tara's thoughts returned to Sanjay, who was probably sleeping on his back, his hands resting peacefully over the gentle heave of his chest. Were his last thoughts before going to sleep about Liz? "Madly, utterly, helplessly in love," Tara repeated softly. Was he a different man with her? Was he soft, gentle, caring? Did he cup her face and whisper sweet nothings into her ear? Did he kiss her; hold her tenderly even when they weren't having sex? Tara rolled over to her side, because the weight on her chest was making it hard to breathe. *If wishes were horses. If turnips were bayonets. If Liz would drop dead. If Liz would drop dead.*

She pressed her cheek to her folded arm and willed her mind to change thoughts. She had to focus on bettering herself. Learning to drive was the first step, even if it meant using up all the money she'd earned. She was glad she had enrolled at Brad's Driving School that morning, but the lesson had been terrifying. Her instructor Brad had taken her to I-285 and her heart had been in her mouth all the way.

"Stay in your lane, speed up, speed up! You are going too slow!" Brad's constant bellowing jangled her nerves. The large trucks and trailers on I-285 were Godzillas. She had come close to veering out of her lane and almost hit an SUV, but Brad had swerved the wheel in the nick of time, leaving her in a cold sweat. Her sixty-minute lesson was a trial that had pushed all other worries off her mind. She hoped it wouldn't be as scary tomorrow. But if it was, what choice did she have but to face her fear?

Driving was just the first in a series of enormous challenges Tara had laid before herself. Once she had a driver's license, she would look for a cheap used car. Then she would start a job search.

It took all of seven attempts for Tara to pass her driving test and get a license. Each time she failed, she had to pay Brad $75, her weekly earnings, for the trouble of taking her to the DMV. The first time, when the examiner asked her to step on the brake lights, she froze in the driver's seat. She had no idea what brake lights meant. The other times, the examiner asked her to take a left or right turn at the next crossroad, and Tara kept going, as if her test were one straight path. Either her mind refused to cooperate or her jelly hands rejected her mind's command to make a turn. The last two times, she had failed the zigzag and parallel parking tests, bumping into the orange cones until they dropped over. Each time she failed, she wept into her pillow, her tears draining her resilience.

"You need practice," Alyona said, with the authority of a seasoned driver. She allowed Tara practice sessions in her Mini Cooper, supervised trips in the by-lanes of their neighborhood, gave her directions in a series of sharply barked orders. "Speed up, slow down, turn left, turn right." She set up make believe cones at intervals—a wicker basket, a stool, a few bricks—and had Tara weave through them, or bring the car to a stop in a space between them, until she had perfected the techniques of zig-zag driving and parallel parking.

After two months of practice, Tara was coaxed to try the road test a seventh time. This time, Alyona took her to the DMV south of Atlanta, over thirty miles away. She had asked around, done extensive homework in finding a center that had no reputation for fussy examiners. It helped, psychologically at least. The examiner had a benign face, and that propped up Tara's confidence. She turned when she had to, tipped over no cones, and brought the car to an almost perfect position while parallel parking. She came out of the DMV, a wide smile slathered across her face, eliciting whoops of joy from Alyona. She could finally drive. No one would comprehend how big a personal hurdle she had crossed. She had driven to the top of Mount Everest.

Derek had broken up with Alyona earlier that fall. The post-breakup routine was a set one—dripping tears on Tara's empathetic shoulder, sipping her soothing cardamom chai or chamomile tea, and secluding herself in her apartment for a week. Then, Alyona was back to being Alyona. By December, she was going out with Brian McKenny, an energetic, buffed up Georgia native with sandy-brown hair, who owned an auto repair shop in Tucker. Again, Brian was everything that Derek was not, and she was in love like she had never been before.

It was Brian who helped Tara find her first car. He told Alyona about the white, two-door Mitsubishi Lancer, which had been offered to him by his pawnshop owner friend in Stone Mountain. Brian didn't need the car, but he had checked it out, and it seemed to be in good running condition. Alyona wasted no time in taking Tara to see the car. The pawnshop was a shocking museum of guns, gold, and gadgets, and the owner was a surly Santa with a flowing silver beard, but the Lancer was a stroke of good fortune. The girls took it for a test spin around the block, Alyona behind the wheels, evaluating its mechanical wellness— lights, brakes, accelerator, tires, air, heat, music. The car smelled like cigarettes and cleaners but seemed to be in fine fettle.

They headed out an hour and a half later, Tara steering her Mitsubishi Lancer down the main street, nervous and excited. She was finally in control of something, even if it was an old piece of junk purchased at a pawnshop for $675.

Chapter 12

Tara tried to avoid Sanjay as much as she could; they lived in precise compartments of her design. She stayed in her room until he left for work, and retreated in there when she heard him open the front door at night. It was a cage, but the inconvenience was of her choice, and it wasn't really all that difficult, given that he left early and returned late. She had enlisted Alyona's help in getting a membership at the county library. It was a shame she had waited this long to do something so simple. Books brought the world to her cage, as they had done in her childhood.

At Shanti Nilaya, ironically, it was Zeenat, who did not speak or write a word of English, who was responsible for Tara's acquaintance with books.

Grandfather Madhava caught Tara with the Beary girl on a Sunday afternoon, playing hopscotch behind the mango tree in the backyard. He silently confiscated their marker, a flat piece of stone, and gruffly ordered Tara back into the house.

"Have I not told you to stay away from that girl? As long as you live in this house, you will maintain propriety." His voice was a growl, his face dark like a thundering cloud. An irritated grandfather was worse than a grandfather who treated her like one of the walls of the house. Tara disappeared from his view behind the veil of Grandmother Indira's sari *pallu*, and stayed there through his dressing down.

"She won't play with the rickshawallah's daughter again," Grandmother Indira weakly assured her husband, but it was Uncle Anand who miraculously appeared on the verandah to save Tara.

"Come with me," he said, putting a hand over her shoulder, ushering her out of the house. "We'll find you new playmates."

He asked Tara to hop on his bicycle. They were going to Second Bridge, he said. She rode pillion, clutching the sides of her seat with an iron grip, keenly aware that the breeze was blowing her hair into a feather duster, and wondering who her new playmates were and how Uncle Anand had stumbled upon them.

But they arrived at a library. NEW ENGLISH LIBRARY, said the sign outside the door, painted in red letters on a white background. Tara was met with book-lined shelves covering three walls and dividing the room into three rows, and a small laminated checkout counter where the library owner sat, poring over the day's newspaper.

"I think miss will like the Enid Blyton books," he said in English, pushing his glasses down his nose to peer at them. Uncle Anand agreed and led her to the far end of the room, to shelves stacked with books by the English author. He picked *The Magic Faraway Tree*. The blue cover had an illustration of three children atop a tree.

"Here. This is your new friend," he said. "Read this book. Then come back for more. Read. Read. Read. Learn about people in England and America. Who knows? One day, you might even go there."

Tara nodded. She didn't want to ever go to England or America. She wanted to go to Dubai, to be with Amma. The last books Tara had read were two thick volumes of the *Fairy Tales*.

But that was in another life, a long time ago, when her own life had been a fairy tale, and her friends Pippi, Leenika, and Runa were impressed with her ability to string words and read whole sentences. She remembered the thrill of living the lives of Cinderella and Snow White and Rapunzel and Red Riding Hood over and over again until the stiff books had turned limp in her hands.

She felt the familiar stirrings of excitement when she looked at the cover of *The Magic Faraway Tree*. Three naughty children looked back at her from up a tree, beckoning her into their world, promising an adventure she would love. She came back the following week, completely smitten with Enid Blyton, and itching to say *hallo* and *queer* and *shan't*. Soon she had devoured *The Magic Faraway Tree* series and graduated to the *Famous Five* and the *Secret Seven* books. She craved English tea and fresh-baked scones with strawberry jam every afternoon.

Several evenings, from her upstairs room, through the grilles of the rectangular window, Tara saw Zeenat waiting for her in the backyard. A couple of times in the morning, from the inner sanctum of the house, she caught Zeenat peeping into the verandah from the topmost step that led into the house. Tara could have disobeyed Grandfather Madhava again because he didn't always keep watch over her, but she no longer felt the need for Zeenat's company. Zeenat said things that made Tara sad; Julian, Dick, Anne, and George of the Famous Five only made her happy. It was easy to decide whose company she preferred. So she stayed indoors, hidden away from her only friend at Shanti Nilaya, until she stopped seeing snatches of a voile veil by the mango tree.

A couple of years later, when Uncle Anand started to go crazy, it was a bunch of American teen detectives, Nancy Drew and the Hardy Brothers, who rescued Tara from a life of near isolation.

It was the ten-day Dassera festival. Every now and then, the beat of drums filled the air, sometimes distant, like the roll of thunder, sometimes reverberating from close quarters. The beats came from *huli vesha* groups. A bunch of teenage boys from the neighborhood got together in troupes, and went from home to home, dancing the traditional tiger dance for a few coins.

When the first huli vesha visited Shanti Nilaya, Tara watched from the verandah as the troupe members, stripped down to their gold satin knickers, painted head to toe in yellow varnish with black stripes to resemble the national animal, pranced and twirled, crouched and leaped to the beat of the drum. Even their faces looked so remarkably tiger-like—painted whiskers and all. They had on headgear made of papier-mâché and raw wool that resembled tiger fur.

And then, when they started to enact the killing of sheep, Uncle Anand undressed hurriedly on the verandah steps, discarding pants and shirt, and joined the dance. It was a strange sight, a fake among the pride, dancing out of line in blue-and-green-striped boxer shorts, and the members of the huli vesha split open their black lips to laugh.

"One too many, Brother?" the leader of the pride asked, pointing a yellow thumb toward his mouth, but Uncle Anand only crouched and leaped, crouched and leaped, his face in deep stupor, until Grandmother Indira ran into the yard and slapped him on his back.

"Stop!" she screamed, and he did at once, hunkering down, burying his face in his crossed arms. The drumbeat and the dance of the tigers stopped too.

On the ninth day of the festival, after lunch, Uncle Anand disappeared. A fretting Grandmother Indira, her brow knitted, peeped out at the hilltop repeatedly from the corner room window, but Uncle Anand did not suddenly manifest under the banyan tree like he sometimes did, no matter how many times she looked. By early evening, she could no longer ignore the dread in her chest. She sent Tara down the T-junction to look for Uncle Anand.

"Don't go too far" she said. "Only up to Beary store. Ask if he was there this afternoon."

Tara didn't have to ask, because she caught a glimpse of Uncle Anand just beyond the Beary store, surrounded by rowdies and little boys. The drumbeats of the huli vesha filled the air from somewhere in the neighborhood, and Uncle Anand was dancing again, shaking his head like a tiger and prancing in frenzy. Tara watched with a pounding chest, not knowing how to penetrate the thick ring of rowdies in their printed shirts open at the chest and flared pants, who were jeering, clapping, whistling.

"Anand Circus has come to Morgan Hill," the one in the gaudy yellow shirt yelled between catcalls.

When Tara returned with Grandfather Madhava, the crowd had dispersed. The beat of the huli vesha drums was only a rumble further down the road. Only Uncle Anand remained, on his haunches, his back against the compound wall, sweat pouring down his face and wetting his vest. Around his neck was a twisted coir rope with a small bell that he was struggling to undo.

Tara wished Uncle Anand would go back to being the Uncle Anand he once was. She missed their evening sojourns to the Beary store, the snacks he bought her. That night, he was in the mental ward at the hospital in Kankanady. It was schizophrenia, Grandmother Indira said. He'd had the same symptoms some years earlier, before Tara was born. Earlier in the evening, a decision was made. There was no more leeway for hoping, praying, pretending, or brushing the matter under the carpet. Uncle Anand desperately needed help. Zeenat's father Hamabba's rickshaw was summoned, and he came with his cousin Idinabba to coax a stiff, silent Uncle Anand into the rickshaw for their difficult ride to the hospital.

When Uncle Anand returned home from hospital, the monsters in his head had not disappeared. During his good days, he stayed silent; on his bad days, he often targeted Tara.

One Wednesday, returning from school, Tara was met by a *mundu*-clad, smiling Uncle Anand who filled the front doorway.

"Uncle, let me pass," she said.

Uncle Anand moved aside, and when Tara attempted to pass through, her spine prickled in warning. A chill clamped down on her chest when he grabbed her hand and walked her out again to the middle of the yard where he had assembled firewood like a small pyre.

"Divine Mother Sita," he said, prostrating himself at her feet. "Show them your purity, your virtue. A test of fire is what they seek."

Tara knew Queen Sita, wife of Lord Rama from the epic *Ramayana*, was a *paragon of virtue*; Uncle Anand had told her that just last month, when she had to ask him the meaning of *paragon* and the meaning of *virtue*.

"I am not Sita, I am Tara." Her voice trembled as she tried to reason with Uncle Anand.

"Your subjects, Mother Sita. Prove it to them."

Tara watched, frozen, as Uncle Anand bounced up and struck a match into the firewood. The pyre burst into golden flames, hissing, dancing, growing in the afternoon breeze.

"Mother Sita," Uncle Anand implored again with folded hands. "Walk through the fire, I beseech thee. Prove thy virtue."

Tara ought to have run, but it was as if her legs were pegged to the ground. She buried her eyes in her hands and let out a high-pitched cry.

"Aaaaaah, aaaaah, aaaaah!" she cried, even when she felt a pair of hands under her armpits, when she was suspended in midair and then delivered to the safety of the verandah steps. Grandfather Madhava, who had now retired from his job as postmaster, had saved her in the nick of time.

Following that incident, she latched her upstairs room door from the inside every night. She ached to lay her cheek on Amma's comforting lap, to have Amma wipe away her tears with her soft fingers, to tell her that all would be well.

Her mind drifted, seeking happier times, and scenes emerged, montages of another life: swinging on a swing in a lush green yard lined with rose bushes, the wind in her hair; helping Amma decorate her birthday cake with pink frosting and Cadbury's Gems, and then blowing out six candles in a pretty pink lace frock with red patchwork flowers surrounded by her friends Pippi, Leenika, and Runa. Was it all only a fairytale?

Tara did not remain downstairs without reason. She put all her effort into avoiding Uncle Anand, and when she saw him, she averted her eyes. She tiptoed out the back door to school every morning and slithered in the same way, and stayed in her upstairs room all evening until dinner time, away from Uncle Anand's maniacal reach.

Daddy's kinder, more loving younger brother, the one who told her stories and bought her snacks, had disintegrated into a million schizophrenic bits. The one person in her corner had pushed her into complete isolation. Nothing in life was ever absolute. Not love, not trust. Only books remained; they were her only escape from life.

She was relegated to a room again every night, this one across the world, but the solace of books remained constant. A couple of times, Sanjay had knocked on her door and burst in looking for a technical book or a manual from the shelf. It made her self-conscious of her new one-piece gown that barely reached her knees and left her slender shoulders and arms almost bare. He had brought in his manliness and the faint smell of shampoo—it stirred and stoked a longing in her, to be touched, to be caressed, to be loved; it morphed to anger when she remembered what had become of their marriage. She had her eyes fixed on the book, Salman Rushdie's *The Ground Beneath Her Feet*, and he was out as soon as he had found what he was looking for, impervious to her presence, her longings, her anger. How wretched she was, to still cry for his love.

As the months wore on, and her initial shock and anguish plateaued, her imagination sometimes went into overdrive. In her spare time, her mind crafted little fantasy tales. They all ended the same way: with Sanjay realizing his folly, recognizing Tara as the true love of his life, falling on his knees, seeking her forgiveness, taking her with tender passion.

She yearned to tell him that she was the proud owner of a car, which was parked in their common apartment parking lot; that she had the license to zip around in her prized possession; that she could drive and change lanes; that she had even merged on the interstate once. But she knew he didn't care. She lurked only as a minor inconvenience in a corner of his apartment. Like a roach.

"I don't care!" Tara whispered under her breath, but it was a rather loud whisper, and the corners of her mouth drooped after she said it. The sexy lingerie, it was certainly not to catch his attention. She dressed better in mall-bought clothes, got highlights in her hair, touched her eyelashes with mascara when she went out—they were self-improvement exercises that uplifted her sagging self-esteem. She didn't do any of this for him, and certainly not to come up a few notches in comparison with an evil blonde bitch.

Chapter 13

Tara had seen little of her brother at Shanti Nilaya. The first time he returned to Mangalore with Amma and Daddy during the summer of 1979, he wasn't even the brother she had said good-bye to. He was a four-year-old boy with curly hair who called her *Akka*, big sister, but said he didn't know her.

A week into their vacation, Daddy took his family to the Summer Sands beach resort in Ullal. They stayed at a luxurious red-tiled villa with soft beds and a palm-fringed pool, the vast expanse of the Arabian Sea before them. An idyllic weekend, so far away from her reality. Daddy looked every bit a Gulf resident in his gold-rimmed aviator glasses and swimming trunks. He was in a good mood too. He ruffled Tara's hair and joked about its unamenable nature.

"Thank God, it is only your hair that is wild," he said.

Amma, lovely Amma, whose fashionable chiffon sari billowed in the warm seaside breeze, shook her head, blinked her eyes at Daddy to make him stop teasing. "We'll get a haircut next week," she said, as if her hair were wild too. It wasn't.

Daddy asked Tara about school, but nothing about home where Uncle Anand was doing a good job hiding his paranoia from his Dubai relatives behind a stony face and deep silence.

"How is school?"

"Fine."

"Are you studying hard?"

"Yes."

"I am expecting you to be the first doctor in the family."

"I want to be a writer."

"A writer?" Daddy laughed. "All romantic notions in that head, eh? Reading is good, but writing is not a real career. Writers go hungry."

Amma shook her head again and called Tara her little Shakespeare. "Not all writers go hungry," she retorted. "Your room wouldn't be lined with books if they did."

Tara looked at her little brother as he sped from the pool to the golden sands to the ocean's cool edge to marvel at the frothy blue waves. She knew he would grow up to become a doctor or engineer. He would make Daddy and Amma proud. Even now, at four, he was a curious child and asked unending questions.

"My intelligent boy," Daddy said with pride, when Vijay wanted to know if the waves that licked his feet at Summer Sands traveled all the way to Dubai. The wind carried sea water across great distances, Daddy explained. So it was possible the water would one day reach Dubai.

Later that day, Tara helped Vijay mold wet sand into a castle. "Who lives in the castle?" he asked.

"Amma, Daddy, Vijay, and I," she replied.

"No. Amma, Daddy, and Vijay. You live in India."

"But I am your sister. We should all live together, no?"

Vijay contemplated this for a while, then shook his head. "No, you are the dragon. You are in the attic, locked up."

"Why am I the dragon? Why should I be locked up? I am your sister."

Vijay made curved claws of his chubby hands, stuck his tongue out, and made guttural growling noises.

"Do this, do this," he cried.

Tara ducked from the attack of Vijay's wet tongue. Then momentarily, the dragon was inside her as she gripped the back of Vijay's head and pushed his face into the sandcastle. Seconds ticked. The castle crumbled into wet sand. The palm of her hand felt his panic as he struggled to push his head up, get his face out of the sand. His legs thrashed about. When she released him, she realized that she had held her breath as long as she had denied her brother air. She used the edge of her frock to wipe the wet sand from his eyelids, and off his face. When she held him in her arms and kissed his cheeks, they were salty with tears.

"That man did it," she said to Vijay, pointing a shaking, guilty finger at a stranger's silhouette in the far distance. She didn't know if Vijay believed her, because he only bawled in return.

Vijay never called Tara a dragon again. After her family returned to Mangalore in 1982, he had no need for the protection of his big sister. Every evening, she stood watch as he played with other little boys and girls in their community, riding his bike or playing cricket or "catch the pillar." Whenever he fell off his bike, he picked himself up without crying. He was outgoing, talkative. She was quiet, introverted. At eighteen, Vijay had moved out of their home to live in the dorm at his engineering college in Mysore. Since then, they'd had little opportunity to bond because, after getting an electronic engineering degree, Vijay had moved to California to complete his master's in computer science, and then taken up a job there.

When Daddy got together with his drinking buddies, he never ceased to brag about his bright son whose zest, drive, and intelligence were unmatched in his eyes. He would sigh, a little tipsy from the scotch, his voice slurring mildly, and repeat his desire to be alive to see all the wonders his son would accomplish in his life.

Amma bragged about Vijay too, but always remembered to

add a good word for her daughter. "She is so creative. She writes beautifully."

At twenty-eight, Vijay was already director of business intelligence in a large healthcare company. At thirty-four, Tara still cleaned offices three times a week. And it was she, the big sister, who needed him now. She called Vijay late one afternoon and gave him an overview of her circumstances.

"I knew there was something crooked about the asshole," he said. "Something just didn't add up."

Vijay visited her one weekend and helped her write her resume. He was only an inch taller than Tara, but he had inherited Amma's translucent skin. His face shone brightly and was crowned with thick, curly hair. She didn't want him staying in the apartment, so he checked himself into the nearby Holiday Inn. In his hotel room, she settled into a moss-green upholstered chair and watched sullenly as he worked his contacts in the Atlanta area, hatching the best route for Tara to build a career in IT.

Soon, a plan emerged, after long tele-conversations with faceless, seemingly knowledgeable techies at the other end of the phone. A path was laid out for her. The first step would be to enroll in an IT institute run by an acquaintance of Vijay's in Norcross, to train in quality assurance. Once she had the QA certification, the acquaintance would help place her and take a cut from her salary each month.

Vijay was pragmatic and operated like the engineer he was. In his world view, problems were always material and had solutions. Tara was grateful to Vijay for the support, and for helping with the fees at Anil Rajgopalan's Qvision Tech Institute. And yet, even when he berated Sanjay, not once had he put his arm around her or asked how she was coping with her situation.

"You need to get out of the victim mentality," he told her matter-of-factly before leaving for California. "Focus on bettering yourself."

She resisted the urge to snap back at him, to return his check that she was holding in her hand. It was the same hand that had pushed his head into a sandcastle all those years ago. From where she stood, it was important to put things in perspective. At least Vijay had cared enough to rush to her aid. She smiled a thin smile and said nothing in return. She prepared herself mentally to go back to tech class, despite her poor aptitude.

The road to QvisionTech was littered with obstacles, like merging from the ramp onto interstate I-85, then getting into the third lane that took her directly to Jimmy Carter Boulevard, peering into her driver's-side mirror, making sure—then doubly sure—no other car was within disaster range in those lanes. Once she had passed the busy Spaghetti Junction, which looked like a massive, impossibly complicated intertwining of roads that left her awestruck, she then had the task of moving over to her right, which was trickier, with the traffic merging from I-285. She breathed a little easier once she was safely off the interstate and on the relatively non-overwhelming Jimmy Carter Boulevard. Overall, though, driving wasn't nearly as nerve-racking as she had imagined it to be. Or maybe fears became easier to grapple with when not facing them was no longer an option.

Her instructor, Samuel Varghese, was an amiable, stocky, bespectacled Indian. The first day of class, he took the time to learn the names of his eight students, seven of them Indian, and the eighth a Hispanic guy. He then introduced himself, waxed eloquent about his wonderful years of experience in QA, four of them at Qvision, and chatted with his students, asking each of them about their backgrounds and their former careers. Tara learned that most of her classmates had minimal knowledge of computers, and were, like her, wide-eyed, anxious, and looking for new careers. Her classmates had gleaned little about her, except that she had a background in print journalism and she had never worked in the US. The embarrassing bit about her job at the cleaning agency she kept to herself.

Tara willed her mind to be receptive as Samuel started his first class with the basics of software quality, the difference between software testing and software quality assurance, and the necessity of testing. When she loosened her grip over her thoughts, her mind wandered, but it was surprisingly stripped of emotion. Her mind created fleeting snapshots—Sanjay and Liz having lunch at a fancy Italian restaurant, giggling, holding hands; Sanjay and Liz kissing in his car; Sanjay saying "I love you" to Liz—and still, she felt no emotion. She pushed her stray thoughts away and brought her focus back to Samuel. He had progressed to bug reporting, bug tracking, and release certification—what they meant, she had no clue. She saw a teenage girl in a blue skirt and white shirt, her head bent, eyes moist, a report card in hand, and Daddy yelling in the background, "You are only fit to clean pots and pans."

She snapped out of the scene. *Tara, focus,* she reprimanded herself. *Daddy, I will prove you wrong.* Her mind had to stay on Samuel, on his full lips as they formed words, on his slight Kerala accent, on the words he had written, in neat round letters, on the blackboard.

Tara's days were divided into class mornings, work afternoons, and study nights, each segment filled to the brim with a routine that she was slowly getting used to. She got home from class, kicked off her shoes, changed into her comfortable work uniform, and waited, a bit impatiently, for the honk of Nadya's horn. She cleaned offices with the same zest—Nadya now trusted her to clean entire offices on her own—and her mind was filled with thoughts that did not always involve her husband the Romeo and his beautiful Juliet. Often, they involved recent experiences of the morning and new challenges of the evening assignments.

Sometimes, Sanjay and Liz came to the fore, and sometimes they lingered on, but she could will herself to think of other things.

She spent three hours of her weekday mornings at the institute, where she and the three other Indian girls in class ended up forming a clique. Shyamala was a housewife who was anxious to start a career in QA. Her two kids were in middle school and no longer needed her all the time. Anita had given up her job as a teacher's assistant at the county school system to get into the better paying IT world. Yasmin had been a doctor in India, who didn't want to go through the three-year residency program and the strict US medical license requirements, after she married and moved to Atlanta. Sometimes, the all-girl clique went to the nearby Indian mall for lunch after classes, where they gossiped, poked fun at the way Samuel held his chalk up like a school teacher and started almost every sentence with a singsong "see," and sighed at the assignments they had to work on every night. They were a motley crew, richly different from one another. Shyamala was traditional and took pride in her home, kids, and kitchen. Anita was outgoing, fun-loving, and talkative. Yasmin was graceful, health conscious, and spent a considerable amount of time every day on yoga and exercise. But their differences didn't matter as they bonded over QA and *dosas*, tests and kababs, virtual bugs and Chinese Indian lo mein at the food court.

Some days, after lunch, the girls walked the mall at a leisurely pace, stopping at the display windows at the stores. They oohed and aahed at the colorful, embellished salwar suits, saris, and jewelry that beckoned, and raised their eyebrows in exaggerated horror at the price tags. "Better to get from India," they said. Still, they walked in and looked around for good deals. Tara never bought anything and seldom contributed to the excitement of the window shoppers, but it felt good to just hang out with her new friends. Once, on a whim, her three friends draped a rose pink, crystal-encrusted, chiffon sari around her pink blouse and jean-clad self. She giggled as they marveled at her tall, slender figure, and went a little red when they wondered aloud if she had been a sultry model back in India.

To her family, she was too tall, too thin, and her complexion was two shades darker than Amma's. It amused her to think that her friends were marveling at these very flaws in her appearance.

Chapter 14

It was a regular weekday when, after a particularly boring class, Anita had a deep craving for *chaat*. The rest of the group agreed that tangy chaat was exactly what they needed to spice up their day. They trooped to the chaat corner at the Indian mall, chit-chatting, waiting for their orders to be called out.

As was usual with Shyamala, the topic veered around to her difficult mother-in-law who was visiting from Hyderabad. Anita had pitched in with relish, about how conservative her in-laws were. Yasmin said little, but laughed at the girls' stories with delight. She had never known her in-laws; they had passed long before she married. Tara didn't know her in-laws much, having spent less than a week with them. In the earlier days, when Sanjay called them once or twice a month, she spoke to them briefly, only exchanging pleasantries. Sanjay was rather brusque, cutting them off midway through their reports on family matters, offering them no glimpses of life in America. Tara felt sorry for her in-laws and wished Sanjay would show some love toward them. Now, she did not participate in the in-law bashing; she only raised her eyebrows and shook her head at appropriate junctures.

At first, when the lean, bearded guy with the thick, black-framed glasses approached their table and said, "Hello, miss," she didn't even realize he was talking to her. She pushed a whole *pani puri* into her mouth. It took a nudge from Yasmin for her to notice that the man had extended a hand in her direction. She shook it, mildly confused, her mouth full.

"Hi, I'm Abhi. I have a photo studio at the mall, Picture Me Photography. You may have seen it, it's in the left wing." Tara blinked and chewed surreptitiously, covering her mouth with her hand.

"Miss," he said, undeterred by her lack of response, "one of our clients, Raj Jewelers, the largest Indian jewelry store in the Southeast, is planning an advertising campaign in the local media. I am in charge of the photography for their creative. I've seen you a few times at the mall, and I think you have the perfect face for the kind of look I have in mind."

He stressed *perfect*, using his long lean hands, turning them ninety degrees at his wrist in her direction.

Tara was stunned, tongue-tied, and her mouth was still pretty full. What was the guy even trying to tell her? Was he kidding? Was he a weirdo? He did look a bit like one, with his unkempt, salt-and-pepper beard and wild hair. She swallowed her pani puri, almost gagging on the sharp juices.

"Miss, would you model for Raj Jewelers? It is a just a day's job, and you will be compensated well. This is a prestigious campaign. Say yes, miss."

Tara shook her head, bewildered, wondering how to get out of the situation. "I'm not into jewelry," she said.

"It doesn't matter."

"What would it involve?" asked Anita. Abhi pulled over a chair, sat down, and made himself at home with the girls, propping his elbows on the table.

"Just a series of still photos in beautiful clothes and expensive real jewelry. That's all. You girls can keep her company if you wish. My wife will be there too."

"Do you own Picture Me Photography?" Shyamala didn't seem certain.

"Yes, madam." Abhi dug into his pocket and fished out a few business cards, glossy ones with a glamorous Indian bride on the front. He distributed them among the girls, like he was dealing cards.

"Picture Me Photography," it said. "Glamour photos, portraits, weddings, events."

Below was the salt-and-pepper guy's name, Abhilash Sorte, and his contact details. Shyamala studied the card and raised an eyebrow at Tara, whose blank eyes gave no answers.

"Give us some time. She will get back to you tomorrow," Shyamala said, taking charge.

"Sure. Take your time. But please, miss, say yes. You have a perfectly divine face. I picked you out from a mile away."

Tara looked at the photographer. Her eyes flickered as a memory came rushing back. Divine face. Someone else had once said that to her. That voice rang in her ears again, after all these years. Her mind raced back to the summer of 1982, placed her atop Morgan Hill, then led her down the road that led to Saldanha Villa where her childhood isolation had ended, just as she stepped into her teens.

School was out. After lunch every day, when her grandparents rested, Tara slipped out and ran up the hill to her new friend Annette Saldanha's house. She always remembered to carry a couple of books with her; it gave her an excuse for her absence—she was at the library to exchange books. Of course, this meant that she never had time to actually *go* to the library, but it didn't matter. Daddy's bookshelf had enough English, Russian, and American classics to last her a few more years. Besides, she didn't read much that summer because she had become a hoarder of words. When she was in her room, she read stacks of *Reader's Digest* that Daddy had subscribed for her, focusing on the section, "It Pays to Increase Your Word Power," learning the definitions of new words such as *egregious* and *malign* and *anachronistic*, and storing them all in her brain. Then, each afternoon, she took her stock of words with her to Saldanha Villa.

Annette was tall, with a silky bob cut that framed her rather square but attractive face. She was Tara's senior at school, but they had become friends after Annette had offered Tara a ride to school from the bus stop in her chauffeured foreign car. The car rides had quickly become a regular affair. Annette talked nineteen-to-the-dozen all the way to the school gates, and called Tara a sweet angel for being an attentive listener.

Tara's new friend lived in a sprawling, traditional Mangalorean villa near Second Bridge. The villa had a warm ochre frontage and was enclosed in a high, white-painted compound wall that shielded it from outside pedestrian view. The front yard was large, and the red brick driveway that led up to the house cut through manicured lawns lined with pretty rose bushes.

The Saldanhas were Catholic. Annette's father, Roy, owned vast coffee plantations in Coorg. Her mother, Mariette, stayed back in Mangalore and helped manage their two luxury hotels. She was on the board of an education trust and a children's orphanage, and was a regular presence in the local newspapers for her philanthropy. Big brother James was broad shouldered, and had the square Saldanha jawline. But it was his friend Cyrus, who lived next door to the Saldanhas, who threw Tara into a tizzy these days. She lived in a constant, conflicted state of self-consciousness and abandonment.

Cyrus was tall, rakish, and all of sixteen. Tara had learned from Annette that Cyrus's father was Catholic, his mother a Parsi. Cyrus hadn't seen his mother since he was a baby because

she had run away with a Punjabi businessman and was not heard
of again.

Tara knew that the Parsis, who followed the Zoroastrian
faith, had migrated to India from Persia several centuries earlier.
The Parsi gene, perhaps, explained Cyrus's fair skin, but his eyes
remained unexplained. Often, Tara went home and mulled over a
burning question of earth-shaking importance. What color were
Cyrus's eyes? Brown, hazel, green, gray? They could be any of
these colors. Each time she stole a sidelong glance at him, they
appeared a different tint. Someday, she would muster the courage
to look at him eye-to-eye, and then she would know for sure.

Cyrus was gregarious, and his voice had broken fully. When
he laughed at his own ribald jokes, deep dents appeared on his
cheeks and made Tara wonder how he could be so happy when his
mother had abandoned him. He had a mop of straight hair that fell
over his forehead and covered his right eye, which he tossed back
nonchalantly every so often. A couple of times, Tara had felt his
gaze on her, and she had wanted to disappear. But why on earth
would he look at her? And why couldn't she be more worthy of
his exotic gaze? Why hadn't she inherited Amma's hair and light
skin? Every afternoon, when she got to the villa, she stopped by
the gate and tamed her hair with her fingers, pursing her lips hard
to draw some color to them. Yet, in his presence, she couldn't help
but freeze like an ice maiden.

During the holidays, two of Annette's cousins came visiting
from Goa. Angela, the older of the two, was in the ninth class. She
had big breasts and an eager face that lit up often. She laughed a
lot, and even more loudly so at Cyrus's jokes. Michele was thin
and pretty, with a heart-shaped face and a pointed chin.

Every afternoon, the Saldanha cousins hung out in the large
verandah, sipping orange flavored Tang and polishing off Shrews-
bury biscuits that the maid brought out. English songs played on
low volume in the background. They argued over what record

to play. James wanted to play Bob Marley songs. Annette liked the old Beatles hits. But Cyrus was a disco music aficionado, and his constant demand was for "Funkytown." He was voted down more often than not, because "Funkytown" was too loud for the afternoon. It might wake her mother up from her siesta in the inner chambers of the villa, said Annette.

They also played Ludo or carom. At other times they formed two teams of three each to play a word game. One team would pick out words from the *Reader's Digest* feature, "It Pays to Increase Your Word Power," and the other team would have to explain the meaning of the words. Then, the teams switched their Q & A roles. The team that got the most words out of ten correct won the game.

Tara discovered she was good at the word game, better than everybody else. Her team always won, no matter how difficult or rare the word. Soon, they all wanted her on their team.

"Tara, Tara!" Cyrus would chant loudly, making fist pumps and jumping up and down every time she charted their team to victory. "Tara and Cyrus make the best team."

The other girls giggled. Annette winked at Tara. Tara blushed and looked down at her hands, her heart always pounding inside her chest. Her reaction embarrassed her. She knew her face went red every time he cheered; she could almost feel the blotches emerge on her cheeks. Why couldn't she be confident and nonchalant like the other girls?

Once, he looked at her, and addressed her directly. "Tara means star, no?"

She froze.

He repeated his question. "Oy, Tara, Tara means star, right?"

She nodded. "Also, the Buddhist goddess of compassion who emerged from a lotus," she whispered. Her alarm grew when he dramatically threw his head back, closed his eyes and sang, his arms stretched like in prayer, swaying from side to side:

"Star light, star bright,
The first stargoddess I see tonight;
I wish I may, I wish I might,
Have the wish I wish tonight."

Stargoddess? She suspected Cyrus had made that word up. She released her breath when he finished and mustered a shy smile. The girls burst out laughing. Even James grinned from ear to ear. She wished her dumb heart would stop thudding like a drum; she was afraid he'd hear it beating.

For many days after that, Tara could not get that scene out of her head. A rogue clad in light blue denim and black T-shirt, his eyes closed, singing and swaying cockily. He kept her sleepless for long hours, and when sleep came, he claimed her dreams.

Was he teasing her? Should she be offended? Tara was in entirely new territory and had no clue how to respond. What if Amma knew? Tara had no doubt that Amma would forbid her from going to the Saldanha home again. She hoped Cyrus wouldn't tease her again. But she hoped he would. Why was she so happy? So tormented?

Amma, Daddy, and Vijay bid adieu to Dubai and came back to Mangalore for good in mid-April. She would have been happier if she hadn't been consumed with thoughts of Cyrus. For a while, her wretched heart had even been disappointed at their arrival. What if she couldn't slip out for her afternoon adventures? What was she going to tell Amma, who would see through the bogus "going to the library" story in no time? Tara stayed home for two days, worrying and fretting, and appeared so withdrawn that Amma wondered if Tara had a fever coming on. On the third day, she could stay away no longer. She decided it was wisest to tell Amma the truth.

"Amma, I have a friend at Second Bridge. Her name is Annette Saldanha. We meet in the afternoons to play word games. It helps us improve our English," she said.

Amma arched her eyebrow. "A Saldanha? What does Annette's daddy do?"

"They have coffee plantations in Coorg. Annette's mummy owns Villa Mahal and Gateway Hotels," she said. "Her photo was in the paper last month," she added for good measure.

Annette's family background seemed to please Amma.

"Oh! My daughter has learned to make high society friends and all!" she teased.

She gave Tara permission to carry on her visits, as long as the girls did something constructive and educational and did not go out on their own.

"See if you can play games to improve your math skills," she said. "And be back soon. Vijay gets bored all by himself."

Tara didn't tell Amma this, but she didn't care much about Vijay's being bored. He was six now, the same age she had been when they had moved to Shanti Nilaya, and her life had started to fall apart. She spared no thought in his direction as she sped up the hill on lightning feet. She was late, so she burst into a sprint all the way to the front gate, the surge of wind in her hair. She could hear the Saldanhas erupt into cheers when they saw her open the gate, so she couldn't stop to catch her breath, to tame her hair. They clapped as she walked the red brick path up to the house, breathing heavily through her mouth. She looked up at the group. She caught sight of Cyrus. Strangely, he just stood with his hands in his pockets. No cheering. No clapping. No comment said in jest. The dip in her spirit was automatic; she couldn't help but be disappointed.

"We wondered what had happened to our sweet angel," said Annette. "Why didn't you come the past two days?"

"My parents came from Dubai," she said softly, as if that were explanation in itself.

"Oh! We got worried."

"We are glad you are back," said Michele. "You have to help me win the word game today."

"No way! You were on Tara's team last week," Angela protested.

Tara was pleased they had missed her. Nobody had ever made her feel this wanted before, not even Amma. Yet, her heart sank. Cyrus had still said nothing.

Annette noticed. "And what's wrong with Cyrus today? Why so quiet, old chap?"

Cyrus brushed his hair back with his fingers and flashed his dimples.

"All is well now, isn't it? Aren't we going to get the game started?"

Tara's torment multiplied that evening; her questions occupied every nook of her brain. Why had Cyrus been so quiet? Why had he not insisted on being on her word power team? Why had he not teased her when she won the game?

When she took Vijay up Morgan Hill for a stroll at Amma's insistence, her answers to his incessant inquiries were absent-minded, curt. She wished she could confide in somebody. But who? Annette was always with her cousins these days. That night, her diary entry read:

> *O capricious heart,*
> *Will thou ever tame?*
> *O agony, bittersweet,*
> *What is thy name?*

Tara's poetic frame of mind ended when Cyrus returned to his gregarious self, which was the very next day. Then she only had to worry about how she appeared to him, about the effects of his teasing on her cheeks. And it wasn't only teasing. Sometimes, he tried to engage her in conversation.

"Do you read Alistair MacLean?" he asked her one day, while the conversation was on books.

Tara wasn't sure the question was directed at her.

"Star," he repeated. "Do you read Alistair MacLean?"

He had called her Star, the English translation of Tara. She shook her head, blushing a beetroot red.

"I've read two. *Guns of Navarone* and *Where Eagles Dare*, both about World War Two. Great books," he said.

"I'll look for them at the library," she managed to whisper.

"What book are you reading these days?"

"*Jane Eyre* by Charlotte Bronte." Her choice of books seemed suddenly ridiculous. She wished she were reading a spy novel or a thriller. Was Cyrus disappointed in her choice of books?

"Did you get that at the library?" No sign of disappointment.

Tara shook her head. "They are from my Daddy's collection of English classics."

She wished she had the courage to look into those bewitching eyes, rather than at the wall or the floor. But he was seated too close, his T-shirt was too stylish and the fall of his hair too charming over his forehead. Later, in the safety of her room, she would imagine brushing it back with her fingers, peering into his eyes, reflecting on their magical color; she would cross the threshold to immorality at leisure.

"She's read all the classics. Can you imagine?" Annette said. "By the way, we are planning to see *Chariots of Fire* on Friday. Tara and Cyrus, I hope you two will come."

Cyrus was in without a second thought. Tara whispered something about having to ask Mummy.

"Tell your mum our driver, Uncle Lobo, will take us to the theater and back. There is nothing to worry about," Annette said.

"Tell Mum Cyrus will be your bodyguard. He will guard you with his life," said Cyrus. Tara looked down at her hands as the others giggled.

Of course, Amma said no. She said Daddy would not allow it. She was too young to go out with friends. They had not met the Saldanhas and knew nothing about them. They would all go to Ideal Ice Cream Parlour in Hampankatta and have tall glasses of gadbad instead.

Tara escaped to Morgan Hill with Vijay and moped.

"So old-fashioned!" she complained to a rock, of her family.

Chapter 15

By mid-May, Daddy and Amma had found the perfect house. It was in Falnir, a nice neighborhood in the heart of Mangalore city, where fancy terraced houses blended with large traditional homes. Their home was on Model Street, in a colony of twenty-four houses, all painted white, with neat rose bushes in the front and a little patch to grow fruits and vegetables at the back. Pretty bougainvillea trees lined one end of the compound.

Daddy said they would move in by the end of May. Amma was thrilled that things had fallen so beautifully in place. Tara searched for some fragment of relief, of happiness in her heart. Day after day, year after year she had yearned to be reunited with her family. And yet, now, she found only despair. She wished for time to stand still, for the days to stretch on infinitely. She wished the end of May would never arrive. Falnir was so far away from Second Bridge; it seemed like a different world. How could she ever come to Annette's house? If only Daddy would change his mind and take his wife and son back to Dubai.

She continued to run up to the Saldanah house every afternoon, but said nothing to her gang about moving. Every day, she counted the days left to be in Cyrus's proximity. Would he miss her at all? Just a tiny bit? Even though she didn't belong to his world of attractive, self-assured girls—girls who became class monitors and excelled at badminton and participated in school debates and danced gracefully in his arms at the Saldanah ball.

The day she dreaded came too soon; the more she wanted it to go in slow motion, the more it galloped to the finish line. That final afternoon, in a low voice, she told Annette that her family was moving to Falnir the next day.

"What!" cried Annette. "You bad girl. Why didn't you tell us before?"

"Sorry."

"Oh, I will miss you so much!" Annette wailed. "You will visit us, no?"

"I will try."

The group continued to play their board games in silence. Cyrus refused to look up. His focus was entirely on his Ludo board, even when Annette sighed, and said, "Tara dear, you've made me so very sad today."

"I wish you all the best, Tara," said James, looking up from his board. "Annette, stop being a drama queen. Wish her good luck."

That afternoon, Tara stayed as long as she could, through the anxious hours of being ignored by Cyrus. Eventually, she had to leave, or she would get into serious trouble at home. The girls hugged her. Even Mrs. Saldanha came out to say good-bye.

"Good-bye, sweet friend," said Annette, planting a kiss on Tara's cheek. "You are the nicest girl I have ever met. I am going to really, really miss you."

Tara prepared to leave, then decided to linger a few minutes longer. Did she have the courage to say good-bye to Cyrus?

Annette noticed. "Cyrus," she yelled. "Stop being a donkey, man. Say bye to Tara."

Cyrus raised his head from his game and waved at Tara.

"Bye," he said.

"Bye," she whispered. There could be no more stalling. She embarked on the excruciating walk to the gate. So, this was it. She wondered if she should allow the tears she was holding back to flow. He hadn't even said a proper good-bye. He had acted like she was invisible, like she didn't matter, like all that teasing and wanting to be on her team was a joke. Yes, that is what she had been to him. A stupid, insignificant, irrelevant joke.

She pushed open the gate and fastened her pace once on the road. The sun was in the far west, the paved road that led to Morgan Hill almost deserted. She had gone a few yards down the street when she heard footsteps. They were close behind her, she could tell. She looked over her shoulder, too consumed with her turmoil to even be alarmed. Then, her breath caught in her chest. What was he doing following her? She stopped and looked at his tan shoes in utter bewilderment.

"May I walk with you till the end of the street?" he asked. She said nothing.

"May I?"

She nodded.

They walked in silence. The sound of their footsteps on tar amplified. She wondered what Grandfather Madhava or Daddy might say if they saw her walking down the street with a boy.

"God, why do you have to leave?" he said after a while.

"Because my family has come back. . . ." she started to say.

"Oh, I know that. But why do they have to move you so far away?"

She didn't know how to respond to that.

"Star, I will miss you."

Tara looked down at her feet, dumbfounded.

"I like you. Very much." The intensity in his voice shocked her. She said nothing, her tongue was in knots.

"Do you like me?" he asked.

She opened her mouth to say something. But what? What was the appropriate thing to say? She felt his fingertips on her elbow. She recoiled; it was her stupid reflexes again. How was she going to muster enough courage to not behave like a completely terror-struck idiot?

Cyrus let go of her elbow. "Okay, okay, don't be scared," he said.

They continued to walk in silence, two unlikely figures in the early evening light. They were almost up to the end of the paved street, and the Pentecostal Church at the northern end of Morgan Hill loomed into view. He couldn't possibly walk with her beyond the church. She stopped, and in a sudden burst of urgency, the courage she was searching for finally came to her lips.

"Yes," she said.

"What?"

"Yes."

"You like me?"

"Yes."

From the corner of her eye, through her moist lashes, she saw Cyrus smile. It was the most heartwarming, disarming smile she had seen on a human face. He touched her cheek softly with the palm of his hand. This time she did not recoil.

"Can you look at me for a minute? Please?" he implored. She obeyed. He dropped his hand from her cheek, stuffed it in his pocket. "I've always wanted to tell you a little story. I will make it fast," he said. "When I was little, my nanny had a framed picture of the Madonna in her room. It was a small print of a Renaissance painting, I think: Madonna with son, on a throne surrounded by white lilies. When I first saw you, Star, I was stunned. You look every bit like the Madonna in that picture, the same divine face. Unfortunately, Nanny took it with her when she left, or I would have brought it to show you."

Cyrus touched her cheek again, then gently cupped her chin. She closed her eyes. She hoped nobody from her neighborhood would see her like this. She wished she could still the trembling of her foolish lips. She wondered if there were women at the nearby water station. She wished for the warmth of that hand to never leave her.

"You have an aura around you of deep peace. You are so different from the other girls, so unique. Don't ever change, okay?"

Tara nodded. She, the Madonna? Aura of deep peace? He was wrong, of course. He had equated silence with peace. Little did he know that the sea was calm in the doldrums. Perhaps this was a dream. She'd wake up any minute and see that none of this had actually happened, that it was her heart's yearnings creating foolish fantasies while she slept. She kept her eyes closed.

"Will you be in touch?" she heard him say. She nodded. The gentle pressure of his fingers moved back up to her cheek. Then she felt his breath on her face, warm and moist. She snapped her eyes open in alarm. His face was just an inch away from hers. She looked straight into those eyes, the magnificent prisms that reflected light so eloquently, and then turned and fled down Morgan Hill. She didn't look back once.

She had the rest of her life to replay this scene a million times in her head, each time with a different ending.

The photographer's eyes danced with hope when she said a definitive *okay* to his request.

"Okay? You mean, you will work on the campaign?"

"Yes."

Shyamala, Anita, and Yasmin looked at her in surprise, while Abhi punched the table in triumph, his lips cracking wide open to reveal glistening teeth.

The photo session lasted several hours on a Saturday afternoon. Abhi's wife, Sania, who was a beautician and owned a salon at the mall, worked on Tara's makeup and clothes. Shyamala and Yasmin could not make it to the shoot, but Anita stood guard outside the dressing room. The clothes were from the nearby Hi Fashion Boutique. Tara posed in a variety of saris and salwars, Abhi gently goading her to pull her shoulders back, to stand erect, to look into the camera, to get the expression right. Then they dressed her as a demure north Indian bride, a red silk embellished *chunni* over her head, gold jewelry in the parting of her hair, a large nose ring. After they were done with the second shoot, Sania washed Tara's face, wiped off all the residual makeup, and worked afresh to create glamour. She held out a royal blue off-shoulder gown, causing Tara to almost back off from the shoot.

"I-I'm sorry, but can I wear something else?"

Sania sensed Tara's problem. "Don't worry, this is not revealing, just off-shoulder to show off the jewelry."

Tara hesitated, stalled. She couldn't imagine leaving her shoulders uncovered.

"Don't be a prude, Tara!" Anita urged, from outside the door. "You are so slim, you can carry it off. Even I wear off-shoulder dresses."

The majority opinion won, and Tara surrendered her inhibitions to the camera. During the shoot, she kept pulling her dress up at the bust, much to Sania's chagrin. "Your dress is hiding the choker, stop pulling it up." She glowered at Tara, like a teacher would a disobedient child, while Abhi only laughed.

"Focus here," he said, tapping at the camera on the tripod. "Forget everything else. Trust me, you are going to look beautiful. Who knows, Hollywood might come calling." He guffawed at his own joke, as he moved the spotlights closer to his subject.

Chapter 16

The girl on the billboard smiled coyly, a thick, ruby encrusted, twenty-two-carat gold choker around her long, swan-like neck. She looked striking. Hair perfectly coiffed into a top knot. Nose sharp under the spotlight. Rosebud lips painted red. Doe-like eyes highlighted with mascara, kohl, and blue-black shades of perfectly blended eye shadow. Her face and creamy bare shoulders dominated the billboard, with the advertiser's message occupying minimal space in the right-hand corner. "Shop our new collection at Raj Jewelers," it said, fancy white font against a dark background, then the address and phone number, in smaller size.

Tara cupped her hand over her mouth and squealed, "Oh my God, oh my God! No!"

Alyona, who stood next to her in the parking lot of the strip adjacent to the large billboard in Decatur, laughed excitedly. "No? You mean yes. You look like Cleopatra!"

Tara cracked her right eye open, and all she could see was her bare shoulders and the tiny hint of cleavage. "I wish they hadn't chosen this photo. Oh my God, I look like I have no clothes on."

"Don't be silly. Nothing is seen except your shoulders. You look like a million dollars, my dear. And look at that nose. You have perfect nose."

Alyona grabbed Tara by her shoulders, shook her excitedly. "You are going places, girl. You are a model now."

"You think Sanjay will see it?"

"Of course he will see it. A lot of other handsome, rich men will see it, too." Alyona winked.

Tara cupped her cheeks, shook her head. "I still can't believe how all this happened." She hoped Sanjay would see her, looking alluring. She tried her best to make that happen. When the same ad appeared in all the Indian publications in town, she picked up a copy of the largest circulated magazine, where her face stared out of the glossy back page. She laid the magazine on the coffee table. She agonized over whether she ought to leave it backside up. Would that seem too obvious? A tug-of-war ensued, in which humility finally triumphed over vanity. She left the magazine face up, but cleared her coffee table of recent issues of *Time*. Surely, Sanjay would pick it up, read it, then turn over to look at the back. Surely, he would.

That morning, at the institute, Samuel had been a little more attentive toward her, turning in her direction often during class, smiling widely, even a little lustily, said the girls afterward. If Samuel's attention embarrassed her, there was more to come at the Indian mall, where people turned around to look at her a second time.

"We are in the company of Atlanta's celebrity," said Anita. "Soon people will be asking you for your autograph."

"Stop," Tara laughed. An elderly man sitting adjacent to them at the food court held up the back page of the magazine for the girls to see.

"You are in the magazine," he said loudly, pointing to the page, causing everybody else within hearing range to look in their direction. He grinned broadly.

"Old man is letching after you," whispered Anita. The girls broke into peals of laughter. Tara's cheeks turned warm. She kept her gaze on her plate through the rest of the meal. This was all so unreal.

Not that she ever wanted or expected Hollywood to come calling, but the attention felt so good. She desperately wanted Sanjay to see the advertisement, preferably on the billboard, where she looked larger than life.

He did. On a Thursday afternoon. Tara, who had just reached home from the institute, was warming up a Lean Cuisine sandwich in the microwave for lunch. The girls had decided not to go to the Indian mall that day because Shyamala's daughter was sick, so she had to rush home after class. Tara thought she heard the creak of the front door, then footsteps in the corridor. She stood still, listening, preparing to take flight into her room. But he was at the open kitchen doorway in no time, blocking it with his towering presence. He looked ominous, furrowed brows on a dark face, arms by his side, fingers curled tightly into his palms.

"Why are you on the billboard?"

She should have been thrilled that he had finally seen her in her glamour avatar, but the hiss in his voice caused her heart to flutter nervously.

"I was selected to model for Raj Jewelers."

"Did it occur to you to ask me first?"

Tara looked away. She could think of several sharply worded retorts, but none came to her lips. She shook her head.

He took a few steps forward and loomed above her.

"You filthy whore, you posed nude on a billboard? Are you that desperate for attention?"

Tara closed her eyes. Indignation welled inside her. "I was not nude. You are just angry because I look more beautiful than your whore."

She heard him suck in air; a second later, a sharp shooting pain spread across her right cheek. She reeled, almost lost her balance in shock. He had actually struck her.

"Don't ever call her that again." He was a few inches away from her, a corner of his mouth dribbling fury. She clutched the edge of the counter for support, held the other hand over her burning cheek. She had never seen so much anger on his face before.

"Liz broke up with me today because of you and your filthy advertisement."

"Was she jealous?" She looked at him squarely.

She felt another blow, this one was more vicious; it made contact across her ear and temple. She winced in pain, her ear rang, eyes watered. She looked at him again. He trembled in rage, yet her anger was stronger than her fear of him.

"The guys got talking about the billboard, and Avinash Godbole who had seen you at Target congratulated me, said he had seen my wife on the billboard—and Liz was right there. Right there. There was no getting away from it."

"So, Liz didn't know your wife's in America and living with you? Too bad." Tara laughed hysterically. She sounded, to her ears, like the hyenas from *Lion King*. "So, your double life got busted, huh?" She bent over in pain as she felt the impact of his shoe on her abdomen, then another. A series of blows rained on her face and head; she wiped the moisture off her upper lip and saw blood on her hand.

Suddenly, it dawned on her. She could die right there, a victim of Sanjay's rage if she didn't get away. She made a dash to the front door, tried to unlock it, but he was right behind her. He yanked her hand from the knob, twisted her arm until she screamed in pain.

"You are not leaving now. I am not done yet," he barked.

"Sanjay, please. Don't hit me, please," she pleaded. "How is it my fault if Liz found out?"

"How is it your fault? Yeah, it was my fault. I felt sorry for you, allowed you to stay here, provided for you. Totally my fault. I should have sent you packing a long time ago, before you had the guts to drop your clothes for public entertainment. Do you even have the body to show off in public? *Hijra!* Eunuch! Yes, that's right. Do you know that's the first word that came to my mind when I saw you at Hartsfield–Jackson airport?"

The insult implied that she was unfeminine, the third gender. It stung. She fluttered her eyes shut as a rush of raw emotion clutched her throat. He moved away, flopped on the sofa, holding his face in his hands.

"Oh God, you destroyed me today, bitch. I've lost the only person I've ever cared for. She patched up with her husband and is packing her bags to leave for DC as we speak. I've lost everything. Everything."

Tara said nothing. A thick silence followed, punctuated with sniffs and sighs from Sanjay. "You know what?" he said after a while, raising his head. "I think you better leave. I don't think I could bear the sight of you anymore. I'm sorry I married you, I'm sorry I was kind enough to give you refuge all these years."

He strode to the front door with purpose, walking past Tara who lay in a heap on the floor, and opened the door with a jerk.

"Leave."

"Sanjay, please."

"I said leave."

"Sanjay, please, I have nowhere to go."

"I said out, woman! If you stay, there's no telling when I might be tempted to kill you."

Tara picked herself from the floor. She walked up to the door slowly, hoping he'd mellow, change his mind. He didn't.

"Take your purse with you," he said.

Tara walked to her closet, found her bag, and walked to the front door again. For a second, she had contemplated locking herself in the bedroom, but she didn't trust her instincts; her mind was too frozen to execute a plan. She pleaded again. This time, he grabbed her sore arm and pushed her out the door. She shuddered when he slammed it shut in her face.

She sat on the top step of the stairwell a long time, hoping Sanjay would open the door, but knowing she'd be too afraid to go back in there if he did. She tried to focus on what to do next. She rummaged through her purse, and luckily, found her cell phone which still had three bars. She tried calling Alyona at work, but got her voice mail. She contemplated calling Vijay, but decided against it.

Finally, it was time for the yellow-and-black school buses to drop off the elementary school kids back home. When the parents who walked down the stairs to receive their children gave her questioning looks, she pulled herself up and got out of the way. Such an ordinary day for so much drama, for her flimsy semblance of a life to collapse.

The sun bore down on her, scorching her sore face. Her head throbbed, and her limbs ached. She didn't know what hurt more—the beating or his insults. She let her feet lead her; her mind was still too much in shock to think of recourse.

She found her way to the seventh pew, near the side aisle, where she felt as invisible as she wanted to. She had never seen the inside of West Hill Baptist Church before. The sanctuary was a large hall with rows and rows of pews, the backs of which held copies of the Bible. There was one right before her, with a black cover that she touched with light fingers. The pews faced a red-carpeted, two-level pulpit. The lower platform had a table, some chairs, and a lectern. She noticed a piano in the upper level. Her eyes scanned the raised levels, looking for a figure of Jesus on the cross or of Mother Mary with her son. She saw none, only a bare cross high up the wall.

Tara closed her eyes and found herself in her school chapel, where she had prayed ardently for her mother to be happy again.

She saw the gentle face of Mother Mary. She saw Jesus, nailed to the cross at the wrists and feet, a crown of thorns on his head. Jesus who had suffered for everybody, who would make it okay for little Tara's Amma.

She fluttered her eyes open. She saw no point in stepping back in time, but stepping ahead was a mystery too dark to see. The nasty ache in her head was an impediment to any clarity of thought. She focused on her breath, on the air that struggled to get to her aching belly and flow out of her burdened chest. The sanctuary smelled mildly of wood and candles, like harmony and warmth. The stained-glass windows, several of them around the hall, filtered the glare of the afternoon sun, bathing her in soft light. And so she sat, a lone lost bundle in the seventh pew, making no plans, thinking no thoughts. When she felt a gentle tap on her shoulder, then another, she was slow to open her eyes. It took her several seconds to remember where she was. Then she saw her—sparkling green eyes on a happy face, a crowning glory of cottony hair. She was peering down at Tara, a buoyant smile on her pink lips.

"Oh my goodness! Did I scare you?" Tara had heard the Southern drawl on TV, but never from a real person. She shook her head.

"May I sit beside you? Do you mind?"

Tara shook her head again. She almost wanted to take flight, embarrassed at being caught in a place where she didn't belong, but something about the elderly woman—in the way warmth reflected in her eyes, in the glorious creases of her face, in the geniality of her words—made her stay.

"It's a beautiful day, isn't it?" The woman sank into the pew beside Tara, examining her face. "Are you hurt?" She took Tara's limp hand in hers, and patted it softly.

"I am Ruth Murphy. What's your name, darling?"

"Tara," she whispered.

"Can you spell it for me?"

"T-A-R-A"

"Tara," Ruth repeated, although it sounded more like *Terror*. "That's a pretty name. Where are you from, Tara?"

"India."

"I've heard so many good things about India. I've always wanted to visit, see the Taj Mahal. Have you seen the Taj Mahal, Tara?"

Tara shook her head.

"So, what brought you to our church today?"

Tara hesitated, ran her free hand through her hair, and, when a sharp pain hit her across her temple, she blurted, "My husband threw me out."

She felt a warm, white hand, crisscrossed with translucent green veins, squeeze hers. "Bless your heart. He hurt you before turning you out, didn't he?"

Tara nodded.

"Would you like me to call the police?"

Tara's eyes widened in alarm. "No, no!" she said emphatically. "Not the police. Please."

"All right, all right. We are not going to the police." Ruth's voice was reassuring. "Do you need to see a doctor? Are you hurt? We can go to urgent care. It is just two minutes away."

"No, no. I am all right. I just need a painkiller for my headache."

"I could take you to CVS, but I have a better plan. How about we go to my place, have a bite to eat, take a painkiller, and relax a bit?"

Again that rich drawl, words stretched in upward curves beyond Tara's comprehension. "I beg your pardon?"

"Let's go over to my place, my house."

Tara understood this time, but wasn't sure how to respond.

"Doodlebug will be thrilled to meet you. She loves company."

Tara looked at Ruth, a question mark on her face.

"That's my little doggie. She loves to meet people."

Tara nodded. It was not like she had other options. Alyona was still at work. She didn't feel close enough to her QVision Tech friends to seek their help.

Chapter 17

Ruth Murphy lived down the street in a two-story, four-bedroom Cape Cod cottage with a steep pitched roof and dormer windows. The front yard was a vibrant bouquet—like the owner of the house, thought Tara. Gerbera daisies, azaleas, and day lilies nodded in the light afternoon breeze, secure among the oaks, magnolias, and dogwoods. Ruth pulled her red Oldsmobile up the paved driveway into the two-car garage. They entered the house, past a short hallway, into the kitchen, where polished pine wood met Tara's eyes, and the mild smell of cinnamon wax and baked bread greeted her senses.

Tara had never been inside an American home before. Ruth ushered her into the family room, a charming interplay of wainscot paneling and old-world furniture, with a glass-and-brass enclosed fireplace that occupied the far wall. Tara slipped into the comfort of a soft fabric sofa and strained her neck to stare silently at a quaint town square scene on a large frame that adorned the wall behind her, as if the clues to her future lurked in the painting.

Later, after Tara had lunched on pickled cucumber and cream cheese sandwiches, washed it down with coffee so strong it felt like a tall mug of bitterness, finished it off with a large square of homemade brownie, and popped two Advils for her pain, she felt more human again.

Doodlebug was a child with an ever-smiling face, her mom insisted. To Tara, she was a friendly Yorkshire terrier with a glossy blue-black-tan coat and a moist black button of a nose. Together, dog and woman lounged on a wicker chair in the screened-in porch that overlooked a dry creek and woods past the grassy backyard. From the adjoining deck floated the herbal aromas of potted rosemary, thyme, and parsley, smells so foreign compared to the coriander and mint bunches of Amma's garden.

Doodlebug jumped from Tara's lap to her feet and back, madly wagging her tail, begging to be indulged, which Tara did, stroking her soft head, petting her under her chin. Doodlebug responded with happy noises and a dripping tongue, and Tara smiled as if she didn't have a care in the world.

The back porch opened into the family room where Ruth spent time making calls, talking to the church pastor, and then, based on his references, to some other folks. Tara watched the older woman's animated face from her vantage point, at the way she blinked her eyes in rapt attention, absentmindedly tapping her wooden pen on her writing pad, then responding with a stream of words spoken with wide-mouthed cadence, words utterly lost on Tara.

It shocked her, every now and then, that she felt no earth-shaking fear or sadness, as if her problem were too enormous to infiltrate into her. Each time the horrors of the day started to play back in her head, Doodlebug would put a paw on her knee or a wet nose near her arm, and reality would go over to a corner and wait.

When Ruth finished her calls, Tara walked up to her and said, "Miss Murphy, my friend Alyona must be back from work. Would you please drop me to her place?"

"Call me Ruth. Make me feel young." Ruth's warm smile crinkled her eyes. "Where does Alyona live?"

"She is my neighbor."

"Does she live on the same floor as you?"

Tara nodded.

"How about we invite Alyona over for dinner tonight? I am sure she will enjoy my pot roast."

Tara hesitated. "I've already troubled you enough."

"Doodlebug and I love company, don't we, Doodlebug?" The Yorkshire terrier wagged her tail happily. "We don't know what frame of mind your husband is in. We are not sure you are safe walking into a place where he can see you. How about you give this old woman company tonight? Tomorrow, we will find you some legal help."

Tara strained to understand Ruth, she watched her lips intently. "Legal help?"

"Yes, I just spoke to Joe Crawley, an attorney known to our pastor, David. Joe says there are several groups in DeKalb County that offer free legal help to victims of domestic abuse." She took Tara's hand and motioned her to sit beside her. "I have a couple of numbers. Tomorrow, we will fix up an appointment, pay a visit to one of these centers."

And suddenly, the boulder that stood waiting in a corner came rolling toward Tara. She shook a little as she tried to grapple with the complexities unfolding before her. She felt ignorant; she knew so little, understood so little.

"Will Sanjay—my husband, Sanjay, will he be in trouble?"

"He deserves to be in trouble, don't you think?"

Tara shook her head vigorously. "Will he be arrested? I don't want him to be arrested, please, Miss Murphy."

Ruth patted her forearm kindly. Doodlebug, sensing Tara's agitation, licked her face.

"He has never hit me before. This was the only time."

"Do you want to go back to him?"

Tara contemplated the question. She closed her eyes. An

image appeared before her, like an apparition. Sanjay, unhinged, his face contorted in rage, spewing insults. "Hijra! When I saw you at Hartsfield–Jackson airport, that's the first word that came to my mind." She felt his kicks to her abdomen, the blows to her head, to her face, the twisting of her arm, her screams. She covered her face in her hands, shook her head.

"It's okay." Ruth stroked her hair. "It's okay, honey. Do you have a job?"

"I work only part time cleaning offices." Somehow, the embarrassing secret that she had kept hidden from her family and Indian friends seemed safe with Ruth. She didn't think Ruth would judge her, look down on her, or laugh at the menial nature of her job.

"Do you make enough to live on your own?"

Tara shook her head. "I go to an IT training institute in the mornings. I am training to get certification in quality assurance."

"So, until you are certified and get a job in computers, you will need help to begin afresh. That's what we will discuss with the advocate at the legal center."

"So, Sanjay will not be arrested if we seek help from the legal center?"

"Not unless that is what you want. We will only discuss your options. You don't have to act on any of them."

Tara nodded. Her instinct told her she could trust sweet Ruth, a stranger until that morning, to do what was best for her. "All right, Miss Murphy."

"Ruth."

Tara managed a feeble smile. "Thank you, Ruth, for everything."

At supper time, Tara was helping Ruth set the table for dinner, laying floral, gold-rimmed china over green-and-wine maple-leaf-patterned placemats, when Dottie Payton, who lived next door, walked in through the kitchen door. She studied Tara with curious eyes before stretching out her hand.

"Hello, hello! I am Dottie; nice to meet you."

Dottie reminded Tara of Agatha Christie's detective, Miss Marple, with her perfectly curled salt-and-pepper hair, crisp sea-green pant suit, flat tan pumps, and inquisitive blue eyes. Before the end of the evening, Tara had learned that Dottie and Ruth were as thick as thieves—but they belonged to different poles. Dottie was yin to Ruth's yang. Ruth was impulsive, Dottie weighed matters carefully. Ruth was the doer, Dottie the thinker. With Ruth, words flowed in a rapid torrent, or so it seemed to Tara. Dottie spoke slowly, enunciating each word, so Tara understood her better. But they concurred over one thing—that their opposite natures were an advantage in their daily adventures. They argued, teased, and laughed at each other's expense, but "it was all in good fun," insisted Ruth. Dottie fussed at Ruth for leaving her behind at the church clothes closet that morning, while she drove Tara home.

"She left me behind to do all the sorting, folding, pricing— all the dirty work by myself," she complained.

"Well Dottie, it seems like God favored me over you, didn't he? He put me at a place where I could see Tara. He knew I needed to be with her."

Dottie grudgingly agreed.

At six thirty, Alyona bustled in with Viktor. Tara was relieved to see them, familiar faces in a sea of newness. She threw her arms around Alyona, sinking her face into her shoulder. She felt weepy in Alyona's comforting bear hug.

"You are not going back to him. You are not," Alyona said. Tara nodded in agreement.

Chapter 18

Tara slept fitfully during the night, waking up in a cold sweat in Ruth's guest bedroom, repeatedly tossing aside the wine-colored blanket, then covering herself. Like an old scratchy tape recorder, her mind kept returning to the big events of the day. The bigger shock, however, was to wake up again and again and find herself in a stranger's bedroom—a stranger so far removed from her normal existence.

She dozed off again when dawn began to break. Sanjay was back, towering over her, peering down into her wide-open eyes, face blazing dark red, as she cowered under the sheets. He pinned her down on the bed, pressed her chest with his bare hands, until she could breathe no longer.

"Hijra," he whispered in her ear, then roared in laughter, as he squeezed all air out of her lungs. "Die, Hijra."

Tara tried to scream, but the guttural sounds died in her throat. She tried to move, to get away from him, but her arms were paralyzed.

"Terror," he laughed. "Terror."

"Tara!" Tara opened her eyes with a start. Ruth had drawn open the pretty floral curtains to allow a golden day into the room. She was bent over Tara, gently stroking her moist forehead.

"There, there. It's all right. Did you have a nightmare?"

The strong smell of coffee and the warm aroma of sausage and eggs wafted up, rekindling Tara's senses, slowly waking her up. She wasn't able to eat much though, her nerves and the churning of her gut getting the better of her.

By the time she approached the women's legal center with Ruth and Dottie later that morning, her nighttime apprehensions had subsided, and she was eager to get it over with, whatever it was that had to be gotten over with. Her heart still beat like a boom box, nonetheless. They were at the right number, but there was no sign displayed anywhere that told them they had arrived at the correct address. Besides, the building looked like a single-story home, not a legal center, and the front door was locked. The only giveaway was the intercom mounted on the front wall beside the door. Ruth buzzed the intercom and spoke into it. It turned out they were at the right place.

The women's advocate at the center, who went simply by the name Kendra, was a thirty-something African American woman, with shoulder-length hair that was styled straight and a cobalt blue blouse over a black pencil skirt. A warm smile lit her face, but her manner was businesslike. Ruth and Dottie took turns explaining Tara's case to her. Kendra listened with patience, made notes on her pad, and asked Tara a few pertinent questions before coming up with a plan for her.

Her solution: filing a civil restraining order against Sanjay. "That's the best way to get an early court date," she said.

Tara knitted her eyebrows in concentration. "Restraining order? But I don't expect him to come after me."

"It doesn't matter. We are trying to get you financial compensation as quickly as we can."

"Will he be arrested?"

Kendra shook her head. A restraining order was not a criminal case, it would not affect Sanjay's records, she said. "Once you file the order at the county courthouse, you will be directed to the magistrate's court, where a presiding judge will read the petition and hear your version of what happened. In your case, he has no reason not to grant you a temporary restraining order. The judge will set a date for a court hearing, which will be within the month. If you have personal belongings that you need retrieved from your house, talk to the judge about it, and a sheriff's deputy will accompany you there on a set date. I will let you know of the procedure in detail later, but in short, once the order is signed by the judge, your husband will be served by a sheriff's deputy, following which he will be required by the law to stay a hundred yards away from you, and also to be present in court on the day of the hearing."

Again, a mild bout of panic. Sweat beads on her forehead. "All this—I mean going to court and all—will it affect his job or career?"

"No, sweetheart. Once again, this is a civil case. This will not affect him in any way, other than the fact that he has to stay away from you, and appear in court."

"Will you represent me in court?"

"Yes, absolutely."

"What will happen at the hearing?"

"The judge will grant you a restraining order which will last a year. Also, he will determine whether you should be granted financial compensation and support."

Dottie pressed Tara's hand and nodded, and her pink lips mouthed "Yes." Tara turned to look at Ruth, who rubbed her arm and flashed her happy smile.

Tara looked down at her bitten nails. She wondered what Amma and Daddy might say of her new adventures. She could imagine Amma's precise words: "*What kind of wife takes her husband to court?" That's what our neighbors and relatives will say. Daddy and I will have to bear the brunt of such loose talk.*

The neighbors and relatives need not know, Amma. You need not know, Amma. Tara rubbed her face with both hands, and when she looked up, she shocked herself and everybody else when she said, "Yes, madam. Where is the courthouse? Can we file the papers today?"

She felt Dottie to her left and Ruth to her right, press her arms in approval.

"I'm so proud of you!" Ruth leaned in to whisper into her ear.

Some of Kendra's businesslike manner disappeared when she flashed a sunny smile. "I am afraid it's too late today. I suggest that you go to the courthouse first thing Monday morning."

Tara spent the weekend doing whatever Ruth did, following her around like a child in oversized clothes—brown pants and a navy knit top from the church clothes closet that Dottie had picked out for her. They, along with Dottie, devoted themselves to a church project—filling care packages with hand sanitizers, wet wipes, deodorants, laundry detergent sachets, and candy to be dispatched to soldiers in Iraq, remembering to insert Ruth's thank you note, written in her childish handwriting, into the bag. They dropped off the packages at the church and then went visiting Ruth's friends.

On Saturday, they brought flowers and a card to a woman dying of cancer at the hospice off Clairmont Road. Martha could not say much, as she had tubes that helped her breathe and eat, but life still lived in her pale gray eyes. Ruth held Martha's bony hand and gossiped about people they knew in common. Tara sat on a stool and watched, as Ruth lost herself in an embellished account of how Jane Moore's daughter had finally admitted to her parents that she was lesbian.

"Now, that's all right, Martha. God loves everybody. It's not for us to judge," she added.

Tara noticed how the story spread life from the dying Martha's inquisitive eyes to the rest of her face.

Later that afternoon, they visited Sally Andrews, a junkie hooker at the county jail. They left their cell phones and purses behind in Ruth's car because those items would not be allowed in, Tara learned. They went through the security search and then waited in line to deposit an envelope filled with crisp dollar bills into Sally's personal account. They awaited their turn to take the elevator up to the little room with dividers and phones. Sally appeared, beaming into the glass of the divider, a weathered expression clinging to the last vestiges of what once must have been a striking face. She waved at them and eagerly grabbed a phone.

Tara marveled at how Ruth knew what to say to a woman dying of cancer and to a woman who was incarcerated for being a public nuisance. Her silly banter told them what they wanted to hear: that they weren't alone in the world, that she cared.

That night, after they had dined on homemade chicken walnut salad and cornbread, Ruth settled down in the family room with a book. Tara relaxed on the carpet cross-legged, Doodlebug next to her. Her eyes fell on a small, framed black-and-white family photo on the side table, in the shadow of the lamp that stood behind it. A young couple and a boy of about seven stood in the front yard of a house, smiling into the camera. The man was immaculately dressed, his hair neatly brushed back. The woman wore a form-fitting dress that ended an inch above her knees, and had a sixties-style bouffant. The boy had his hands on his hips, a naughty smile on his lips.

"Ruth, is that your family?" Tara pointed to the photo. Ruth nodded.

"That's my husband Joseph and son Charlie. And me, of course. This was taken outside our home in Augusta. I forget which year. They are both with God. Joseph passed two years ago. But Charlie left us first."

For the first time since she arrived, Tara saw the effervescence on Ruth's face flatten and fade.

"I'm sorry," she said.

Ruth folded her reading glasses. "Life has to go on."

"Yes."

"When Charlie died of cancer, my life fell apart. I had just retired after teaching at the county school for thirty-five years. I knew no other life. My only son was gone. He was divorced and didn't leave behind any children. My life had lost all meaning. I prayed every night for guidance, to make sense of the loss. One day, I decided to make peace with my life. I discovered that making others happy made me happy. And so, every day, I wake up with the intention of making one person a little happier. You know, my dear, as they say, joy is contagious. It rubs onto me."

Ruth lived a charmed life despite her losses because she made herself useful to others. Perhaps, to Ruth, Tara was just another beneficiary of her kindness. But Tara couldn't help but see Ruth as a surrogate mother and not just a kind woman who was helping her out because that was her nature.

On Sunday afternoon, they went shopping to buy three bras, a pack of cotton panties, and a cell phone charger for Tara, whose phone had died on Friday. Ruth insisted on paying for everything. When the phone was sufficiently charged, the first thing that lit the screen was a message from Sanjay.

"Tell your mother to stop calling my home number."

My home number. Like she didn't live there anymore. Like she had no part in his life anymore. Like he hadn't wasted even a moment to wonder what had happened to her. Tara felt a twinge of sorrow. What did she expect? Remorse? Guilt?

She knew Amma would be frantic, but she wasn't ready to tell her anything yet. She didn't respond to the text message, but she emailed Vijay that night, telling him she was out on a trip with Sanjay, to tell Amma not to worry about her. It was a vague email with no details, but she would worry about filling in the facts—real or made up—later. She hoped fervently that Sanjay had not picked up the phone and told Amma everything.

On Monday, Ruth accompanied Tara to the courthouse. When she was finally ushered into the chambers of Judge Greg Thomas for the ex parte hearing, Tara had clammy hands, and her throat felt like it had been rubbed with sandpaper. Sitting in the outer hall, she had imagined Judge Thomas to be an imposing man with a gruff manner, someone like Grandfather Madhava. She had worried incessantly about freezing, not being able to even open her mouth to make her case. But she had imagined wrong. Judge Thomas had kind brown eyes and a warm voice. He read the petition, then asked her questions, and his sympathetic manner put Tara at ease. She recounted, in brief, what must have seemed to Judge Thomas a sad story of domestic abuse. He had no hesitation in granting her the temporary restraining order she sought against Sanjay. He set the court date for two weeks later. A sheriff's deputy would serve Sanjay at his apartment, he said. Sanjay would have the opportunity to make his case during the second hearing.

Ruth had decided they had to celebrate Tara's win even before she was out of Judge Thomas's chamber. So, they drove over to B&B Cafeteria, where they made plans for the next two weeks over fried chicken, green beans, collard greens, sweet potato soufflé, corn bread, and iced tea. Tara would have more privacy in Dottie's finished basement, where she could come and go as she wished, cook her own meals, and watch any TV show.

"This can be a permanent arrangement if you wish," Dottie said kindly.

When evening came, Ruth helped Tara pack a small tan suitcase with clothes from the church closet—mostly tops and skirts—and her underclothes and toiletries from the guest bathroom. A cardboard box from Sam's Club was filled with rudimentary utensils—a pot and pan, two plates and two mugs, some forks and spoons, a kitchen knife. There were also cans of soup, baked beans, and cut vegetables from the church larder. Ruth remembered to bring a loaf of bread and a box of homemade brownies from her kitchen to drop into the box.

"Now, visit me any time you feel lonesome or feel the need to talk," she reminded Tara. "You can walk in anytime. Anytime."

Four days after being thrown out of her apartment, Tara was settled into her own personal space in Dottie's basement, a rectangular room with a sea-green tiled kitchenette and bathroom that overlooked the grassy oak-leaf hydrangea-and-magnolia-scented backyard. Tomorrow, she would muster courage to go back, but only to bring her car. Thereafter, she would get back to classes and work, to a whole new vision of a normal life.

Tara lay wide awake on the green-and-white-checked sofa bed, barely watching the small TV that was set to CBS News. She had cut the volume, so all she did was stare absentmindedly at the flitting images. The day had been rather uneventful, at least by her recent standards. Ruth had driven her to the apartments to bring her car back that morning. She had spent the afternoon working with Nadya, who now knew to pick her up from Dottie's front yard. Alyona had visited her in the evening, bringing two containers filled with homemade pasta and egg salad, which they had eaten over noisy conversation.

She stared languidly at the hands of the old wooden clock that was mounted on the far wall, at the *tick-tock* of the passing seconds. It was 11:17 at night. It would take her a while to get used to her new home, to discard the vague feeling of being marooned on an island. She needed to shift her awareness, to focus on all that her newfound independence would bring—bonding with Ruth and Dottie, filling the space with laughter and conversation, even just breathing freely. She would never lack for companionship here. When she thought of home with Sanjay, she thought isolation, prison, purposelessness, betrayal. And yet, severing bonds, ruffling feathers, defying the established were hard things to do.

Sanjay was served that morning. She imagined what the scene may have looked like. Did Sanjay's jaw drop at the sight of the crisp, khaki-uniformed deputy? Was he furious? Had he expected her to go away quietly, so he could forget her like a bad dream? Was he plotting ways to get even with her? She was dying to know what he was thinking.

Close to midnight, her cellphone, which lay on the cherry wood desk by the sofa getting charged, lit up like a hundred-watt bulb. She jumped up and grabbed the phone in a spurt of reflexes. It was Sanjay's message.

"I am sorry. Please come back home," it said.

Tara read the text over and over again, as if a hidden message or a new insight might pop up the fourth or fifth time. She had to control the urge to run upstairs to Dottie, to seek her advice on how to react. Was she supposed to feel happy, relieved, suspicious, angry?

Right now, all she felt was a colossal storm of confusion that submerged all rational thinking. She paced the long stretch of her room, taking baby strides to make her route last longer. She felt the sudden urge to pee. She ran to the bathroom and sat on the commode for what seemed like eternity. When she returned, her cell phone was lit up again. She stumbled to the desk, flipped her phone open.

"Tara, come back, darling. I am so sorry I hurt you," his second message said.

A sob constricted her throat. The phone dropped from her shaking hands. She scrambled to pick it up, afraid the fall might have somehow deleted his messages. She read the message again, then again and again. Her feelings were grouping, forging in one direction. They seemed a lot like sympathy, or at least a mixed version of it. But when she resumed pacing the room, now with more vigor, those feelings changed. One minute, Sanjay was a pitiable character, the next, a demon.

She had spent months imagining this—Sanjay apologizing, accepting her as his wife—and yet, the circumstances were so different now. His messages didn't warm her heart. She knew he had perceived the court case as being a threat to his job, his career, and his life in America. He was scared enough to want to take her back. She felt stupid to feel sorry for him. And yet, her feelings were out of control; they had a free will of their own.

It was another hour before his third message came.

"We will work at being happy together. Text me. *Please*."

She did not text him, even though it took every ounce of her will to refrain from providing him with some solace, some respite, from the churning of whatever emotions he was feeling because of her.

At nine in the morning, she got a call from Vijay, who had just received a phone call from a remorseful Sanjay. An hour later, Amma called on her cell, but it was Daddy who spoke to her. Her personal crisis had become a crisis for the family.

Chapter 19

"You are kidding. Please tell me you are kidding." Ruth made no attempt to coat her disappointment in Southern charm. "You don't have to do that. You'll be okay. We are here for you."

Tara drew in a long breath. Daddy and Amma's sage advice—all of which made perfect sense to them—was so hard to translate for the benefit of her American friends. Sanjay had called Daddy and pleaded with all the skills he could muster. He was a reformed man, he would make marriage his first priority, he had promised.

Daddy and Amma had insisted that she go back, give Sanjay another chance. Now that Liz was gone, the playing field was hers to claim. A grown man, a proud man had groveled at their feet. Groveled. She would have to be hardhearted to not give in.

"My parents want me to give Sanjay another chance," she told Ruth feebly.

Ruth grabbed Tara's hands and sat her down on the sofa. "And what do you want? Do *you* want to give Sanjay another chance?"

"He has promised to change, to make marriage his first priority." Tara looked down at her hands, away from Ruth's probing eyes. "Separation is not easy. It would bring shame to my family. My parents would have a hard time in their community."

Ruth sighed. "I wish I could understand this better."

At night, Tara stayed awake, probing her decision to go back. At some point in the night, she uncovered a deep truth. Being wanted had always been the biggest challenge of her life, and of greatest import. She had to see if Sanjay would now want her, love her. It mattered, even though, to her own shock, when she searched her own heart for some love for him, she came up empty-handed.

When Tara got into Ruth's Oldsmobile for the ride back to the apartment she shared with Sanjay, her chest felt like a block of granite. She felt no eagerness to return, despite the uncovering of her truth. She knew she had opened her palm and let it fly, that which she had in her grasp for a minute. She knew the pangs of forfeiture would stay in her heart for a long time.

Ruth insisted on coming in to meet Sanjay. Even though he looked haggard with a two-day stubble that stuck out of his chin like prickly weed, Sanjay returned Ruth's cordiality, even offered to make her some coffee, which she politely refused.

"Take care of my girl. I'll come get you if you don't," she said to Sanjay on her way out, a plastic pink smile on her lips.

"Of course," he promised, with a hollow laugh.

He was quick to shut the front door behind Ruth, as if to put a lid on an embarrassing drama. Tara shuddered, as if she were a rat caught in a trap. She had expected to feel righteous, for the balance of power to have shifted. Yet, when Sanjay towered over her, she couldn't help but sink into a corner of the sofa to stop the trembling of her legs.

He took the loveseat. She could see him struggle to get the appropriate words out. "You must be hungry," he said at last. "Let's grab some Indian food. I hear that a new *desi* restaurant has opened in Decatur. Their tandoori chicken is supposed to be the bomb."

She nodded. Sanjay didn't like Indian food. This was his way of making up. But it was so inadequate, so ineffectual. She escaped into the bathroom, where she stayed for a long time, giving in to all that emanated from her chest. On the other side of the door was her reality. Her return was as much a compromise for Sanjay as it was for her. Nothing had changed between them.

Sanjay kept his promise to Daddy and Amma. In the spring of the following year, they moved into a house in a neat subdivision called Stone Crest in Dunwoody, a different part of town, away from her friends. The house was bright and warm, especially in the summer when the sun toasted its red brick front and made the grass in the little front yard seem greener, the roses redder. Two of the three bedrooms had plenty of sunshine, and the third Sanjay used as his study. They bought a new sofa set for the formal living room. Alyona helped Tara pick the sheer curtains and tan faux silk valances for the windows, a fact that Tara did not care to tell Sanjay.

A month after they moved, Tara found a job as a tester— through her QA training institute—at Alpha Tech, a software company in Suwanee. She didn't enjoy bug testing, but it was better than the alternative: to stay in an empty home. Besides, at $25 an hour, the money was good. Over the weekends, she still made plans to hang out with Alyona or with her friends from QVision Tech. She still accompanied Ruth and Dottie on their church projects.

Sanjay ate at home every weeknight. She wished he didn't. Cooking every night was a tedious chore, especially after an entire day spent finding bugs in software, and then driving home from Suwanee. She had five standard Italian and Mexican recipes, which she rotated with little enthusiasm, one for each day of the workweek. On weekends, they either ate out or resorted to takeout dinners.

At the kitchen table, they sat shielding their thoughts with small talk. Often, they gave in to silence, after struggling to find common ground. He had not once mentioned Liz in the time since she had returned home, but it was evident Sanjay still missed her—in the fine lines on his forehead, in the forlorn, faraway look that haunted his eyes as they watched TV or when he drove them around town. Three times a week, he worked out at the neighborhood LA Fitness. But exercise did nothing to change the brooding, solemn expression that had become his permanent feature, as if he had resigned himself to a loveless life with a woman who had dared take him to court.

Sanjay had stopped using condoms, although starting a family was never discussed. Tara would have liked that too, starting a family, if only because that would give her some purpose in life. But she froze each time Sanjay kissed her, worked on her body. She still had trouble getting *LizSan* out of her head; when she managed that, Sanjay's insult poured ice over her body: *Hijra. That's the first word that came to my mind when I saw you at Hartsfield–Jackson.*

As the year went on, they stopped having sex. Behind the shallow small talk, a dull silence hung over them like a shroud.

"You have a beautiful home, a green card, a full-time job, and a husband who earns well. All you need is a baby to complete your life," Amma reminded her happily from time to time. If only Tara could feel some of that charm; if only the dream-like quality of her life would percolate into her heart.

Amma and Daddy came to visit when the white hydrangeas were in full bloom in the front yard. Initially, most evenings, Sanjay and Daddy sat watching TV, sipping their glasses of Glenlivet or Black Label, a bowl of nuts and minced goat meat kababs or chicken 65 on the coffee table, making small talk, which often centered around politics and corruption in India or the complexities of its rambunctious democracy, while Tara and Amma busied themselves cooking dinner. Tara cooked a dish that Sanjay would eat, because he now joined them at the dinner table; Amma cooked for the rest of them.

Amma had fallen in love with the large kitchen, with its granite countertops, chocolate-glazed maple wood cabinets, the island that held a cooktop, the trendy stainless steel appliances, and she made the best use of them, cooking up a storm three times a day. Once a week, Tara drove her parents to the farmers' market, where Amma, her face fuller but striking, the middle-aged spread more obvious in her faded denim pants and knit top, went berserk selecting vegetables and exotic fruit on sale. She was equally excited at the Indian grocery store in Decatur, looking for spices and condiments and frozen seafood to make Tara's favorite dishes. Often, Tara came home from work to the robust aroma of *rohu* fish marinated in turmeric and fried in mustard oil for *macher jhol*, a recipe Amma had learned from their Bengali neighbor before they had moved to Shanti Nilaya. Amma would always remember to set some *misthi doi*, sweet curd, in a clay pot for Tara to relish after dinner every night.

When they first arrived, Tara's parents had been severely jet-lagged. Daddy was also bored. He had nothing to do all day and could not venture out on his own. By the end of the second week, however, he had acquired a new hobby and established a routine. He picked up a few books on gardening at the library and everything else that he needed from Pike Nurseries. He set about creating a little vegetable patch in the backyard, where he planted tomatoes, eggplant, green peppers, and squash in neat rows. Every morning, after a late, leisurely breakfast of omelet, buttered toast, and hot tea, he spent time nursing his babies, while Amma cut store-bought vegetables or marinated fish and set the pressure cooker with rice and dal on the stove for lunch. When he wasn't gardening, he read the day's copy of the *Atlanta Journal Constitution* from cover to cover. When Tara got home from work, the three of them went for a walk through the subdivision. Sometimes, if the weather was right, they ventured out of the subdivision to Morris Road and strolled up to the library a mile and a half down the road. They sauntered through the library, flipped through the magazines—it was a welcome, cool break before their return journey home.

Tara's parents had no trouble stopping to talk to the neighbors at Stone Crest, Amma more so than Daddy. Within weeks of their arrival, they had made friends with doctoral candidate Valentina Bernacki and their next-door neighbor, Susan Myers. Tara had never even seen her neighbors before her parents' arrival. Valentina, who was from Colombia, lived in a larger house by the entrance. She was married to the head of the physics department at Emory University. Susan lived right next door to them, a stay-at-home mom to three little kids, the youngest one, a six-month-old baby girl named Samantha whom Amma carried and bounced and cooed to in Kannada.

It rained sparsely during Amma and Daddy's three-month-long stay. But every evening, the atmosphere thickened a little when Sanjay got home. Tara watched like an outsider as Daddy's demeanor got stiffer, politer; as Amma hushed and relegated herself to the kitchen. In the morning, when Sanjay left for work, they shed the restraints, and Amma rushed to draw the curtains open to let the sun in.

A month into their visit, Sanjay started staying out after work, and when he was in, he preferred to stay in the bedroom, watching TV there. He came down for dinner and made perfunctory efforts at conversation with Daddy alone, but the strain showed on everybody.

Amma, like many Indian women of her generation, had mastered the art of dichotomy.

"What a strange man. He acts like a paying guest in his own home," she grumbled. "What to do, Tara. This is an Indian woman's life. We have to accept what we cannot change. At least he is perfect in every other way."

Without a pause for breath, she added, "When my friend Savitha visited her daughter in San Diego, her son-in-law treated them with so much love, like they were his own parents. He even took them on a road trip to Seattle and Vancouver. Our ears grew ripe listening to her stories." Then, shaking her head, she added, "Not that I want to travel. I'm just saying. Men of your generation are not like the old timers. They are more understanding. Your husband, he is still an old timer, no doubt about that."

Tara said nothing to Amma. Yet, every day, observing her parents' behavior toward Sanjay, she was reminded of her own dysfunctional relationship with him. Like them, she was happier when Sanjay wasn't around to stifle her spirit.

At the end of their three-month-long visit, Tara dropped her parents off at Hartsfield–Jackson airport. They were flying to San Jose to spend a month with Vijay, before heading back to India.

They said their good-byes at the security check line. Amma burst into tears, hugging Tara, mouthing gibberish, making Tara choke with frothing emotion. Surprisingly, even Daddy, who admonished Amma for creating a scene, gave Tara a long, warm hug.

"Take care of my vegetables," he said, eyes glistening, hands gripping her shoulders. "And take good care of yourself."

Tara was too late to stifle a sob; it escaped her throat and wet her eyes. She dug into her purse as the tears flowed, found a pack of tissues, offered one to Amma, whose nose had turned red, and dabbed at her eyes with the second one. She stood waving until she could see Amma and Daddy pass the security check; then she twisted her neck from side to side to catch a last glimpse of them.

The emptiness hit her in the chest on her way back home. Love, warmth, and companionship had quietly taken the place of pain, resentment, and reticence. She had not snapped at Amma, and there had been no awkward silences with Daddy. Her parents had never been on her team before, united against an opposing force. All her life, they had been the others, the abandoners. Now, with them gone, she was left stranded alone in the hollow space of her American dream.

Her shoulders hurt from the simple act of driving back in thick, crawling traffic on I-85 north. By the time she reached home, Sanjay had reclaimed his spot in front of their family room television. She flopped on the couch, carelessly discarding her shoulder bag on the floor.

He did not look at her or greet her. Perhaps it was the realization that, with her parents gone, he didn't have to put on an act anymore. Perhaps her parents had reminded him of the lacerations to his ego when he had to grovel with them for Tara's return. Perhaps he had reached the breaking point, like she had. The silence gnawed into her ears, despite the CNN reporter's inflected summary of news from Washington DC.

"God, I miss them already," she said at last, to the ceiling, rather than to the man next to her.

"They are not taking over my house again." She hadn't been expecting a response, any response. She looked at his hard face, stunned.

"Your house, Sanjay?"

He didn't respond, save for the tightening of his jaw. They continued watching CNN: underwater shots of a Roman shipwreck found in the Mediterranean, an ancient wreck languishing on the ocean floor for centuries. She tried to make sense of the find, of the silence between them, of similar evenings that lay ahead of them. It was as if she were suddenly on the seafloor herself, the water filling her lungs. She couldn't breathe. She rushed to the backyard, to Daddy's little green patch, where life grew in neat little rows, taking in large gulps of air through her mouth. She bent over to pull a rogue piece of crabgrass out by its root, her eyes dripping large pearls over it. She had promised Daddy she'd keep his patch alive. But she was consumed suddenly with the need to find life for herself.

She rushed back in, as suddenly as she had rushed out to the garden, and stopped a foot away from his recliner, hands balled into fists, nails digging into her palms.

"It was a mistake, Sanjay." Her voice was quavering from all that was churning inside of her. "How I wish I had never come back."

She watched his mouth harden into a thin line; heard the sharp intake of his breath.

"You ungrateful bitch." He jerked up from his seat and loomed over her in a giant stride. She knew what was coming—the savage fury she had seen before. She took his first blow calmly. The second one sent her sprawling on the floor again.

"Sanjay, think of the consequences. I will call nine-one-one," she part implored, part threatened, her eyes streaming with pain.

"I'm beyond caring. I'm a dead man anyway." She felt his foot in her abdomen, kicking again and again, then a series of blows to her face, her head, her arms, until she wished she would just pass out and feel nothing.

"You are sorry you came back? I was kind enough to take your ugly ass back in, you worthless piece of shit," she heard him bark through the fog in her brain. She looked around for her sling bag, remembering that her cell phone was in it, but her vision had blurred, she could see only a haze, and through it, a bare foot repeatedly and violently assaulting her. She closed her eyes and gave in to Sanjay's relentless rage.

He stopped when he had had enough. Or perhaps, when he realized that the physical pain he was inflicting on her did not assuage his bruised ego. She was alive, conscious, and free when he left the room.

It was still dark when she emerged from upstairs into the family room, dressed in a bright yellow blouse and blue jeans, a small suitcase in her hand. He had dozed off on the recliner, a half empty glass of vodka on the side table. He woke up with a start when she called out his name. His face darkened, as recent events of the night flooded his mind.

She hesitated, but only for a moment before she embarked on her short leap of faith to the garage door. There, she turned around to face him a final time. His eyes had been on her back, but he quickly looked away.

Her voice was placid when she said, "I am not worthless to me, Sanjay."

She shut the door behind her, not waiting to see his reaction.

Chapter 20

Her new apartment was on the third floor, in a sprawling community of corn-yellow and green buildings called Sanctuary Hills that looked deceptively small from the road. Before moving in, Tara stopped with Ruth and Dottie at Target, only a quarter mile away, to pick up a single bed-in-a-bag in bright floral print, a shower curtain and toiletries for the bathroom, and basic necessities for the kitchen. Her car was already loaded with a new box mattress, knick-knacks from the Indian store, and a suitcase filled with her new clothes.

Alyona was waiting for them in the parking lot when they got to the apartment community. They lugged the new buys to her apartment. Tara boiled milk in a new stainless steel pot in her small kitchen, and let it gush over the stovetop. An Indian housewarming tradition to signify the flow of prosperity, health, and happiness into the new house, she explained to her friends. She was careful to mop the mess with sheets of Bounty before sweetening the milk with some sugar and filling three cups a quarter full for her and her two friends to sip.

Tara smiled brightly through the pain in the various parts of her body, and her utter exhaustion. The ivory walls of her own little space were bare, but when she opened the blinds to let the sun in, its dappled glow felt magical. She turned around to face her three dear friends, their radiant faces overflowing with happiness for her. For a moment, she felt like she were with Pippi, Leenika, and Runa, as if the first six happy years of her life had come back to her.

She woke up the next morning on the box bed, glad to be able to turn her face this way and that, and yawn, and stretch her arms over her head with no rock sitting heavily on her chest. She remembered waking up on her first morning in America, realizing that her near stranger husband had never come in, weighed down with the burden of making her marriage work. She let it sink in, the awareness that she no longer carried that fear of failure.

Every evening, after work and over the weekends, Tara scoured discount stores, flea markets and yard sales, Ruth or Alyona in tow, buying things for her apartment—a fawn plush sofa bed, a tiny oval dining table for four. She remembered her first purchases at a thrift store in Decatur, and Sanjay's utterly vain reaction to her visit there.

She felt liberated spending hours foraging for used stuff, choosing a large Picasso print of *The Three Musicians* or a vintage corner stool on which she placed Ruth's beautiful gift, a dried fall foliage and wheat straw arrangement.

She chose to tell her family she had moved out only when Amma and Daddy's California vacation was coming to an end. Until then, she had kept up with Amma's banter, knowing that her newfound solidarity with her parents would end soon, yet not wanting to ruin their vacation.

"Why, Tara?" Amma cried, her disbelief rushing across the phone waves.

"You and Daddy saw how bad it was."

"It wasn't so bad, Tara. We women make peace with our circumstances," Amma's voice was breaking.

"He hit me, Amma. He kicked me. Repeatedly."

"What will we tell people?"

"Tell them, Amma, that your daughter also deserves a life."

"What life can there be without a husband?"

Tara responded only with a deep sigh. She felt no urge to even snap at Amma.

"I'll ask Daddy to speak to Sanjay. We'll make him promise he'll never raise his hand to you again." Amma's distressed voice was making plans for her, as always.

"I am not going back, Amma. Not now, not ever. Call me when you can accept the fact."

Amma called again from Mangalore two weeks later, after the shock of the news had dissipated somewhat, catching Tara during her drive to work. She had found out that Sanjay hadn't shared the news; not even with his parents. Her call to Sanjay's mother had confirmed this.

"Daddy says it might not be a bad idea to separate for a while. It might put some sense into Sanjay's head, make him realize your value."

"I am enjoying my new life, Amma. My apartment looks really pretty now. I'll email you some photos."

Amma ignored her response. "Just make sure nobody finds out that you moved out. We don't want people to gossip unnecessarily."

"I was planning to invite all those gossipy people to my apartment for dinner."

Amma's voice rose in anguish. "Don't joke, Tara. People can be cruel; you have no idea. They are like wolves looking for a lamb to tear apart."

Tara was grateful that her social circle did not consist of wolves. Two weeks after Diwali, she found a day that was suitable for all her friends to celebrate the victory of light over darkness, of good over evil. She shopped for groceries and cooked a lavish Indian meal—chicken curry, sautéed spinach with *paneer*, garbanzo beans in light gravy, *naan* and biryani. She piled her new crystal bowl, a gift from Dottie, with sweet cashew and pistachio *barfis*, and lined packs of tealight candles on her new antique console table.

In the end, only Alyona, Ruth, and Dottie came. Victor was in middle school and rarely accompanied his mother anywhere anymore. Anita, Shyamala, and Yasmin didn't show up. Maybe it was Tara's fault. She had expected her Indian friends, who all lived far up north, to drop everything to be at her party. They had their reasons—the distance, kids, tight schedules, something unexpected that had come up. She had received apologetic text messages from all three of them earlier that evening.

"They are no friends of yours," declared an indignant Alyona. "They should have been here to show their support."

"They are wolves in friends' clothing," Amma would have said. But Tara wouldn't allow those who weren't in her apartment to affect her equilibrium. She was suddenly reminded of what Amma had told her a long time ago, weeks after they had arrived in Mangalore. Exasperated over Tara's fearfulness, Amma had said: "Remember this Tara. You are a *Kshatriya*. You belong to the warrior caste. Hold your head high. Always."

Tara had pulled her shoulders up that day, but her spirits had sagged like a punctured balloon. She had so many things to deal with in a new town, she couldn't even count them—lizards, spiders, a dungeon-like kitchen, new people, and the worst of all—a new school. She had wondered if Amma had gotten it all wrong, and she were actually at the bottom of the caste pyramid.

"Hold your head high, Tara," she reminded herself, as she invited her friends who had taken the time to be with her to light the tealight candles. Together they created rows of sparkling light outside the doorstep, on the mantle, the breakfast ledge, across the coffee table. The collective glow of the candles was magical, as if there were a cosmic revelation hidden there.

She packed Ziploc bags of biryani and curry for Alyona, and sweetmeats for Ruth and Dottie to take home. The rest she divided into sandwich bags for herself to have over the course of the week, for lunch and dinner.

Tara was not a believer in the caste hierarchy; that humans are born unequal. But Amma's words to her six-year-old daughter now held new meaning. Not because Tara was born a Kshatriya, but because she needed to feel whole.

Tara still did not enjoy finding bugs in software. But her paycheck paid her apartment rent, filled up her car with gas, and enabled her to eat out with Alyona every weekend. But it was always at the back of her head that she had to find a way to get back to writing. Sometimes, she dreamed of holding her own hardbound book, her name in bold engraver's font. She subscribed to twelve issues of the *New Yorker* magazine. She scoured the Internet for writing courses in Atlanta. She found one at Emory University, but it was too late to register for their upcoming term. She brought home Stephen King's *On Writing: A Memoir of the Craft* from the library. She read it, and then stayed up all night crafting a short story about an Indian restaurant manager who falls in love with an exorbitantly priced painting of an aristocratic woman. Pleased with her creation, she emailed it out to online literary journals.

Her mood was sullied in the morning, after she found a rejection in her email. Strong storyline, the editor conceded, but the principal character was too one-dimensional, the treatment of the story too simplistic. *Read books on character building*, was the editor's all-knowing advice to Tara. She logged out of the new Gmail account she had created for her literary work and snapped her laptop shut.

The next evening, at the library, she came across a *Marie Claire* feature written by a *New York Times* bestselling author: a personal account of despair and persistence through basket loads of rejection letters from publishers, and her ultimate triumph when a little-known literary agent had agreed to represent her.

Inspired, she wrote again. Submitted again. When the rejections filled her inbox, she wrote again. Submitted again. When her first short story got published in the *Rosebud* online literary journal, it felt like the sweetest victory, as if she had won the Man Booker award.

It shocked her that she thought so little and so fleetingly about Sanjay these days. She felt no anger, no pain, no neediness; every emotion she had ever felt for him, she had left behind in her suburban dream.

He appeared briefly on her mind one evening, on her drive back home from work on I-85 south, when a billboard caught her eye as she passed Jimmy Carter Boulevard. Instinctively, her foot hit the brakes. Her steering wheel trembled, as it decelerated from sixty-five to fifty mph, causing the black Mercedes Benz behind to almost bump into her. As the driver changed lanes and whizzed past, he pulled down his window. He shook a fist in her direction. *Shit!* Tara looked ahead, shaken. She would have to come back to see herself on the billboard, now in bridal wear, looking demure, a red silk dupatta covering her hair, a second-time model for Raj Jewelers.

It brought back memories of the storm that the first photo had brought into her life, and before that, her desperate hopes for Sanjay to see the advertisement and find her beautiful and worthy of him.

How unworthy of her he had been all along. How blind she had been not to see it that way. She turned back to catch one last look at herself in her demure bride avatar. If nothing else, it served as a reminder to her to put a legal end to her marriage saga.

The divorce came quickly. It was uncontested. She asked for nothing, not even the meagre belongings she had left behind. The only thing she carried over to her new life was her legal status as a permanent resident of the United States. It amazed her how easy change had become, once she took the leap of faith.

Chapter 21

Tara pulled up a sling patio chair to a warm corner of her balcony which overlooked the road. She put her feet up on the chair, her long maroon, polka-dotted pajama-clad thighs taking on a V-shape. She rested her mug of tea on her right knee, holding it lightly. She enjoyed these peaceful Saturday morning moments, thinking up a storyline, creating characters, feeling their emotions.

She took a sip out of her mug and closed her eyes. She felt the warmth of the dappled sun on her eyelids. There was so much to be absorbed through the other senses when the eyes were closed. Birds chirped with enthusiasm. A car revved to life. She heard the patter of little feet running, a child's voice saying, "Bye, Mom." The mom responding with, "Bye, sweetie. Love you."

She wondered why Americans felt the need to say *I love you* to their loved ones every single day. She wondered why Indians had so much trouble saying *I love you*. Amma and Daddy had never said *I love you* to her. Ever. She doubted they had even expressed their love for each other with those words. She wondered if she could manage an essay on this topic. But really, what did she know about love?

She'd see. She lowered her legs, slipped her feet into her pink plush bedroom slippers, walked lazily back into the kitchen, fixed herself a bowl of Quaker Oats in the microwave, and took it to the living room. She propped her legs on the edge of the coffee table, slipped a soft red cushion into the concave of the sofa to buffer her lower back, and set her laptop on her thighs. She worked on the bowl of oats as she waited for the laptop to boot.

She logged on to Hotmail first. She couldn't remember when she had last checked her personal emails; it was at least two weeks ago. Nobody ever wrote to Hotmail anymore, anyway. She had lost touch with almost all her friends at the *Morning Herald*, and she didn't use MSN messenger any longer. Still, her inbox was inundated with emails, the kind she either did not bother to open or deleted immediately. There was a notice from the library reminding her that Vikram Seth's *A Suitable Boy* was due, a cell phone bill from AT&T, sale notices from Macy's and Target, a 20 percent off coupon from Border's bookstore. Ensconced between the mostly junk emails was one from C. Saldanha, which she almost deleted but chose to open instead, if only because the name Saldanha meant something to her. It was dated September 28, 2005, almost a week earlier. The subject line simply said, "Hi!" Junk, she thought, but opened it anyway. It read:

> *Twinkle, twinkle little Star,*
> *How I wonder where you are!*

She read the two lines, and instinctively knew.

> *Twinkle, twinkle little Star,*
> *How I wonder where you are!*
> *I saw you on I-85 this morning, sparkling like a diamond, causing accidents. You almost got me killed! I am in Atlanta for a few days. I hope I can see you."*

He had signed off with just his first name and cell phone number.

She put a hand to her chest when she Googled his number; it was a San Jose area code. The email had been sent exactly a week ago. Was she too late seeing his email? Was he back in San Jose? She was shocked that he still remembered her, that he had recognized her on the billboard, that he had reached out, that he had retained his wit.

But did she want to write back? What was she to write, anyway? What was to come after *Hi Cyrus*? She shut her laptop and changed to go for a leisurely walk instead. She had hoped to develop her essay on the verbal and nonverbal expressions of love, but her thoughts kept coming back to the email.

"I don't need this type of distraction," she murmured. What she needed at this point was the peace to heal, to rediscover herself. Yet, her hand was pressed to her chest when she returned to her apartment, her heartbeat erratic. She had no idea how long she had walked, only that it was a sunny day and she was thirsty. Still, her feet took her to the laptop in the living room rather than the kitchen to quench her thirst.

Again, she wondered if she should simply delete the email. But what was the harm in meeting him once, an opposite force reasoned. She was curious to find out where life had taken him, how he had turned out, if his eyes had changed color. Eventually she replied, after sending three drafts to the trash bin. The first one was too cold, the second one too friendly, the third just didn't sound right.

"Hi Cyrus," her email said. "So good to hear from you. I'm sorry, I haven't been regular at checking my Hotmail. I just saw your note. Hope you are still in town. Would you like to do lunch at the Cheesecake Factory, Perimeter Mall tomorrow? Is 12:30 good? Looking forward to catching up. –Tara"

She had no reason to stay on Hotmail, but she did. In a few minutes, her inbox had a new email from C. Saldanha.

"Star, you are late but lucky. I am still in town. Can't wait to see you tomorrow! How did you know I have a weakness for cheesecake?"

She smiled from ear to ear, lips stretched across her face. The cocky charm. He hadn't lost it.

Tara drove over to Alyona's apartment that afternoon, and gave her the news and its backstory, taking care to suppress the nervous energy that was spiraling inside her chest. When Alyona's last relationship with Amir Rezaee, an Iranian who owned a Persian restaurant in Roswell, ended two months ago, she had vowed to stay off men forever. "Men are dogs," she had proclaimed then. "I am through with dogs."

Maybe Alyona was right. Maybe she just needed to hear from another person that she ought to stay away from Cyrus.

"Girl, you are full of surprises," Alyona exclaimed "And Madonna face? Nobody has said nothing like that to me before."

"It was a long time ago, Alyona. We were kids."

"You are kids no more. You be careful, girl."

Tara nibbled a fingernail. "I'm sure he is happily married. Maybe I'll get to meet his family soon."

"If he was married, he would not have contacted you."

"Should I cancel the lunch?"

"Meet him, have sex if you want to. Just don't fall in love."

Tara shook her head in exasperation. "Alyona. I don't plan to have sex, nor fall in love. I don't need any complications in my life."

"Yeah? Then why are you getting your hair done?"

"Why shouldn't I look nice?"

Alyona bustled about setting up her tools to wash and tame Tara's hair. "Why you bite your nails like rabbit? How terrible they look," she admonished. As they waited for the dark golden mahogany tint to seep through Tara's hair, she trimmed the nails to one length and buffed them until they shone.

Tara smiled at a memory as Alyona blow-dried her hair. Her thirteen-year-old self was taming her unruly hair with her fingers and pressing her lips hard to get color to them, before going in to spend time with Cyrus and the Saldanha gang.

The Saldanha gang. She had lost touch with them all when she changed schools after moving to Model Street. Her new school had been within walking distance of their new home, but figuratively, she had walked many miles before she could adjust to her new circumstances.

Her new school uniform—blue pleated skirt and white shirt—were of fine quality fabric and pressed to perfection by the iron-wallah. Her black leather shoes glinted in the sun every day. But she had no friends. The first six months, she sat alone during school lunch break, nibbling little conscious bites out of the four-tier stainless steel tiffin carrier in which Amma packed a full meal. When the other girls played throw ball during PT, she sat on the grass and watched. There were at least four other girls of her age group in the colony where they lived. She saw them every evening, hanging out on the steps of one house or the other, their voices loud and their laughter unrestrained. They reminded Tara of Annette, Michele, and Angela, but unlike her friends, this gang seemed unapproachable.

She tried to take pleasure in resting her head in Amma's lap like old times, to have Amma run her slender fingers through her rough hair every night. But her heart had very blatantly shifted loyalties. It felt nothing except the overpowering pain of separation from Cyrus.

She returned to Shanti Nilaya of course, always day visits with her family to celebrate *Ugadi* or *Dassera* with her grandparents, but the visits were never long enough that she could slip out on her own. She hoped for a glimpse of him, craning her neck when their car passed by Second Bridge, but she was always disappointed.

Her final year in high school, he ceased to occupy her mind all the time. Yvonne became her best friend at school. The neighborhood girl gang of four was not so haughty after all. They included Tara in their group. She moved on to other infatuations—movie stars, a thick-mustachioed guy in the neighborhood who rode an Enfield Bullet and didn't know she existed, and one summer, an IIT student with light eyes who came to spend a couple of weeks with his aunt next door. The infatuations lasted a few months each; then they waned without ever being realized. The searing intensity of her adolescent feelings for Cyrus, she had never experienced again. She didn't think she could feel that potency again as an adult, not even for Cyrus.

When she pulled into the parking lot of the Cheesecake Factory and checked her face in the visor mirror, it still seemed too much: the retro gloss lipstick, the eyeliner. She dug into her purse and pulled out a pack of wet wipes, dabbed off the eyeliner, and patted her lips clean of some of the color. She checked her watch. It was past twelve thirty. She had to get in. She closed her eyes and took a deep breath, held it, exhaled slowly. Then she walked toward the restaurant.

She had had a last-minute change of heart about a floral dress she had picked out the previous night. Instead, she wore a rather plain white blouse, a khaki A-line skirt, and flat tan ballerina shoes. She walked up to the hostess and hesitated. She didn't know if he was already there. She tilted her head and scanned her eyes across the tables. How was she going to recognize him?

"Miss, are you looking for me?"

She whirled around. How could she not have recognized him? His eyes were the same, as was his dimpled smile. After twenty-three years. Only his hair was shorter, darker and brushed back away from his forehead. He wasn't exceedingly tall, perhaps just a couple of inches taller than she. He looked lean in his khakis and dark blue polo shirt.

He held his hand out. She shook it, embarrassed that hers was cold and clammy. He covered it with his free hand, his skin warm on hers.

"Hi!" she said. Her throat felt dry. "I was looking for a graying, pot-bellied, middle-aged man, ha-ha." She hoped she hadn't sounded rehearsed. The words had tumbled out in a sudden release of nervous energy. He threw his head back and laughed. He had even teeth, and his dimples were deep.

"You dig pot-bellied men?" He looked around, still holding on to her hand. "Not hard to find one at the Cheesecake Factory."

"No," she said with a laugh.

Once they were seated, she had a sip of ice water. The pounding of her heart had come down a notch, allowing her to talk without seeming breathless.

"So, how did you recognize me?"

"Who doesn't? You are a famous model." The dimples were back.

"Oh, the billboard," she waved her hand dismissively. She told him she was a QA professional by day, that the modeling was a one-time thing.

"But how could you tell it was me? I mean, I was just thirteen when you last saw me."

He tapped the left side of his chest. "That face, madam, is etched here."

She blushed, drank a sip of water. He watched her, mirth in his eyes.

The server brought a plateful of fried calamari and their drink orders to the table, a classic margarita for her with salt on the rim and a chilled Bud Light for him. She took a sip of her margarita, the salt causing her face to pucker involuntarily. He watched openly, and laughed.

She cleared her throat. "But how did you get my email address?"

"I have my ways."

"What ways?"

He took a swig of beer, rested his elbows on the table, and told her of his search. A couple of years back, during his visit home, he had come across an old copy of the *Morning Herald* in his Dad's study. It was a comprehensive, well-researched article on the minuscule Parsi community in Mangalore. He had read the article, of course, but what caught his attention was the byline. The article was written by a Tara Raj. He'd called the *Morning Herald* office, only to be told that Tara Raj no longer worked there.

"And that was the end of my search, until last week, when I saw you on the billboard, causing accidents on I-85. I went straight to Raj Jewelers, who put me on to the photographer who had shot the campaign, and he gave me your email address after I promised to hire him for my wedding."

"Wedding? You are getting married?"

"No."

She slipped a casual glance at his sleek fingers—no ring. Of course, that didn't mean a thing. Indian men did not wear wedding rings. She wondered if she should ask him about his marital status, but he beat her to the question.

"So, Tara, forgive me for sounding like an Indian aunty, but what does your mister do?"

"He doesn't. I'm divorced." She took a tiny bite of crunchy, fried calamari, not watching his reaction, quickly changing the topic. "So what brought you to Atlanta?"

"Destiny," he laughed. He and his partner, Tony Kaputo, owned a video gaming company, Playable Media, in San Jose. They were in the middle of negotiations to buy over a smaller company, Peach Street Games, in Atlanta.

"Does that mean you will be visiting Atlanta often?"

"If all goes well, yes. And now, I have one very good reason to hope it does."

She smiled, rather stupidly, put her elbow on the table, and rested her chin on a cupped hand. "Where's your wife?" she asked.

He shrugged. "No wife. Been married twice, though. The first one is up there. The second one is probably in New York."

"Oh, I am sorry."

"You knew her. The first one, I mean."

"Oh, you married Angela, Annette's pretty cousin!"

He grinned. "Wrong answer."

"Michele?"

"Wrong answer again."

"Oh my God, you married Annette Saldanha? But she was family!"

"Hmm. Yes, but she was in the family way."

"What?" Her elbow dropped from the table. But why? she wanted to ask him. "You were cousins!"

"When you're young, you do stupid things."

A thought then hit her, what he had said earlier about his first wife being "up there." "What happened to Annette?"

He cupped a hand around his beer bottle, and tilted it along its axis; the smile on his lips waned momentarily when he said, "She died of meningitis. Just two years after we got married."

"And the baby?"

"He was stillborn."

"Oh!" She instinctively leaned forward, squeezed his free hand across the table. Her hand was no longer clammy or cold. He held on to her hand, his fingers curling into hers. A tenderness spread across his face, mellowed its features. With the smile gone, she could see that he was older, that time had matured him, that life had thrown curveballs his way, as well.

"I am so sorry," she said. "So sorry to hear about Annette and your baby."

He nodded.

Their lunch orders arrived. They ate, and the chatter around the restaurant seemed louder, as if they'd just realized there were people around them.

"The second wife. Who was she?" she asked.

"Patricia. I met her at NYU Stern where we both got our MBAs. Five years down the line, we realized it was a mistake and went our separate ways."

It had taken him a while to move on, he said, but he had recently started dating again, a woman named Giana.

She tried hard to appear nonchalant. "Sounds like an Italian name."

"She is."

"This is good," she said, pricking a plump shrimp blackened with pepper and a chunk of juicy pineapple on her fork, hastening to change the topic of their conversation. "Would you like to try it?"

"If you'll let me."

She leaned forward to drop the shrimp and pineapple goodness on his plate. Without looking, she knew his gaze was on her, not on his plate.

She stayed at the Cheesecake Factory, across the table from him, until people started to arrive for early dinner. Often, it was her own voice reaching her ears, animated and wordy. She told him about Ruth, Dottie, and Alyona, referring to them as her Atlanta mothers and sister. She talked about her newly renewed passion for writing. He filled her in on his interest in yoga and meditation, his charity work. He ran the Annette Saldanha Home for Children in Mangalore with his father, a shelter for abandoned kids.

When he offered to walk her to her car, it seemed likely that he would miss his return flight to San Jose, unless he drove to the airport like a formula one racer.

"Well then," she said, leaning awkwardly against her Toyota Camry. "Drive safe."

He touched her shoulder lightly. "Don't old friends deserve a good-bye hug?"

She took a step forward and leaned in toward him. His outstretched arms enveloped her as if they had been waiting for this moment for decades. He felt warm, familiar; as if they had embraced a million times before. She was awash with long forgotten feelings. When he finally drew back and touched her cheek lightly, much like the scene from twenty-three years ago that she had replayed a million times in her head, her instructions to herself had flown out of her head. She gazed unabashedly into his eyes.

"Thank you for not running away this time," he said playfully.

It wasn't a long drive home. Or perhaps it was. There wasn't much traffic inside the Perimeter. Or perhaps there was. She had no idea. When she turned the key in the lock to open her apartment door, she wondered for a second how she had gotten there. Which route had she taken?

She glided into the bedroom, dropped on the bed in a ninety-degree-angle fall, face up, arms stretched out. Her cheeks were still flushed. She closed her eyes and imagined again, the warmth of his embrace, their long conversation. She had been wrong in her assumption that her adolescent feelings for Cyrus were dead. Those feelings were back with the same intensity.

She smiled at a memory. After she had slid behind the wheel and rolled down her window, he had leaned in, his face and shoulders filling her view. She had noticed his thick eyelashes, how they accentuated his unusual eyes, and a little cut high up on his jaw, below his right ear, where he had probably nicked himself shaving that morning. She had noticed her own immense desire to put her hand out to touch it, to touch him.

"I have a confession to make," he had said, looking into her eyes. "I was not in Atlanta when your email arrived yesterday. You made me take a red-eye from San Jose."

She had simply stared at him in disbelief. "It was worth it," he had said.

"Yes, it was nice reconnecting," she had mumbled.

There was something else he had told her that made her heart smile now. "I stood at the spot until the sun went down," he had said of that last day so many years ago. "I kept coming back to the spot, even walked past your grandmother's house for weeks in the hope of seeing you. Annette said you changed schools and she never saw you after that last day."

"Oh, really!"

"Oh, really? Is that all you're going to say?" He had laughed.

"I'm sorry. I was so timid."

He had leaned forward and given her a peck on her cheek, a gentle brush of his lips against her skin. "Please don't make me wait a quarter of a century to see you again."

Her eyes closed at the memory, her face arching up involuntarily. Maybe she shouldn't have met him. Already, the calm she had spent months building inside of her, around her, had been invaded with ocean waves of emotions.

Chapter 22

H is email arrived on the sixth day. The Atlanta deal had come through and he'd be back in town next week, he said. She deleted the email, but let it rest in the trash folder. For two restless days, she resisted the urge to resurrect the email, filling her free time with grocery shopping and elaborate Indian cooking, reminding herself of the pitfalls of rushing into something she wasn't ready for.

On the third day, she allowed a shift in her thoughts, pondering the purpose of her resistance, her attempt to block the splendored sunshine from flooding her life. Why was she living in the past, in the future? In the present, Cyrus's return seemed like her karmic bonus for taking care of herself, for not allowing her past to harden her heart.

She found the email, hit reply, and typed a simple *Congratulations!* She slept easy that night.

He asked her, via email, if he could take her out to celebrate the Atlanta deal when he visited the following week. She met him for dinner on a Thursday evening, driving straight from work to a small café in Buckhead. She had taken care that morning to wear a blue sheath dress that flattered her slim figure. She congratulated him again in person with a quick sideways hug, taking in how the white of his shirt and the deep red of his tie made his face glow, his eyes sparkle, even in the dim interior of the café. In between bites of his chicken panini sandwich, he told her he had broken up with Giana the week before. She knew she sounded dishonest when she mouthed, "Oh, I'm so sorry. I hope you are okay."

He said he was fine, they had only dated a few weeks.

She met him for dinner each time he was in town, which was at least twice a month. They found ways to make the dinner stretch, never running out of things to share. He updated her with news on their three mutual friends. Angela had been a flight attendant for Lufthansa until she retired and married a Delhi-based pilot. Michele was a gynecologist who worked in a Bombay hospital. She had married a cardiologist across town and had two kids. James, who remained his best buddy, had taken over his father's coffee estates after his parents' death.

She told him what a disappointment she had been to Daddy when she joined the arts stream in college, opting to major in literature. He'd had plans for her to become the first doctor in the family. Just before she graduated with a master's, she had applied for a sub-editor's post at the *Morning Herald* on a whim, with no background or training whatsoever in journalism. She had been the first one from her class to get a job.

"I bet your daddy was finally proud of you," he said.

"Yes, but he was also quick to add that if I had applied my gray cells a little more, I could have passed the foreign service exam."

"That's a typical Indian parent's reaction. But you stood your ground to do what you loved, so you were quite the rebel."

She had never seen herself as a rebel, and it tickled her pink that he thought of her as one.

Every waking moment, her mind hopscotched through thought after sweet thought; waiting, endlessly waiting, for their next meeting. By the end of the fall, Cyrus said he was going to be spending a considerable amount of time in Atlanta, overseeing operations of Peach Street Games. It made sense to look for an apartment, to feel at home, rather than stay cooped up in a hotel room. Tara thought he would opt to be near the trendy Buckhead nightlife or the midtown skyline, but Cyrus wanted to be close to nature. He settled for a two-bedroom, top floor, furnished apartment a few miles away from Buckhead, with a large patio that overlooked a thickly wooded park. The patio was perfect for his morning yoga sessions, and the park was ideal for his daily conversations with his inner self, he said.

In the second week of December, a little after Christmas lights began to adorn the city, he moved into Sherwood Park. After he had unpacked his suitcase and duffel bag, the first thing he wanted was a Christmas tree. Tara had bought hers, a seven-foot, Slim Arizona last December at Garden Ridge. She offered to take Cyrus to the same store where, together, they chose the tree, a red reversible skirt, strings of lights, red and silver baubles, and assorted ornaments. He picked an eye-catching five-point star of Bethlehem to top the tree from high up on a shelf. His eyes were trained to spot stars, he said, as he pressed it to his heart. She laughed and slapped him on his shoulder. But beyond his playfulness, she sensed his need to make her part of his Christian family tradition, to involve her in the unwrapping of his new life.

After their shopping expedition, Tara helped him assemble the tree, string the lights, and put up the ornaments. Cyrus heated some spiced apple cider, which they sipped out of large brown ceramic mugs as they worked. When they were done, they settled together on the sofa and looked at their creation: the ornaments, spaced out, yet glimmering delicately in the glow of the lights.

The tranquil, mellifluous strains of the *santoor* gently filled the living room. Tara cast a glance at Cyrus's Bose home audio system on the entertainment console.

"Pandit Shiv Kumar Sharma? What happened to the guy who insisted on playing 'Funkytown' every afternoon?"

He laughed. "He got lost in transition."

"Hmm. Lost in transition. That's clever. Yoga, meditation, santoor. It is amazing how much you have changed, Cyrus."

He said he had learned his lessons the hard way, after the Wall Street slump depleted him completely several years earlier, and, after a particularly weary day, when he had taken a flight out of New York to San Francisco where a friend lived, minus his wife of five years. She had moved out just that morning, and he had nothing to lose, nothing to stop him from starting over.

She began her story at a tangent, telling him about the nightmares and sleep paralysis that had started when she married Sanjay. He wanted to know more, so she gave him images of her life in Atlanta to piece together like a montage. When she was done laying bare past hurts, she looked into his moist eyes and smiled. "Thankfully, it is all in the past."

"What a crazy man." He leaned forward and took her hand, fingers entwining with hers. "I'm so sorry you had to go through so much pain, and I admire you so much for standing up for yourself."

She looked up into his eyes, and saw herself, shining, in the middle of two honey pools.

"I love you, Star." His voice was soft, yet ardent. She opened her mouth to respond, but only silence flew out. She needed to tell him, she was desperate to tell him, so she lunged forward and claimed his mouth. Her eyes closed of their own accord, not seeing the emotions that passed through his face. But she felt them, in the burning of his tongue as it discovered her moist mouth, exploring new territories; in the grip of his hands that cupped her face; in his mildly cinnamon-scented breath, laden with yearning. When she finally pulled back, he ran his hand through her hair, and let her in to the thumping of his heart. She lifted her face to gaze into his eyes; wet, luminous pools in the soft glow of the Christmas tree and the fading daylight.

"You have a wonderful way of saying things," he said. His voice was gentle, happy, still breathless.

She looked away smiling, suddenly shy. It was as if the years in between had never happened. She melted in his warmth as he kissed her forehead, her eyes, her cheeks; as his hand found the gap where her black T-shirt ended, as it explored the small of her back. He claimed her mouth again, then her long swan-like neck, catching the vibrations in her throat. His hand was climbing up her back, making her spine tingle with longing.

She arched back, pulling him down with her. They made love in the glow of the twinkling lights of the Christmas tree. He kissed her shoulder afterward, as they lay in each other's arms, spent. "I love you, my precious Star," he said tenderly. "I have loved you from the time we first met."

"I love you too, Cyrus," she said softly, turning to kiss the tip of his nose. She had never, ever, in her life, said those three words to anybody; not to Amma, Daddy, or Vijay. They finally came to her lips now, those three profoundly magical words.

They planned an August wedding. It was a natural progression of their relationship. Exactly two months before her big day, Tara telephoned her parents to have the most difficult conversation of her life. She dialed with clammy hands, after considerable phrasing and rephrasing in her head, knowing how upset they still were with news of her divorce.

"I am getting married, Amma. I'll be happy if you and Daddy will come."

She was met with silence. She strained to hear a bit of her old mother; the rush of emotion, the sob, the sigh. She heard nothing. The shock of the news had been too much.

"Amma."

"You seem to have planned everything yourself. You don't need your parents anymore."

Tara fought a wave of guilt before responding. "Please come, Amma. You know I need you and Daddy." She wasn't being entirely truthful. She didn't need them around as much as she needed peace with them. She told them about Cyrus—what he did for a living, how much he respected her, how well they got along.

"Cyrus? That is a Parsi name," said Amma.

"His mother is Parsi, but his dad is Mangalorean Catholic."

Another long silence. "Is he making you convert?"

"Of course not, Amma."

"His family might insist on it."

"Amma, his family doesn't care what religion I follow."

"At least you could have found a Hindu. Our people will never accept this marriage."

Tara tried again, two weeks later. This time she offered to make all the arrangements for their travel; they only had to get to the airport. But Amma was brusque in her response. "Daddy's blood pressure has shot up. We can't travel now."

She understood the insinuation. "Is he regular with his morning walks?"

"We don't go anywhere anymore. Already people are gossiping about your divorce. How long will it be before this scandal hits Mangalore? It is our punishment for being parents. . ." Her voice trailed off, words left unsaid but implied. Punishment for being her parents. Laying guilt came so naturally to Amma. Tara crumpled the calling card, fingers curling over the thick paper in her palm. "Can't you be happy for me, for once?" she cried.

Amma was quick and elaborate with her answer. Real happiness lay in selflessness, in sacrifices, in putting the family before oneself. A good woman sought a life of character and dignity, not willful pursuit of her heart.

Tara asked to speak to Daddy. He refused to come on the line. Tara disconnected with shaking hands. She took deep breaths, found a magazine to fan her inflamed, sweaty face. She still had to call Vijay, and was eager to get it over with. She gave a moment for her overwrought nerves to calm down, to compose her thoughts, before she dialed his number.

"You bailed out," he said.

"Vijay, I expected you to understand."

"Have you ever thought about what dad and mom must endure on your behalf in Mangalore?" His voice was cold. "You didn't hesitate to throw them to the wolves."

"It seems like that because they are part of the pack," she cried. "You all are."

Falling from grace wasn't easy, just as being rejected wasn't easy, no matter how many times it happened. She was an outcast, like Uncle Anand before her, for bringing her family hurt and shame. Suddenly, she went from feeling hot to cold. She wrapped herself in the aqua chenille throw on the sofa, yet she shivered, guilt racking her insides. She must have dozed off from sheer exhaustion, because when her eyes opened, Cyrus was in her apartment, kissing her forehead.

She sought his arms, the beat of his heart against her ear, and believed him when he said time was a great healer, that her family would eventually come around, that they had to accept her decision to seek happiness for herself.

"They will welcome me with open arms once they see how much I care for their daughter," he said. She nodded. Somehow, in his arms, her family's reaction seemed to fade in its importance, like a miracle balm healing a knife wound instantaneously.

Chapter 23

Tara and Cyrus took care of the arrangements themselves, finalizing a time slot for the wedding, making sure the priest was free for the ceremony, buying bags of rice, lentils, and clarified butter to be donated to the temple kitchen, filling little goody bags with favors—white metal bowls, nuts, and Indian sweets—to be distributed to the guests. Cyrus and Alyona went flower shopping, looking for marigolds and roses. When they finally found the flowers, much to everybody's relief, Alyona offered to string them into garlands to be exchanged by the bride and groom after the ceremony.

Cyrus's dadda, Terrence, flew in for the wedding. Annette's brother, James, came with his wife, Lily, and their two kids, eight-year-old Anna with the infectious smile and two missing teeth, and five-year-old Johnny, a cherubic mini-version of James. They all stayed in Tara and Cyrus's new four-bedroom house, a noisy group of happy, excited people.

James and Lily helped Tara and Cyrus in the kitchen, with the cleaning, with the laundry. James towered over everybody else in the house. He was balding, sported a goatee, and wore loose Hawaiian shirts, which his wife said were a futile attempt to cover his beer belly; but he had the same quiet, gentle disposition that Tara remembered. Lily was the opposite—petite, talkative, gossipy, with small hands that kept everything around her neat. They seemed to get along fine, and James was happy that his best buddy had finally found his Star.

They were all in the large kitchen the evening before the wedding, sipping wine and beer, munching on trail mix, prepping for the chicken *vindaloo* and soft *idlis* fluffed with yeast, the kind Cyrus loved. The kids had made themselves scarce, which wasn't difficult when they could play video games in the family room.

"To find you on a billboard in America, after all these years! That's a miracle, man, simply a miracle," James said, shaking his head, laughing, as they stood at the counter, slicing onions, garlic, ginger and tomatoes for the vindaloo. He set the knife down on the board to pat Tara's shoulder. "They ought to make a Bolly-wood movie out of your love story. I am so happy for my Cyrus."

"Tara, dear, thank you for making my boy happy," Cyrus's dad pitched in from his post on the bar stool near the marble-topped kitchen counter. His gray-green eyes were a little glazed from too much wine, and his salt-and-pepper mustache, upturned at the ends, had specks of dust from the trail mix. He wiped a tear from the outer corner of his eye.

"Cyrus grew up without a mother's love. There was only so much a father could do, you know. He deserves love. He deserves you."

Tara rushed to give him a hug. He patted her back softly, wiping another tear from his eye. The wine was making her giddy, and the onions were making her teary-eyed, but it was something else too. She caught happy vibrations in her heart. She heard silent meaning in the words expressed—that Cyrus was lucky in finding her, that they loved and accepted her and thought she was the one for him.

The other people in her life who thought she was special and who she thought were special came to the wedding, too. Alyona came dressed in a blue Banarasi silk sari, a gift from Tara, her short hair in an updo and embellished with little white fake flowers. Ruth looked regal in an orange, Swarowski crystal-encrusted chiffon *lehenga* that swept the floor, also a gift from Tara. Dottie wore her navy-blue suit and white blouse elegantly. Cyrus's friend Tony Kaputo came in a black suit with his pretty wife, Ashley, who wore a yellow chiffon sari. There were three others from Peach Street Games, two men in crisp black suits and a girl in a floral, off-shoulder dress, who stood in rapt attention as the priest tried to explain the significance of the rituals to them in English.

Tara wore a red Kanjeevaram silk sari with heavy, gold-dipped silver work through its six yards. She had worn a green one with a red border the first time. Red was in now, said Lily, who had been entrusted the task of assembling the bridal trousseau, much of which she had accomplished with a shopping expedition to Bangalore. Alyona worked on Tara's hair, taming it with iron and gel and spray, coaxing it into an updo, embellishing it with real flowers and a *tikka*, a gold chain with a pendant in the middle parting of her hair. She wore heavy gold jewelry for only the second time in her life. Lily had shopped for most of the collection in Mangalore, but one traditional choker necklace belonged to Annette, and to Cyrus's grandmother before her. Tara had been hesitant to wear it until Cyrus's dad convinced her that Annette would have wanted her to have it, that she alone was the rightful owner of this shining piece of family history.

Tara and Cyrus were married in a simple temple ceremony. The contrasts were many between her first and her second wedding. A thousand guests had borne witness to the first, an elaborate series of ceremonies amid the chanting of Sanskrit *mantras* and a ritualistic pyre. This time round, there were a handful of witnesses and a single ceremony that lasted twenty minutes. Then, she had been scared, stiff, sweaty, and tired. Now, her face radiated its own glow. Then, she had walked around the ceremonial fire seven times with a stranger to signify seven vows that were supposed to spiritually unite them as husband and wife forever. Now, she sat next to her best friend before an idol of Lord Ganesh, the elephant-headed God of all beginnings, the remover of obstacles. She didn't mind joining her hands together in prayer, or repeating the *shlokas* after the priest, because Cyrus wanted a Hindu wedding. He'd had two church weddings, he said—an Indian Catholic Church wedding and an American Baptist Church wedding, neither of which had lasted. This time, he wanted to take his bride to be his wife in this birth and every birth, for all of eternity.

They were seated cross-legged on low wooden stools, their hands folded. A red silk dupatta covered Tara's head for the ceremony. She touched the heavy gold choker. She could feel its weight around her neck, reminding her that she was now part of Cyrus, his family, his history. She stole a quick look at him. He looked so handsome in his beige, embroidered *sherwani* and red pants, a red stole casually thrown across his shoulders. His fair skin gleamed, and his eyes glittered like moonlit lakes. Her heart longed to kiss him. He smiled happily, boyishly every now and then when he turned to look at her. After the puja, the priest directed Cyrus to color Tara's forehead with *sindoor*, vermillion, welcoming her as his partner for life. They exchanged rings, slim bands of gold, Tara's set with a solitary diamond.

"I am dying to kiss the bride," he whispered, after they had exchanged garlands. She clamped a hennaed hand over her mouth to stop the giggles. "There is no kissing the bride in the Hindu wedding tradition," she said. "The priest will be mortified."

The priest, a fair-skinned, young Gujarati man, looked up at her, part question, part smile on his face. She shook her head, and almost choked trying to stifle another giggle.

"Look what you did. The priest thinks the bride is a silly goose," she whispered.

"This gander loves the silly goose," Cyrus whispered back, a fist over his chest. She laughed openly this time.

Two days after the wedding, they went to Disney World in Orlando, the happiest place on earth, where Sara and Johnny suddenly came alive, and she with them. They went from attraction to attraction, Sara and Johnny talking nonstop in their excitement. They soared over Agrabah on Aladdin's magic carpet, Tara working the controls that made them tilt back and forth, Cyrus ahead of them in the front row with Anna, who had the controls that made them fly higher and lower at her whim. Up and down, back and forth they went, Johnny next to her, screaming with joy, his young face lit with pure thrill. She closed her eyes, felt the wind in her hair. She saw a little girl of five or six on a tall red-and-blue, shoe-shaped slide, squealing with joy on its downward spiral, three other friends riding, screaming behind her. She turned around, straining her neck to peer into their faces. Their eyes were closed and their mouths open; the wind had blown their hair over their faces, but she recognized them. It was almost as if she were back at the place where she had been playing—in the grassy grounds of a clubhouse where happiness lived a long time ago—with Pippi, Leenika, and Runa. She opened her eyes and looked at the man ahead of her. The wind had forced his hair onto his forehead. She saw the sharp nose, the face titled upward to catch the wind, the thrill. Life had indeed come full circle. "Touch wood," she whispered to herself. "Touch wood."

Their house was a pristine, white, four-bedroom structure with a three-sided porch held up with white columns, a sloping gray roof, and a beautifully landscaped yard dotted with magnolias. Her fairy tale house. The backyard was large and overlooked a lake and woods beyond. In the middle of the backyard, in a giant oak was their magical getaway, a treehouse that Cyrus had commissioned a couple of months earlier, a little after they moved in, after he had asked her, during a conversation on fantasies, what hers had been as a child. To live in a nest, she had confessed, like a bird. His fantasy had been to soar in the sky, like an eagle.

Their fantasies came together inside the tree house, a ten-by-twelve-foot, oak-paneled room with a view of the lake that was fringed by wooded walking trails at the far end. When it caught their fancy, they sat in the tree house on little folding chairs, next to the stump of an old oak that served as coffee table, sipping hot tea. Sometimes, as the day's light faded into darkness, they folded the chairs and stacked them in a corner, pulled out a thick red mattress, and fooled around. Sometimes, they made love in daylight, surrounded by singing birds.

Through the year, Cyrus spent most of his time in Atlanta, building and fortifying Peach Street Games. He still went to San Jose a couple of times a month, but only for a few days at a time. He was up at the crack of dawn for his yoga and meditation sessions. Then he fixed breakfast. She cooked dinner. At night, they lay curled on the couch, his arms around her, their legs entwined under a plush velvet throw, watching TV or a movie, midway through which his eyes would close, his chin sinking into her face, heavy in peaceful oblivion.

They hiked most Saturday mornings, through summer and fall, and then again in the spring. They traveled through Europe once, and around the States when they could. Between them, silence was never an impediment, conversation never a problem.

Tara still kept up with Ruth and Dottie, joining them for leisurely cafeteria lunches and trips of compassion. Alyona, however, was starring in a new love story, her resolve to never date having died at Tara's wedding. This time it was Casper Eskandarian, a teetotaler who owned a bartending school in Doraville.

"Your beautiful story made me believe in love again," she had sighed. "I want what you have, girl."

Tara wanted that for Alyona, too.

Tara was sold on the immense benefits of yoga and meditation. Every Saturday morning, she and Cyrus drove up to Unity Church three miles away, where he taught basic yoga asanas free of charge to whoever was interested. Tara stretched, held poses, and worked out along with a motley group of young mothers, college students, a recovering cancer patient, and a seventy-five-year-old retired IRS employee. After yoga, they meditated collectively, stilling their minds, liberating them of thoughts, living in the present. She couldn't help but marvel at how wonderfully unruffled and relaxed life seemed from her lotus position. She quickly learned the art of funneling her energies outward, in positive directions, at the bottom of which lay a tranquil core. When she closed her eyes, she was often in an exuberant flower garden, walking hand in hand with Cyrus, a sublime rainbow arching over them. Around them were Amma, Daddy, Vijay, and Cyrus's family. One day, this too would come true.

Chapter 24

Tara quit her QA job to make time for writing. Her short stories and essays appeared in online journals, local magazines, even the *London Review*. *The New Yorker* proved elusive, but she'd keep trying.

Cyrus registered the Georgia branch of the Annette Saldanha Foundation, a charity he had hitherto run from San Jose. The foundation raised and dispersed funds to run the Annette Saldanha Home for Children in Mangalore. Cyrus's dadda managed the home in India, identifying needs, allocating funds, supervising the staff. Dadda had sold Saldanha Motors—a fleet of buses that plied between Mangalore and nearby towns like Udupi, Karkala, and Kasaragod—to his competitor's son, devoting all his energies to the family charity.

Annette Saldanha hadn't been forgotten. Cyrus had made sure of that. It was her name on the charitable endeavor he and Dadda ran. In death, Annette had achieved a larger-than-life status, a saint-like aura. She was the dispenser of love, kindness, and hope. She gave new life to withered, fractured, abandoned little lives.

Annette had never been the love of his life, but she was the family Cyrus never had. He had admitted this to Tara once, a few months into their marriage, when they lay next to each other on the red mattress in their tree house. A part of him had died with the passing of Annette and her mother, Aunty Mariette. Growing up, they had been his anchors, their villa his home.

"I don't ever remember spending an afternoon in my own house," he had said, staring up at the wooden beams of the ceiling reflectively. "Every day, James and I were picked up from school by Uncle Lobo, who dropped us off at the villa. We three kids, we did everything together. I only returned home late every evening after Dadda got home, and even then, I wanted to escape, run back to be with my buddies, play some more, talk some more, argue some more."

"What if Annette were still alive? I suppose you and I would never have reconnected." Tara had turned to face him.

"I would have still searched high and low for you," he had said without hesitation. "Annette and I should never have married. We both knew that going into it. We didn't have a choice. She was pregnant."

"If you both knew it was a mistake to marry, why did you even have sex, get pregnant?"

A long silence ensured. "He wasn't mine," he had said at the end of it. "My son, I mean. Biologically, he wasn't mine."

Stunned, she had searched his face for an explanation.

"Annette was a stubborn girl. She didn't want to make the problem go away."

"But whose baby was it?"

"Some fool from college who didn't want to own up responsibility and face the wrath of his family."

"So, you took responsibility?"

"Yes, what other solution was there? Mangalore is not exactly America. An unmarried mother would be ostracized there even today."

"Does the family know?"

"No one else knows. Only Annette and I, and now you."

"You are a good man, Cyrus Saldanha," she had said, rolling into his arms, kissing the hollow of his throat. "And all this time I assumed it was raging adolescent hormones."

"My hormones are raging now." He had tightened his grip around her; nuzzled her neck. "It's time that we tried for little stars of our own, no?"

She had grown stiff in his arms, mumbled something about needing a little bit more time to prepare herself mentally to be a parent. She was surprised with her reaction, because theoretically, she wanted children. Was she stalling because she wanted Cyrus all to herself for a while? Or was it the fear of failing as a parent?

His disappointment had cloaked her with guilt, but he had never brought up the topic again. Six months later, she told him she was ready.

He enveloped her in his arms, held her tight when she told him she had missed her period by a week. When her physician confirmed the news, he dazzled the dull room with his smile. Their joy lasted two weeks, until she noticed spotting following severe stomach cramps. A visit to the Emory emergency room made their fear of a miscarriage real. He cradled her in his arms that night, kissing her forehead, sounding chirpy.

It was all right, he said. Miscarriages were common. They would try again in a few months, whenever she felt ready.

When the second miscarriage happened seven months after the first, eight weeks into her pregnancy, she was afraid she had run out of time. But he assured her it was okay. They'd take their time before trying again. They had fifty-three kids in Mangalore who called them Amma and Dadda.

Cyrus was going to Mangalore to be part of the tenth anniversary celebration of the home. Tara helped him pick gifts for the children—pencils, fancy erasers, candy, T-shirts. He had wanted her to join him, but her last conversation with Amma had come crowding back into her head. She didn't feel ready to brave the hostility she would face in her community. She had been humiliated as an abandoned wife. She could only imagine the viciousness that would be flung at her, now that she had dared to divorce her first husband and taken a second, outside the community.

After Cyrus left, her social ostracism felt real.

"I may never be able to visit Mangalore again," she told Ruth as they baked caramel cake for the church sale one evening, but all Tara craved was a slice of Amma's pound cake.

"It is your family's loss that they choose to stay away from your happiness," Ruth assured her. "This is your home, and we are your family."

"Your family don't care for your happiness. Why you should care what they think?" Alyona fumed over a plateful of massaman curry and steaming hot rice at their favorite Buford Highway Malaysian–Thai place the following Saturday.

It wasn't as simple as that, Tara knew. It wasn't just her versus her family. It was also her parents versus the rest of the community. Perhaps Vijay was right. She had thrown her parents to the wolves and left them to defend their family honor while she stayed in the safety of Cyrus's arms.

He had called or emailed her every day, and sent her photos of the tenth anniversary celebration of the Annette Saldanha Home. The best one was of Cyrus with a group of kids standing outside their home, his arms spread across them, complementing their toothy smiles with deep dents on his cheeks. How the sun radiated on their faces. How happy he looked with them. They all belonged to him, and he to them. Seeing the photo, she had felt a twinge of regret for not going, for leaving herself out of Cyrus's big family affair.

But there were unexpected gifts to gladden her heart when Cyrus returned home. He spread them out on the bed as he unpacked. A clay peacock with its feathers spread out, a pink paper fan, a white handkerchief with embroidered red roses in the corners—all artistic creations of the kids. There was even a card addressed to Amma that was signed by all fifty-three children. On the front of the card was a watercolor scene of the sun rising between two mountains and crowned with blue cottony clouds. A stick figure stood on the green grass at the foot of the mountains with an upward curve of a smile. An arrow pointing in the direction of the figure, had "Amma" written on its tail end. Tara laughed at the shaggy long hair that fell to her stick waist; at the way her arms stuck out at rigid angles. She would treasure this Mona Lisa all her life. With so much love from the children, Cyrus could never miss having one of his own. Neither would she.

As the Georgia chapter of the Annette Saldanha Foundation grew, so did the number of people who walked in and out of Tara and Cyrus's home. They came every weekend for volunteer meetings: sipping tea, munching on cookies or masala peanuts, making themselves home with discussions, arguments, unrelated banter, and laughter. She couldn't remember a single time in her life that she had enjoyed large groups. But this group of enthusiasts was different. She nurtured the family—there were eight college kids and two young couples. Only if she nourished the roots would the produce be bountiful. She felt like she was in the center of a mighty giving tree, a bit like the wish-fulfilling banyan tree of

Morgan Hill. This tree was empowering. She stepped out of her comfort zone to solicit corporate sponsorships; but even when she prepared her sales pitch endlessly and worried incessantly until a meeting with an IT company boss or a small business owner was over, she discovered bits of herself that fascinated her.

The first fundraiser that the chapter organized, a 5K run, was a mega success, as the local Indian–American newspaper headlined. The team had raised $25,000 for the foundation's causes through corporate sponsorships and registrations. She helped with the bookkeeping, with the registrations, taking calls, providing information. She got T-shirts screen printed with an image of a group of Cyrus's children smiling their winsome smiles, below which was emblazoned, in red, the words, I RAN TO GIVE THEM HOPE, and below it, in blue, the name of their foundation. She handed out these T-shirts to the runners after the race, a smile of appreciation on her face.

The foundation's team members were energized by the success of the summer fundraiser. They geared up for a winter fundraiser that would set them on par with the West Coast chapter. Of course, it would have to be an indoor event to be successful. A Bollywood musical evening or a play, they suggested. A play, they decided. A play, Tara and Cyrus agreed.

"We have an in-house writer," said Cyrus, without any warning. They all turned to look at Tara.

"Okay, but, fair warning, I have never written a play before."

The team members said they'd improvise on the dialogues during rehearsals. A story appeared on her laptop, a modern-day retelling of Shakespeare's *Romeo and Juliet*. She called it *Jahanara*. It was set in urban India, the India she knew. She interjected the story with Bollywood song and dance, like the movies she had grown up with. She called her hero Jahan and his heartthrob Anara. She made Cyrus read each of the four drafts and write his suggestions in the margin.

When the final draft was ready, it threw open a host of questions. Cyrus, and now Tara, were quite the pros at organizing races, but an indoor event was new territory. Who would direct the play? Who would work on the props, the sound, the lighting? Most of them had been part of school or college plays, but none had been involved with the nitty gritty of putting it all together.

"Nobody is going to come if we don't do a professional job," said Shekar, a lanky, third-year student of mechanical engineering at Georgia Tech.

They needed to find an experienced director, they all agreed.

Devika and Samaresh, the IT couple from Marietta, said they knew the perfect person for the job. All they needed to do was convince her of their cause. Munmun Das taught Odissi to kids in Alpharetta. Tara had seen Munmun's ad for her dance school in the local Indian–American newspaper, striking a pose in her dance regalia, dark kohl-lined eyes on an expressive face. But what got the team excited, when she readily agreed to be part of their project, was the fact that she had a lot of experience directing plays for the local Bengali association during their annual Durga Pujas.

Munmun walked into Tara and Cyrus's lives, graceful in a handloom cotton sari, silver anklets around her pretty feet, thick long black hair cascading down her back like a waterfall. She alighted from her gleaming black Mercedes Benz for their first meeting, followed by her sullen older husband, Dr. Sujit Das, a lean, balding gastroenterologist.

Tara and Cyrus took turns thanking her for her help in feeding, clothing, and schooling orphaned children. Munmun bowed, touched her chest. Her silky voice was self-assured. "Oh, it is my pleasure. When I heard about your cause, I immediately wanted to help."

Tara plated steaming hot *upma* and fixed masala chai for the team while Munmun read the script for *Jahanara* and cobbled together a cast for the play. Cyrus agreed to play Jahan to her Anara. Tara declined the role of Anara's mother. "Somebody has to run the show," she said.

Munmun's silent husband did not accompany her after the first meeting. Every Saturday and Sunday, her bejeweled feet carried news of her arrival even before she appeared, sunglasses propped on her head like a band, her saris or salwar suits always starched and crisp, her tone always self-assured. She knew what she wanted, and she got what she wanted from a team that was eager to please. She divided the rehearsals into sixteen sessions spread over eight weeks. The group met in the finished basement of Tara and Cyrus's home. The first weekend, they rehearsed Act One, Scene One.

Tara watched, seated on the plush carpet, face shining, thrilled to see her words being brought to life. She had written much of the dialogue; still the cast improvised as they went along, laughing as they came up with silly one-liners, then amending them to something that Tara and Munmun approved of.

By the third weekend, Jahan and Anara of *Jahanara* had grown up. Then they held hands to sing a love song. It was a scene Tara had written. Nevertheless, her smile waned as she watched from the sidelines as Jahan serenaded Anara with a rose from their backyard. She dropped her gaze to the carpet as the lead couple lip-synched to a romantic Hindi song that played on Munmun's laptop. When she gazed up for a second, she saw her husband's hand on Munmun's back, on the smooth, dusky skin left exposed by her sexy, deep-cut sari blouse. She heard Cyrus call out her name after the song ended, asking her what she thought about his dancing skills. She gave him the thumbs up sign. Cyrus had grown up dancing at the famous Saldanha ball every year. She had never set foot on a dance floor. In her family, dancing with a man was considered crossing the line of propriety. Right now, she was being as silly as her parents were with their rules.

She pulled herself up from the carpet and ran up the stairs to the kitchen to fix hot *khichdi* for the group. It was not too late to learn. Once their program was over, she would look up dance classes in their neighborhood. She'd convince Cyrus to go with her. She'd learn to dance like the Munmuns and Saldanhas of the world.

The group met for rehearsals again the next day. This time, Jahan and Anara held hands on a make-believe park bench, which was actually two garden chairs set next to each other. He spouted poetic verses about her intoxicating eyes, her silken hair that left him breathless. They were good actors, the two of them. They looked the part of star-crossed lovers. What exactly had prompted her to write a love story? She couldn't remember.

She hated her irrational thoughts, the way they hovered over her like the vestiges of a bad dream. She looked forward to Monday, when life would go back to routine, and there would be no intrusion of silly thoughts. Meditation, breakfast, a brief phone call from Cyrus during his lunch break, a leisurely dinner that she would have ready when he got home, and an evening that would end with them watching TV, their limbs entwined on the couch, his face drooping with sleep on her shoulder.

During the week, she went all the way out of her comfort zone, cold calling businesses for sponsorships, setting up meetings. On Friday afternoon, she convinced her ex-boss Srini Reddy to sanction funds for Alpha Tech to become the platinum sponsor of the play. This was her biggest triumph yet. Now, it would be easier to solicit sponsorships from other IT companies. Cyrus was ecstatic. She was left wondering whether her manic drive was to prove something to herself or to assure Cyrus of her value.

She avoided rehearsals the next weekend, staying upstairs in her office. She had booked the venue during the week, a high school auditorium in Norcross, and registered on Sulekha to sell tickets online, but there was still a lot to get done. She created a checklist—hire a light and sound technician, find somebody to put together the backdrops or find a volunteer, create a design for the flyer and contact a printer to print them for the volunteers to distribute around town. She had the weekdays to get her work done, but she chose to get started right away.

Cyrus poked his head into their office, sweaty from rehearsals. She gave him a bright smile and waved her checklist in his direction. "So much to do," she said. "You run along and put on a stellar show. I'll join you when I finish with all this."

The next Saturday, she cooked a difficult Mangalorean meal—*neeru dosa* and chicken curry with coconut. It was exhausting, spreading watery rice batter across the girdle at least fifty times—enough neeru dosas for the gang—folding each cooked dosa in half before moving it to a hot pot. Neeru dosas for so many people wasn't a very brilliant idea, yet there was something lulling about the repetitive job that had filled two hours of rehearsal time. When she was done, she wiped beads of sweat off her forehead with a napkin, and went down to the basement to invite the gang up for lunch.

The group sat on the carpet, talking, sipping bottled water from the basement refrigerator. Only Cyrus and Munmun stood by the window, away from the crowd, deep in conversation. From where she stood, Tara could only see Cyrus's profile, but Munmun was fully visible. Her shoulder rested casually on the window frame, her hair gathered into a knot at the nape of her neck. The shine on her face, the glint of sweat on her neck, the bright yellow of her handloom sari—Tara absorbed all of this in a glance. The dancer's hands were participating equally and animatedly in whatever she was saying, but it was her enormous kohl-lined eyes that cut into Tara's chest—they were transfixed on Cyrus, as if the rest of the world did not exist.

Enraptured was the word that came to her mind, as she made an about face and walked up the stairs. She was forced to open her mouth to breathe easily as she trudged up another flight of stairs to the master bedroom. She headed to the bathroom and splashed cold water on her face from the faucet. She looked at her mirror image, at her troubled eyes. Why had she fled? Why hadn't she casually joined in the conversation, asserted her position? Why had she acted like *Jahanara* actually existed?

She heard voices downstairs. As she patted her face dry with a soft towel, she forced her mouth upward into a smile. The gang had settled down in the family room and around the kitchen table, a cacophony of voices. She found Cyrus in the kitchen, rummaging through the drawers, a bunch of serving spoons in his hand.

"Star, where were you? The gang's hungry," he called out when he saw her. She resisted the urge to snap back at him, to tell him she wasn't the gang's servant.

They sat crowding the formal dining room, some on folding chairs that they had brought in from the deck. They talked about this scene and that and what dialogue would propel the story forward. Munmun sat between Anita's husband, Manish, and Shekar, discussing a scene, plate perched daintily on a napkin over a crossed leg.

Tara felt out of place, like an outcast in her own production.

"How's the food, guys?" she asked loudly. They turned around to look at her, as if they had only just realized she was present. They were effusive in their compliments. Awesome, delicious, food to die for, they said. Munmun wanted the recipe for the neeru dosas. So soft and delicate, she said. Cyrus pressed his bunched fingertips to his lips and blew her a kiss. But their generous words bounced off her ears. She had to find her peace herself.

She slipped out to the garage, to her silver Camry. She drove over to Ruth's and watched, seated on a bar stool, as her friend blended cake mix, sour cream, oil, water, eggs, and sugar for the sock-it-to-me cake she was baking for her former daughter-in-law, Paula. Tara loved being in Ruth's kitchen; the warmth of the wood paneling, the mild aroma of the cake mix and ground cinnamon were enormously comforting.

Ruth bubbled with excitement. "Paula's birthday is on Tuesday. I plan to drive up to Acworth where she lives, and surprise her with her favorite cake," she said. "I can't let you taste this cake, but I made a batch of pecan brownies. I'll put them in a Ziploc for you to take back with you. Would you please tell Cyrus I made them especially for him?"

Tara smiled. "He'll be very pleased."

Ruth loved Cyrus. Everyone she knew loved Cyrus. What was to stop a sensual dancer with a sad sack of a husband from loving Cyrus? She ran her forefinger across the spatula's silicon head and licked the cake mix off of it. What was to stop him from reciprocating?

"It's wonderful that you have such a great relationship with your ex-daughter-in-law," she said.

Ruth looked up from the large Bundt pan she was greasing. "Oh yes, Paula is like the daughter I never had. She never remarried, you know. She and Charlie reconnected and remained friends in the last few years of his life."

"Why did they divorce?"

"Men are such fools. He had an affair with a coworker, and Paula couldn't handle it. It was totally his fault."

"And the affair? It didn't last?"

"No. It was a disaster. But it was too late for Charlie to go back. Luckily, Paula returned. She was there for Charlie during his battle with cancer. He was fortunate that way."

Tara sighed. "What's it with men and commitment?"

"Not all men are bad, my dear. Our Cyrus, for instance, would never hurt you."

"What makes you so sure?"

"Cyrus thinks the world of you. It's plain as day."

"I know." Tara returned the spatula to the bowl. She watched in silence as Ruth poured the gooey batter into the Bundt pan, as she opened the hot oven to slide the pan in. The longer she swiveled on the bar stool, the sillier she felt.

She remembered deliberately, foolishly leaving her cell phone in the car. "I think I better get back home," she said.

She returned to her car, carrying a large freezer bag filled with Ruth's moist brownies. Her blackberry had no missed calls from Cyrus like she had expected. As she put on her seat belt, she called him. He sounded his usual exuberant self. "Star, where did you disappear?"

Sorry, she said. She had promised to meet Ruth that afternoon. She gave no excuse for slipping out of the house even before her guests had left.

"That's all right. Munmun is helping me clean up."

"And the others?"

"Oh, they all left, lazy buggers."

She sucked in air sharply, mumbled incoherently that she was on her way home. Then she abruptly disconnected.

The house was empty when she returned. Only the strains of Pandit Ravi Shankar's sitar played on their Bose surround sound system. She peeped out of the kitchen door, into the yard.

"Cyrus?" she called.

He didn't respond. She scanned the tree house. She thought she heard faint voices from up there. Then she caught sight of a sari pallu through the window—a splash of yellow inside their fantasy place—inside the love nest Cyrus had built for Tara and Cyrus.

She quickly walked back to the family room, taking the couch, sitting upright, tossing her purse and Ruth's brownies carelessly on the floor. She crossed her arms across her chest to stop its shivering, to stop the complete loss of control that was building inside her, the urge to run up the tree house with her chef's knife and plunge it into the woman who had dared to violate her private space.

He walked in alone after some minutes had passed, looking his usual ebullient self. They had stretched like hours, the minutes she had waited for him. Again and again, weirdly, their own private conversation about making little stars, a conversation they'd had in the tree house, had played in her mind, like a stuck recorder.

"Hey, I didn't hear you come in. Munmun just left." He stooped down to give her a peck on her forehead. "How's my girlfriend, Ruth?"

She resisted the urge to strike him. "What was Munmun doing in our tree house?"

"She said she was dying to see it." He sat beside her, draped a casual arm around the back of the couch, fingers touching her arm. "I didn't think you'd mind."

"Really, Cyrus? The tree house is our personal space. Why would you take her up there?"

"You gave Devika and Samaresh a tour the other day," he reminded her.

That was different, she wanted to tell him. *You did not feel threatened by their visit.* "Do as you please," she said instead, picking up her purse and the pack of brownies. She heard him say sorry, that he didn't think she'd mind, that he'd never take anybody else up to their tree house ever again.

She let him talk to her back, as she walked with purpose to the kitchen sink, and dumped Ruth's brownies into the trash can under it.

Chapter 25

She was vaguely aware that she had been there, in the blackness, for a while. She thought she heard her name being called out. She opened her eyes, tried to move, but her body was tied down to the bed. She heard Amma's voice near her head. Then she appeared, young, her face bright, yellow sari pallu blowing in the wind.

"Tara, forgive us, angel. It's time for us to leave," she said. She wasn't alone. Cyrus was with her. They were on the train that was pulling out of Mangalore station. They waved at her, her young Amma and the present-day Cyrus. She tried to catch a glimpse of their faces as she ran behind them, but it was so dusty. No, it was not dust, it was smoke, huge gusts of dark smoke, billowing into her eyes. *Not again*, she cried. She had to stop them. Tara struggled with all her might to open her eyes, but they were shut tightly. She had lost them again.

She woke up with a start. She was alone in her pretty bedroom, gasping, wet with sweat. The smell of fried eggs filled her with relief. It was a Monday morning, and Cyrus was probably downstairs fixing breakfast. Her hands shook as she pushed her damp hair out of her face, as she rubbed her face. She had not had an episode of sleep paralysis since she had left Sanjay.

She cleaned their house all day, because she could not write, could not come up with story ideas. Her nightmare had seemed so real, as did the fear appended to it. But what bothered her more was the fact that it had come back again, invaded her cozy world. She missed the calm of her two years at Sanctuary Hills, where she had rebuilt her life from scratch; where she had firm control over her thoughts, her feelings. Where every day had been about taking a step forward. She wondered now if she had rushed into another relationship before she was ready for it; if she should have given more time for her lacerations to heal; if she should have enjoyed a bit longer the bliss of being self-sufficient, self-worthy.

She fell prey to overthinking as she dusted the blinds, the thoughts returning even as she attempted to push them away. Had Cyrus been faithful to his two former wives? He had been so casual about breaking up with his girlfriend, Giana. Why have a girlfriend if she meant nothing to him? How many other women had he scored with? How easily he had adopted the American dating culture, while she had not so much as gone out with a guy until marriage. They had such different attitudes about sex.

She paused to gaze out the window, to psychoanalyze her dark thoughts—were they justified, or was she overreacting? She simply couldn't tell; she wasn't an outside observer. She contemplated having a conversation with him. But what was she going to say? That she didn't like him enjoying another woman's company? She didn't want him to play the role of Jahan? She wanted Munmum out? All these options meant ruining the fundraiser. So unreasonable. She sounded like a basket case jealous wife even framing those questions in her head.

On Friday, he called her at four o'clock to tell her he had to stay behind for happy hour with clients visiting from San Francisco. She watched an entire Bollywood movie that evening without seeing a single scene. Was it really clients from San Francisco or the Odissi dancer who occupied vast tracts of her mind these days? That night, when he stretched an arm out to hold her, she moved away, rolling over, her back to him.

"What's wrong?" he asked.

"I am tired," she replied.

In the darkness, she felt the gentle pressure of his warm hands move across her strained shoulder, down her back. "Does that feel good?"

"Go to sleep, Cyrus," she said coldly. "Good night."

Her eyes misted as she became aware of the invisible wall between them, slicing them from one to two separate individuals. She avoided him in the morning, getting out of the house before he returned from his yoga session at Unity church. She headed to Macy's at Perimeter Mall, where she spent hours pushing clothes in the clearance racks forward and backward, ultimately buying a bright red blouse she knew she would never wear.

For the rest of the weekend, and every weekend thereafter, she stayed out of the house. She met the sound and light technician at the food court of the Indian mall, went over to the press off North Druid Hills to get delivery of the flyers. She drove all day long, stopping at every Indian temple, grocery store, and restaurant, dropping a handful of flyers at every location or attaching them to glass doors or walls as other event organizers had done. Fortunately, she had designed the flyers herself. It was the faces of the children the fundraiser would benefit that smiled back at her; not the stars of the show holding hands.

He had become aware of the shift, the night she had moved away from him. "We miss you at rehearsals; please stay a while," he implored several times.

"I have things to take care of," she told him the first time. The other times, she ignored his request. "Is something wrong?" he asked her again and again. When she merely shook her head, he tried hard to lighten the atmosphere with his banter. Let's meditate together, he suggested. Every time, she came up with an excuse.

On a Wednesday, just ten days before the show, he called from work to tell her that he had heard from Munmun. She wanted to adopt some of their children. He hadn't conveyed the news casually. She had detected a certain preparedness in his speech, as if he had known she might not take kindly to the news.

"Great," she replied coldly. "Now, she can be part of our lives forever."

"Why do I get the sense that you are not very fond of Munmun?"

She was embarrassed that he had guessed her insecurity; that she thought of herself as lesser than Munmun. He had reminded her of who she'd been in her previous life. She took a sharp breath, fortifying her defenses with air. "Here's what I think, Cyrus. I think I should never have rushed into this marriage. I was so happy rediscovering myself, putting my life together. I regret letting it all go."

He responded with silence, as if he was too stunned for words. Still, she couldn't stop her torment from bursting out. "Now, it's all about your foundation, your team, your play. It's like I have no individuality left."

She heard him draw in a deep breath. "I didn't impose any of it on you. I thought you enjoyed being part of the foundation," he said finally.

"Heck, no. Not anymore." Her lips trembled as a sob escaped her throat. She had only seen her husband's happy side so far, but she could imagine his eyes clouding, his face downcast as he ruminated over her words.

"I'm sorry, Cyrus," she wept into the phone. "I didn't mean it like that."

It was all right, he said after a long moment of silence. They'd discuss it when he got home.

She was afraid he'd rush home, so she fled, driving on the back roads until she reached Alyona's apartment. Alyona talked more than she listened, her tone light, face shining. She was now engaged to Casper, and tiny diamonds flashed on her left ring finger as she laughed.

"Why you have to think so much? Why you can't be calm for another week?" Her tone was dismissive. It was as if Alyona needed to believe in the magical, permanent nature of their fairy-tale because it had revived her belief in love and led her to Casper. She wanted to believe in her own fairytale.

"Because that bitch has found a way to stay permanently in contact with Cyrus by adopting our kids."

"Listen to me, girl. Don't push him away. Don't send him into her arms."

This was not what Tara had expected to hear from her friend. Her stomach churned as she made her way out of Alyona's apartment with a quick good-bye hug. She wanted to be calm, to feel nothing. She just didn't know how. She drove around aimlessly, thinking nothing coherent, the fear in her gut growing. Finally, she slowed down outside their neighborhood park and found a secluded spot to hide herself. It was early September. It wouldn't get dark until late in the evening, which suited her fine. She was afraid to go back home, to face him, knowing she had wronged him but not knowing how to right the wrong. They were approaching the final week leading up to the staging of the play. Rehearsals were scheduled every evening beginning Saturday. She couldn't bear the thought of living through the week.

Her decision to go to Mangalore was impulsive. It surprised her at first; the pull of the home she had given up claim to, the need to see her parents, to wrap herself in parental love that she had branded wanting. The desire grew as the long day faded. *A storm can be weathered only from a safe spot, not from its eye*, she told herself. She needed time to process her feelings, to think rationally.

She expected to see his car in the garage when she returned, for him to anxiously rush to the door. But he wasn't in yet. She was too exhausted to analyze what this meant, where he had gone, or why it made her heart heavy with fear even though she had run away from him. When he returned, past eight o'clock, she was on the sofa, still wearing the clothes she had spent the day in. She sat up with a start when she heard the garage door open, and her heart gave yet another lurch when he walked in. His smile was steady and his hug long and warm, but his usual easy manner had vanished.

She told him at dinner, as they sat across each other at the kitchen table, leftovers from last night between them. "There is nothing left for me to do. The venue is booked, the tickets are sold, the backdrops are ready, the sound and light guy is hired. You guys won't have any trouble on my account, I can assure you of that."

He reacted with the furrowing of his brows. "When will you be back?"

"I don't know, Cyrus."

"Star, what's bothering you?"

She kept her gaze to her plate. "I need some alone time to figure things out."

"Why do you feel the need to leave?"

"I don't want to discuss it."

"I really think we ought to."

"And I don't."

His face had never been this grim before. She hoped for his expression to soften, for him to implore her to stay, tell her he'd miss her, that he needed her on the big day. And yet she said, "I need to figure this out myself."

Words that ended their conversation.

Her heart was heavy when she went up to the tree house one last time early the next morning. She sat cross-legged on the red mattress looking out into the calm, shimmering lake. She would miss this space, the symbol of their symbiosis, a melding of their childhood fantasies. Meditating, talking, laughing, fooling around; it had seemed possible for a while to be carefree like birds.

He gave her a ride to Hartsfield–Jackson airport on Saturday, acting like all was well in his world, relating his conversation with Dadda that morning—a roof at the home needed repairs; Mira, their four-year-old, was still not talking; the children were in the middle of midterm exams. She listened without hearing, without turning to look at him. His detachment, his lightness of spirit was crushing her chest with its heft. His good-bye hug contained no special sentimentality, or maybe it was she who was stiff. When she disappeared into the long security check line, she didn't turn back to wave at him. She was afraid he'd be gone, that she'd freed him.

Chapter 26

Amma and Daddy had created a paradise right in the middle of the city, in a lane where conspicuous display of wealth was the unwritten rule. The Raj bungalow had lush lawns and flowers in the front and a wide concrete driveway leading to an ornate, carved teakwood front door.

She had windblown hair and a queasy face when she rang the bell. Her return after eight long years should have been a joyful one. Instead, she was a bundle of nerves. She had prepped herself for all kinds of reactions from her parents, but she hadn't been prepared to be met by a houseful of stunned relatives. She smiled weakly at a distant male cousin who opened the door, quickly taking off her shoes and entering noiselessly on the marble floor. She kept her head down, but noticed several relatives lounging on the ornate Italian furniture in the living room, their chatter turning to silence at the sight of her.

Amma was in the kitchen, grating a fresh coconut on a countertop grater and chatting with her younger sister, Nanda.

"Oh, Tara," Aunty Nanda exclaimed, a bejeweled hand flying to cover her open mouth. The coconut in Amma's hand dropped to the floor; a cracking sound, scattering white, moist flecks on the shiny marble. Tara picked the shaggy half coconut off the floor and placed it on the counter.

"Why didn't you inform us you are coming?" Amma asked, eyes wide open in shock, made more dramatic by the dark circles under them.

Tara felt a rush of bile burn the back of her throat. She turned around and fled to the bathroom attached to her room upstairs. She took her time, throwing up, then cleaning herself with a cold shower in the green-tiled bath. Amma was waiting for her, clutching a small metal tray that held a tall glass of lime sherbet, when she emerged from the bathroom.

"Why is everybody here?" Tara asked, without looking at Amma, focusing on lifting her suitcase and setting it on the bed; opening, then unbuckling it to rummage for fresh clothes.

"Why didn't you tell us you are coming?" Amma had recovered from her initial shock, but her voice was still a hoarse whisper.

"I am sorry if I embarrassed you, Amma. I'll leave."

"Don't be silly. That's not what I meant." Amma thrust the glass of sherbet in Tara's direction. "Drink. You will feel refreshed."

Tara accepted the glass, took a sip of the salty-sweet-tangy drink. "Why are they all here?" she asked again.

Amma sat on the edge of the bed, wiped her sweaty face with the pallu of her beige handloom sari. She looked thinner, which made the skin on her face sit a little looser, especially around her jowls. Aunty Nanda's daughter Nina was getting married next week, she said. "Since the family lives in Bangalore, Daddy graciously offered to host the bridal party at our home."

"I thought you said you and Daddy don't go to community functions. How are you hosting a wedding here?"

Amma sighed. "It is a family wedding, Tara. Who else does Nanda have?"

"So, you regained your family honor? By cutting me off?"

"It is not like that." There was no conviction in Amma's words, and she quickly changed the direction of their conversation "I just need to know you are all right. Why did you come alone?"

"I have some work related to the foundation we run." The white lie had come to Tara's lips easily, and with it, a reminder of the work she had abandoned midway. She pressed a white knuckle to her lips to stop their trembling.

Amma sighed. "Take a rest now. I can send your lunch up when it is ready, if you wish. So much left to do. Only four days left for the ceremonies to begin."

Her room did not stir any old attachments in her chest. Maybe it was the new sage green on the walls or the new floral bedspread. She had been away eight years, long enough to erase some memories. There were signs her room was occupied by some of the guests. The dresser was messy; a hair dryer and flat-iron straightener jostled for space with lipsticks, compacts, and eye makeup. Three large suitcases lay flat on the marble floor, clothes peeping out from them. Her own slim Delsey stood out, as if it didn't belong in the room.

She looked out the French window into the garden below. It was a riot of colors: rows of potted marigolds, zinnias, dahlias, petunias, and colorful crotons set against a high, whitewashed compound wall. She looked away, suddenly blinded by the charged memory of the tree house she had left behind.

Amma served an early lunch—parboiled rice, fish curry, and green beans. Tara ate ravenously sitting at the desk in her room, filling the wide-mouthed pit inside her with food. She fell asleep in her old bed, and she was vaguely aware of Amma stroking her hair, kissing her forehead, pulling a light handloom blanket over her feet. Then she fell into blackness, heavy, dreamless. She slept all afternoon, and it took Amma several minutes to wake her up three hours later for tea and snacks.

"Come down," she said. "You cannot stay here all day."

Tara met Aunty Nanda and her daughter Nina, the bride, at the round glass-topped kitchen table, where they were nibbling crunchy banana chips with their tea and complaining about the tailor who had ruined a Kanjeevaram silk sari blouse. She took the spot next to Nina. Amma poured tea from a stainless steel pot, pushed the bone china cup in front of her. Tara's head still felt like it was inside a foggy dark tunnel; she eagerly took a sip of Amma's milky sweet brew.

Aunty Nanda looked youthful in her floral handloom salwar kameez, her thick, slick hair pulled back with a wide barrette. Nina, in tight jeans and a short yellow top, looked nothing like the gawky sixteen-year-old Tara had last seen. Her face was arresting and bright; her hair, inherited from her mother, fell straight down her back like a sheet of black silk.

"What are you wearing to the wedding?" she asked Tara. Her voice had a breathless quality to it, as if her excitement could not be contained.

"Oh, I didn't bring anything dressy. I had no idea you were getting married." From the corner of her eye, Tara caught Aunty Nanda and Amma exchange looks. Shame coursed through her; then anger at feeling shame. She breathed in the hot steam from her cup, a sharp open-mouthed gasp.

"Actually, I am not invited to your wedding, Nina." She smiled a tight-lipped smile at her young cousin. "Didn't you know?"

Nina's eyes widened, she put a warm hand over Tara's forearm. "Of course you are invited. You are family."

Aunty Nanda cleared her throat, as if to get the appropriate words out. "The boy's side is from Bangalore; they don't know the story," she said at last. "Why take risks, we thought."

Why risk inviting an outcast, Aunty Nanda had meant. Tara

turned to look at Amma, who had buried her face in her sari pallu, her shoulders shaking uncontrollably. She wondered if she could find a little bravery inside her to hold her head up, even as shame filled her with no restraint and burned her face.

She strode to the living room. Of the many guests she had encountered on her way in, only a few remained; possibly a late afternoon lull in the flow of people. The television was on local English news, but no one was watching. She recognized one of the three boys who lounged on the sofa, Nina's younger brother Nitin, an engineering student. The other two were probably distant relatives who lived in town and had come to hang out with Nitin. Aunty Nanda's father-in-law, Nina and Nitin's grandfather, sat on a sofa chair at the far end of the room, his face lost behind a copy of the *Morning Herald*.

Tara occupied the slatted teakwood easy chair opposite the TV. Her chest heaved; she could hear her labored breathing over the voice of the TV reporter who was yelling hysterically into the microphone about an income tax department raid at a police inspector's home in Karkala. The repeated close-ups of the thick stacks of rupees discovered in the attic was so irritating that she wanted to stuff them into the screeching TV reporter's mouth. A sob was building inside her, which she tried desperately to quell.

Daddy walked in when the news anchor had moved on to communal tensions in Kasaragod, where a public closing enforced by a local Hindu political outfit had been successful. She stood up in greeting, her hands clasped in front of her like an obedient schoolgirl. He patted her lightly on her shoulder. She noticed his slight stoop, at the way his shirt hung a bit too loose over his shoulders. His face drooped, bearing a sullen expression, but she saw no shock when his eyes fell upon her. Amma had obviously called and filled him in. He stood next to her for a few moments, eyes on the wall, as if struggling for words. For once, he didn't know what to command her to do. His gaze moved to the other occupants of the room. The youngsters took turns greeting him.

She heard the rustle of paper. Aunty Nanda's father-in-law had dropped it on the rug. He was now looking at her intently with magnified eyes from behind his convex glasses. His gray mustache twitched. When Daddy left the room to go upstairs to change, he finally spoke.

"When my younger sister ran away fifty years ago to marry a trader's son, we performed her last rites." His voice was loud, in the manner of one who is hard of hearing.

"Grandfather, times have changed." She saw the shock on Nitin's face, and was grateful for his instant reaction.

"From that day, she was dead to us." Aunty Nanda's father-in-law's words burned her ears as she rushed up the stairs to her room. The slow, deliberate, loud words reverberated inside her head as she snapped her Delsey shut and dragged it down the stairs.

Chapter 27

The mud road with the gaping holes that wound up Morgan Hill was now paved, wide, and clean. There were no goats, no goat droppings. This was a different time and an urban place. The traditional tile-roofed homes were gone, replaced by concrete, modernity, and the demands of real estate. Four-storied apartments in pink, blue, and sea-green piled into each other, right up to the top of the hill. Only Shanti Nilaya remained, and the Pentecostal Church at the top of the hill.

Shanti Nilaya looked nothing like the house of Tara's childhood. Daddy had renovated it several years before, adding a new frontage with large outer rooms where marble flooring had replaced red oxide, and an ornate front door with circular floral motifs carved in wood blocked the outside view. In the yard, only one mango tree and the twelve coconut palms remained, spurting in a sea of cement. The barn was empty; Amba, Appi, and their progeny long dead, now an abandoned outhouse where vestiges of the past lay piled in one corner.

The house was empty too, its original residents long gone. Uncle Anand had left first, twelve years earlier, simply walking out the front door one day and never returning. The search party that Daddy sent out to look for Uncle Anand, made up of employees from his showroom, was not successful in finding him this time. For a year, Grandmother Indira had waited for her younger son to return, walking up to the front gate every day. Then she had given up hope, and her own life. Grandfather Madhava had followed her two years later, his heart quietly stopping as he sat in his easy chair reading the day's newspaper.

Tara had secluded herself at Shanti Nilaya for the past four days. Amma had tried tearfully to stop her from leaving, but Tara had insisted on the keys to Shanti Nilaya, repeating herself like a stuck tape recorder. Ultimately, it was Daddy who had handed over the keys to her and silently driven her to the house himself.

Her emotions had been volatile when she first came here. The first evening, she sat on the top step leading to the house and cried loudly, not caring who heard her in the neighborhood. She now understood what Uncle Anand meant when he said all those years ago: *They worry more when I am around, because I bring them shame.*

The first time Uncle Anand disappeared was the day Tara turned ten. But her birthday had been forgotten amid the anxiety of looking for Uncle Anand. It had taken the search party organized by Grandfather Madhava three days to locate him—unkempt, mumbling to himself in the courtyard of the ancient Kadri temple. He hadn't resisted being bundled into Hammaba's waiting rickshaw and taken straight to the mental ward of Father Muller's Hospital for recovery. Days later, the real Uncle Anand—the gentle kernel of the broken shell—had come home. His sanity, a brief spell, was a respite for everyone at home.

"Why did you leave, Uncle Anand?" Tara asked him one evening, as they walked to the Beary store like old times.

"I was tired of this prison." He bunched and raised his eyebrows every so often, as if to shake off dark thoughts.

"But you had everyone worried."

"They worry more when I am around, because I bring them shame."

Uncle Anand hummed softly, a song from the movie, *Anand*.

Kahin door jab din dhal jaye
Sanjh ki dulhan badan churaye
Chupke se aaye. . . .

As the sun sets somewhere far away,
Evening steals in, like a shy bride.

There was a melancholy note to Uncle Anand's voice as he sang, and when he mumbled to himself on their way back from the Beary store, "When the mind is in shackles, one is truly alone."

She was alone again in the prison of her childhood, a restless ache permeating her being. She had forgotten the power her relatives had over her feelings.

Every morning, she dusted the minimal furniture—a blue upholstered couch and padded wicker chairs in the living room, the old dining table and chairs, and a couple of teakwood beds that had withstood the test of time. Gangamma, the maid Amma sent to clean Shanti Nilaya every day, swept and mopped the floor on her haunches, her handloom sari hitched high, the end of its pleats looped between her legs and tucked into her waist at the back.

Around eleven o'clock, Tara headed to the modern kitchen and cooked lunch with the supplies Gangamma had bought from the neighborhood store. She cut okra into roundels to sauté with cumin, turmeric, and chili powder; sliced eggplants and white radishes for the sambhar. She got the rice and lentils going in the pressure cooker. She ate alone at the bare old dining room table. At night, she slept in a room in the old part of the house, where she had once rocked her baby brother to sleep. Her single bed was hard and creaked all night as she tossed about awake. Tara's childhood room upstairs was now just an attic where they stored old furniture.

She ventured out every day. The first day, she had walked up to the Pentecostal Church, and then beyond it to the spot where a water station, once upon a time, had provided water to the neighborhood. Now, a small, blue-painted shrine to Lord Hanuman stood in its place, a bell chiming every once in a while; rickshaws parked opposite the road, waiting for commuters. She thought of the sixteen-year-old boy who had stood at the spot and said goodbye to her several sunsets ago. She imagined his teenage breath on her face. She often remembered him like this these days; that brief period when her life had shone the brightest in this very house. She pictured him peering through the blue narrow gates, looking for her after she had moved out to another part of town; the deep impression she had left on him. Her heart ached for him every minute.

She passed the Saldanha Villa each time she went into town in a rickshaw. Every time, her heart beat in her throat as she turned her neck to catch a glimpse of the house where she had first met Cyrus a quarter-century before. The house was now hidden from the road, thanks to the monstrous blue-faced, four-story apartment building that had sprung up right in front of it.

The day after her arrival, she had visited the ninth-century Mangaladevi temple, a shrine for goddess Mangala Devi after whom the city was named, which was teeming with people even during the day. She had only one memory of the temple: of standing with the crowds with Uncle Anand at the edge of the road leading up to the temple on Mahanavami, the ninth day of the ten-day Dassera festival. A merry-go-round and a Ferris wheel. A vendor selling colorful jujubes. A festive chariot pulled with thick, heavy ropes through the streets. Craning her neck for a glimpse of the goddess who was in the chariot. Her hands folded in prayer; her lips uttering the words: *Oh Goddess, please take Amma, Vijay, and me to Dubai.*

She circumambulated clockwise around the granite central shrine with the crowd, like the moon around the earth, the planets around the sun. There was something calming about being invisible in the crowd, simply following a pattern. She finally understood why she, a nonbeliever, was at the temple. She perceived the same reason on the faces of the devout nameless people around her. She, like the others, had come seeking hope. Even when had she lost faith, she had not lost hope—the life energy, the center of every existence.

The next afternoon, she had hired a rickshaw to take her to the famed St. Aloysius College Chapel on Lighthouse Hill because that was the only touristy place that came to her mind. She sat in the pew along with a group of Hindi-speaking tourists, and spent time studying the beautiful frescoes that covered every inch of its walls and ceiling. A large sign outside said the chapel had been painted by the world-renowned Italian Jesuit, Antonio Moscheni between 1899 and 1901. She had forgotten Father Moscheni's name, and his works of art looked impressive, as if a part of Vatican City had been ensconced in Mangalore; and she wondered why this stunning edifice of local history had never blown her away before. A zealous warden came in and started asking her questions.

"Where are you from?"

"I am local," she mumbled.

"I've never seen you before."

"I don't live here anymore."

"Your husband didn't come with you?"

She shuffled out of the chapel without responding to the warden's last question. She walked to Hampanakatta, the commercial center of the city. Her throat was parched, and on a whim, she made her way to Ideal Ice Cream Parlor. She ordered gadbad, their famous signature ice-cream sundae, and was glad when the server brought it to her table. It was awkward to just sit when people were turning around to look at her. She wasn't dressed any differently, a white handloom *kurta* over blue jeans. It was probably the fact that she was sitting alone in a place that was teeming with people. In a culture where personal space was still an alien concept, you were never alone except when you died. Or if your parents abandoned you in a crumbling old house with a schizophrenic uncle and elderly grandparents. She wondered why she felt such a deep disconnect with her hometown, like a tourist exploring a new place. Was it because she had left her heart behind in Atlanta?

She savored the ice cream, the creamy strawberry and vanilla flavors, the jelly mingling on her tongue. This was a taste her palette remembered. Cyrus loved gadbad ice cream, too. Like most Mangaloreans, they had found it a topic worthy of discussion. She closed her eyes. It was four days since she had left, and she was halfway around the world eating ice cream alone. She imagined his dispassionate face at the airport. She imagined him driving back to Munmun, and Munmun enveloping him in her arms. She felt the jelly and fruity flavors of the sundae rush back into her throat, tasting sour this time. She gulped down cold water, paid the bill in a hurry, and scurried out of the tiny ice cream parlor.

On day four, because she could not think of a place to visit, she decided to explore her old neighborhood. She set out early in the evening, walking down the hill to the T-junction. Where the roads met, she made a left turn and kept walking, trailing her shadow, the way she used to follow Uncle Anand. The neighborhood had changed so much in eight years. More people on the road, more apartment buildings, a brand-new dental school in a four-story, white structure. Where the Beary store once stood was Hasan's Supermarket, with glass doors that were fogged up from the air-conditioning inside and the humidity outside. She turned back at the end of the road and made her way home. Tomorrow, she would return with her wallet to do a bit of grocery shopping at Hasan's Supermarket. She was curious to see what it looked like from the inside.

Halfway between the T-junction and Shanti Nilaya, she heard rapping, knuckles on glass, and then her name being called. She looked up to her left, in the direction of the sound. A bright face in hijab smiled down at her from behind the grilles of a third-floor window.

"Me, Zeenat," the face said in English, loudly enough that she could hear. "Remember me?"

The tiny but modern kitchen was stuffy and smelled of warm roasted chickpea flour, ghee, and cardamom. The counter was overflowing with pots and pans. An aluminum rack above the counter was stacked with stainless steel plates, glasses, and bowls. Zeenat was cutting a giant-sized aluminum pan of freshly set *Mysore pak* into rectangles. She picked two rectangles from the edge of the pan and put them in a stainless steel bowl. She put the bowl in front of Tara, who sat at a brown-and-white, floral-patterned, Formica-topped dining table that was pushed toward the wall to save space.

"Eat. Very tasty," she said in English.

The fairy of Tara's childhood now had an ample middle-age spread that showed through the thin cotton fabric of her kameez. The moon face was fleshier but had lost its symmetry; her mouth twisted to one side, the result of a brain surgery to remove a benign tumor when she was eighteen. The disfigurement had cost her her chances of winning a prince, because her face and fair skin were supposed to have been her lottery ticket. She had married a local Beary, a grocery store owner who had died only months into their marriage. Her older sisters had tried to help her out, inviting her to stay with them, but she didn't get along with them.

Zeenat had returned to her father's house and continued living there even after his death in 1998. A few years ago, a builder had approached the Beary compound with an offer that nobody could refuse. Now, she had two apartments in the building; one she lived in and the other she rented out. Tara knew most of Zeenat's tragic backstory. The last bit about the two apartments she had learned from Amma during her visit to Atlanta.

The Mysore pak was warm and melted in Tara's mouth. "This is very good," she said in Kannada, licking the rich ghee off her fingers. Zeenat's lopsided smile lit her eyes. "All for catering business," she said in English.

"You run a catering business?"

Zeenat switched to Kannada; she had exhausted her stock of English words. Her voice had an operatic quality to it, changing pitch often. She said the catering business she ran out of her kitchen was in its fifth year. She had started off cooking for families she knew in the neighborhood, but her business had grown through word of mouth. The Mysore pak was part of a contract from a wedding party at Second Bridge that included *halwa* and banana chips also.

"My halwa is better than Taj Mahal Bakery halwa. Come back in the morning. I'll let you taste it," she said.

Tara returned in the morning, drawn as much by Zeenat's face—bright, sparkly, happy—as by the promise of authentic Mangalorean halwa.

Zeenat was just getting started in the kitchen, which was now cooler and brighter, with the sunlight glinting on the pots and pans. Tara watched, enchanted, as the fairy sifted the flour into a large plastic pan, boiled sugar to a one-thread consistency in a thick-bottomed cast-iron wok, slowly stirred the flour, and later the ghee, into the bubbling syrup. She watched as Zeenat's face turned from deep concentration to joy the fifth time she tested, between her thumb and forefinger, a small blob of the thickened, golden-brown mixture that she had plopped on a stainless steel plate. "Done," she said, triumphantly, as she proceeded to add ghee-fried cashew nuts and powdered cardamom to the mix.

Tara tasted a square of halwa after it had cooled and complimented Zeenat on its authentic taste.

"When I cook, I forget everything else," Zeenat said, a little grandly, laughing.

Chapter 28

Zeenat paid her a visit the next afternoon, dressed in a simple cotton salwar kameez, the dupatta loosely covering her head and wrapped around her upper body, carrying a stainless steel bowl with two golden *mithai laddoos*. She watched, mirth in her eyes, face resting on her cupped hand, as Tara ate them both and licked her fingers. The laddoos were a bribe, she said, to hear about life in America. What kind of food do Americans eat? Why do Americans love guns so much? Do all women drive cars? Do they have the freedom to live as they wish?

Tara fed Zeenat's curiosity about life in America. Her own six failed attempts at passing the driving test. Her friendships with Ruth, Dottie, and Alyona, learning to enjoy southern and international foods with them. Hearing about the Virginia Tech shootings in a hotel room in Las Vegas where she had accompanied Cyrus for a convention; their shock and sorrow at the senseless loss of thirty-three lives. Yes, women had freedom, but perhaps not as much freedom as American men, she said. For this answer alone, she did not attach a personal story.

"You love America more or India?" Zeenat wagged a finger at her, laughing, warning her not to attempt a politically correct answer. "Tell me the truth."

"I love America as much as I love India."

"Why?"

"India gave me the power of imagination, but America gave me a taste for freedom." She smiled at Zeenat, who, mouth slightly open, tongue stuck to one side of her cheek, was trying to make sense of what Tara had just told her in English.

"Freedom? I hope it is tasty like my laddoo," she replied in English at last, giggling.

"Yes, like the laddoos and halwas and Mysore paks you so lovingly create. They bring you freedom, no?"

On a whim, she asked Zeenat to accompany her to her childhood room upstairs, lacking the courage to go there by herself. They made their way up the smooth teakwood staircase that Gangamma mopped every day, hands guiding feet. The door to the room was latched and raised a shrill furor when Tara unfastened it. She slowly pushed open the doors and walked into the room, Zeenat behind her. She had not been here in years; perhaps not since high school. It was like walking back in time.

The room was crowded with unused chairs and desks, an old hand sewing machine, and one of the twelve wooden boxes that had arrived in Mangalore a month after Tara's family had in 1975. The sun filtered from a glass pane on the tiled ceiling and fell softly on the dark wood of the dusty floor, giving the room a haunted bungalow feeling.

Tara walked across the room, lightly touching the things she remembered: her desk, the rusty table lamp with peeling green paint, the solitary wooden box painted blue—a reminder of her early childhood. She cupped a hand over her nose and mouth and walked to the shelves on the far walls that still bore the weight of rows of crouching books. They were all still there, every one she had voraciously escaped into. She ran a finger across a set of hardbound Charles Dickens's works. She spied the spot where Leo Tolstoy's *War and Peace* and *Anna Karenina* leaned loosely against each other on the bottom shelf.

"You have never been up here, have you?" She turned to look at Zeenat, who had covered her mouth with the edge of her dupatta. "I spent years holed up in this room because of my uncle's illness. It was like a prison sometimes."

Zeenat coughed in response. Her eyes were tearing up from the dust in the room.

"Are you allergic to dust? I'm so sorry; let's get out of here. I'll get the room cleaned tomorrow." She took Zeenat's arm and quickly led her out.

Zeenat was still breathless when she heaved herself into a rattan chair in the living room. "Why are you here all by yourself? Why aren't you staying with your parents or in-laws?" she asked in a wheezing voice.

"I have some work at the foundation we run for children," she started to say, but somehow, holed up away from her real world, the truth felt easier to tell. "There's a family wedding at my parents' house, and I was in the way." She took the other rattan chair, leaned back sighing.

"In the way?"

"Yes, I am a bit of a pariah. I was ostracized for spoiling my family's good name."

"How?"

"I divorced my first husband, and married again for love outside my community."

"Your family is upset with you?"

Tara nodded. "I ruined their reputation in the community, didn't I? If I had stayed, people would have talked, the groom's family would have found out. It would have been all-round embarrassment for my family."

"People have no work but to gossip." Zeenat spat out her reaction. It had come from her gut. She asked to know more about Tara's second marriage and her reasons for ending her first one. Talking to Zeenat about her Atlanta journey was like lifting a weight off her chest. Perhaps she needed to hear the story from her own mouth, to assure herself that she had done the right thing in marrying Cyrus. The glaring September sun shifted outside, the early evening shadows falling upon the front yard at Shanti Nilaya.

"Let them gossip," Zeenat said when Tara finished. "People can talk, but they cannot take away your dignity."

She spoke about her grocer husband, Abdul, who had treated her like a fairy; who had even managed an LPG gas connection for their tiny kitchen when they could barely even afford fire-wood. When Abdul died, she decided to face her family head on, fighting for independence, fighting to start her business.

"It makes you rise in your own eyes. In the end, what matters is how you feel about you." Zeenat patted Tara's sweaty arm. Her face was still red, eyes watery. Tara couldn't tell if it was from empathy or allergy.

"I am so mad at myself for fleeing, not standing up to my relatives." Tara bit her lower lip. "I'm an escapist."

"You didn't escape. You left in protest, came back to this childhood prison alone. That is no less brave," Zeenat said kindly.

Tara slept well that night, for the first time in days, as if she had had a session with a therapist. She woke up when the sun was only a deep blue glow in the narrow window of her new bedroom. She left Shanti Nilaya early and took a rickshaw to the taxi stand outside the crowded Mangalore Central railway station. It was several years since she had journeyed by train. Maybe she would return tomorrow, make a train trip to the sea-kissed Bekal Fort in the neighboring Kerala state. She had been there once with her classmates, a high school trip, when she had created a fantasy tale in her head about bumping into Cyrus high up in the observation tower overlooking the vast expanse of the Arabian sea.

She hired a cab to take her to Panambur Beach. She had forgotten the sound of the ocean, the feel of golden sand under her feet, the calm of an empty beach. It was too early for the food stalls, the horse rides, the merry-go-rounds, for children frolicking in the water. Only a bright red cargo ship floated where the sea met the sky. She meditated, feeling the warmth of the morning sun in her eyes, the heavy, salty sea breeze running through her hair. She imagined Cyrus by her side, clad in a cool white linen shirt, her head resting lightly on his shoulder; and strangely, for the first time in days, she was not haunted by visages of Munmun. Her own love for him felt enough.

When Tara returned, Zeenat was waiting for her on the edge of the top step leading up to the house. She thrust a plastic shopping bag, its edges knotted tightly, in Tara's direction. "Open it after I leave," she said. Her voice was more tremulous than usual. Tara looked up to see an anxious face; there was no smile today.

She sat below Zeenat on the third step. "A gift for me?" she asked.

Zeenat pressed a folded handkerchief to her lips. "You will see."

"I might as well open it now."

Zeenat drew back her handkerchief, wet her lips as if to thaw them. "Okay, open it," she said.

Tara had trouble untying the firm knots, so she clawed holes in the plastic bag using her fingernails, used her teeth as additional tools. She drew out the *something* that was wrapped in layers of newspaper, each layer secured with cellophane. She peeled them, aware of Zeenat's sharp breathing over the rustle of paper.

"Why sheet after sheet of paper?" she asked, amused.

Zeenat smiled awkwardly, then motioned, with the arch of her eyebrows, the sideway swing of her chin that Tara should keep on with the unraveling of the great mystery. And then, when all the layers of paper had been discarded, and because the quirky working of some karmic law had decided that this would be the moment, she was back in Tara's hand, her lost doll Pinky.

Pinky stared at Tara because she had lost her ability to close her violet eyes. Her hair was matted and dull, her replacement dress of yellow flowers against red had faded with age, and she was barefooted. Still, she had fared pretty well in thirty-two years.

"You took her?" It was not a question, Tara needed no answer. The apology was written on Zeenat's face.

"Truth be told, I have wanted to bring Pari back ever since I took her. But I was afraid I'd be called a thief."

"Pari? You changed her name, too?" Tara's voice was sharp.

"What's her name? I don't know," Zeenat stuttered in English.

"Pinky. Her name is Pinky."

"Pinky," Zeenat repeated. "English name. Very good name." As if being agreeable would make up for taking the doll and keeping it for thirty-two years.

"What was that story about the magic doll your uncle brought you from Kuwait? You turn her left arm, and orange candy appears out of her left palm. You turn her right arm, and lemon candy appears out of her right palm? And all the time you made me wait to see the imaginary doll, you had Pinky at home?"

Zeenat looked forlorn. "What to do? I had no uncle in Kuwait."

Tara smiled through her annoyance. She felt too numb to grasp the significance of Pinky's return, or to freshly capture the vestiges of an old loss. Zeenat laughed too, in relief. Her voice, as she narrated her story, was more stable than the loud voice that had made up the story of the magic doll.

The day after Tara's family had arrived in Mangalore, Zeenat's mother had sent her to Shanti Nilaya, as she did most mornings, to buy a measure of milk from Grandmother Indira. When she arrived at the house, she found the family gathered around the table in the verandah, listening to the Prime Minister on the radio. She was enchanted with Tara's mother, who sat on a wicker chair with her eyes closed, whose face shone like the movie star Hema Malini. All Zeenat wanted to do was look at her lovely saris and makeup. So she walked around the house, slipped in unseen through the back door, and headed to their room upstairs. She spied an unlocked trunk, a grand military-green treasure chest. On opening it, she saw, lying atop the clothes, the most beautiful thing she had ever laid eyes on—a fairy with golden hair and blue eyes. It was all right, she told herself, as she fled through the back door, doll in hand. The little girl's movie star parents would buy her another doll. She crafted a little tale for her father, about the bewitching lady at Shanti Nilaya taking one sweeping look with her almond-shaped, kohl-lined eyes at Zeenat's faded hand-me-down gown and bare, cracked feet. "She put the doll in my arms," she told him.

Tara looked out the window, thinking of the geometry boxes, the nice-smelling erasers with the green tip, the colorful school bags, the bell-bottomed pants and bell-sleeved dresses that her parents sent from Dubai. She was too old for a doll, they had assumed. But she had attached no value to the other things they sent her.

"I never had another doll," she said.

"I know, Sister. Please forgive me. Yesterday, when you took me to your childhood room, I saw for myself what I had snatched away from you. It wasn't just a doll. It was your childhood."

"Why did you bring her back now?"

"Because it was the right thing to do."

Tara accepted Zeenat's apology. "I forgive you," she said.

"Really?" Zeenat's face lit up.

"You were a child too, Zeenat. I hope Pinky brought you a lot of happiness." She meant what she said. The real losses of her life had been intangible; they had little to do with Pinky or Zeenat.

She lay on the sofa after Zeenat left, Pinky propped on the coffee table, sheets of old newspaper still on the floor, waiting to be disposed of. Pinky stared at her, her stiff pink arms lifted as if for a hug.

"Dolls have no heart, they cannot love you back. Only living things can." Uncle Anand's voice rang in her ears. Uncle Anand, her Kafka, who told her beautiful stories when she had lost her doll; whose kindness and imagination had the power to help her forget her loss.

Her eyes wandered to a newspaper sheet on the floor, at the photos that covered the top half of the broadsheet. *The Week in Pictures*, the headline said. She picked up the sheet. The pictures were from around town. Solemn looking brides and grooms in silk finery lined up for a free mass wedding at Dharmasthala. Trawlers at Bunder returning from a deep-sea fishing expedition. A man in a canoe clearing weeds from a lotus-filled pond, holding one end of what looked like a long staff, the other end submerged in water. A snapshot of a *bhuta kola*, an invocation of the spirits, the oracle dancer decorated with elaborate headgear, painted face, and straw skirt, arms stretched high up carrying lit torches.

Her eyes began to close. The sea could be physically tiring. Then, a fearsome apparition imposed itself before her, face painted yellow, enormous eyes accentuated with black paint, the whites bloodshot. The red lips moved to form words in a deep voice, almost a bellow: "Like the purple lotus, rarest of rare, you shall rise from muddy waters to rule the world."

She woke up with a start. Pinky continued to stare at her in astonishment. Tara closed her eyes again, remembering in a flash the face she had seen in her dream, the voice that was like a tiger's roar.

When Tara was close to eleven, she had gone with her grandparents and a functioning Uncle Anand to their ancestral home in Bailur. They had stopped their taxi in the shade of a mango tree at the entrance where the asphalt road ended. Trudging along a mud path that wound its way through vast expanses of rice fields and coconut groves, they had come to the nucleus of the farm, a large country home where some of Grandfather Madhava's relatives lived. The house looked ancient but radiated old world opulence, especially the raised verandah with its sturdy, carved wooden pillars that were so wide they could not be contained in Tara's long-armed embrace. The inner rooms had tiny windows that left them in darkness, in quaint mystery.

That evening, the family gathered with the village kinsmen in a decorated field near the shrine for Panjurli and Varthe, the boar spirits, for a night-long ceremony of bhuta kola, spirit worship. A dancer, who was soon to be the oracle, was dressed in colorful costume, a palm straw skirt around his waist, a multitude of flower garlands around his neck. Black paint accentuated his eyes, as he flashed them to great effect. The rest of his face was painted ochre and red. On his head was a large Japanese fan-like crown that shone under the gasoline light, and around his feet were bells that jingled loudly as he stomped the mud clearing on the field. He carried a sword as he danced and twirled, preparing to self-hypnotize, as the musicians beat the drums and finger bells in symphony, their tempo escalating as the evening progressed. The crowd sat in a semicircle around the mud stage, Tara ensconced between Uncle Anand and Grandmother Indira.

She watched fascinated as the dancer began to tremble, as his eyes began to roll. He was in a trance.

"He is having *darsana*. He is possessed with the spirit of

Panjurli," whispered Uncle Anand. The dancer's voice deepened as he spoke. Grandfather Madhava stood up to seek the blessings of the spirit. He begged the spirit for protection for his clan, for the continued good health of his second son, Anand.

"How does he do that?" asked Tara incredulously, of the spirit dancer.

"It is the spirit, not the dancer," Grandmother Indira replied.

"But how do you know he is not faking it?"

"Don't question beliefs, child."

Tara stared at the spirit invoker in enchantment. How was it that there were no spirits of dead people and animals in the land of Nancy Drew and Hardy Boys, she wondered. Why did they only inhabit little towns and villages in India?

Despite her lack of conviction in the bhuta, she closed her eyes and begged, "O spirit, please heal Uncle Anand. Please reunite me with my family. That is all I ask for."

When she opened her eyes, she noticed that the crowd was making way for the dancer, creating a little path right in front of her. With alarm, she realized that the jingle of the bells on his feet was getting louder; he was moving in their direction. She squeezed Uncle Anand's arm and huddled close to him, hoping the dancer would turn around, stop, have a change of heart. But no, he was looking at her with those massive black, paint-lined eyes; then he came even closer until he was a mere six feet away from them. She buried her face in her cold hands.

"This little girl, she will be queen," she heard the booming voice say. Uncle Anand whispered in her ear to open her eyes and look at the spirit dancer, but she could not be persuaded. "The Daiva is never wrong, never wrong," the roar continued. "Like the purple lotus, rarest of the rare, she will rise from muddy water."

"Rise, Swami?" she heard Uncle Anand ask.

"This pure lotus will rule the world."

"Tara, open your eyes, fold your hands, bow down," Grandfather Madhava commanded. Tara opened her eyes slowly, but kept her gaze at the dancer's mud-caked feet. She brought her hands together before her chest, bowing her head.

The oracle had words of advice for Tara. "Always respect and obey your father and mother; your parents are God in human form." He then turned around and twirled back to the clearing that was his dancing ground, leaving Tara to exhale in relief. She hadn't even realized she was holding her breath.

Later that morning, after they had slept a few hours on woven straw mats and had a traditional breakfast of *kotte*—rice and lentil cakes steamed in jackfruit leaves—and coconut chutney, sitting on a raised wooden plank in the long hall with their extended relatives, they made their way back to the bus stand. They walked through the wet rice fields in single file, Grandfather Madhava leading the way, his wife behind him, Tara trailing behind Uncle Anand.

She tapped his forearm to get his attention. "Why did the oracle say I would rule the world? Nobody rules over the whole world, not even President Jimmy Carter."

Uncle Anand gazed into the cloudless horizon without shielding his eyes. "It's quite simple, little girl. The whole of the universe is inside you. To rule yourself is to rule the world."

Grandfather Madhava was dismissive of the oracle's prophecy. "Utter gibberish," he said. The spirit had said nothing about Uncle Anand's precarious mental health, made no assurances, commanded no *poojas* to appease the gods for a permanent healing. What a waste of time the trip had been.

"Facing is healing, isn't it?" Uncle Anand said, his face immobile, expressionless, like it mostly was. He looked again at the burning sun without squinting. His words made no sense to any of them. Grandmother Indira turned around and shot him a worried look, hoping it wasn't the beginning of yet another difficult psychotic episode.

Tara couldn't remember if that was the beginning of an episode, but there had been many, each progressively longer and more severe, in the years that followed. She heard Uncle Anand's voice in her ears; a memory of a deep bellow: *I am the creator, the preserver, the destroyer. I am Brahma, Vishnu, Maheshwara. Do not argue, for I am the wholeness of all creation.*

Her grandparents did not ever argue or reason with Uncle Anand when he had a god complex. That only aggravated him. And they had nowhere to escape an angry god, not even Tara's sanctuary upstairs. Life had been unkind to her grandparents, but even more brutal to Uncle Anand.

She wondered now how he had coped with being shunned at weddings and engagements and naming ceremonies. How had he faced the madman label that preceded his arrival even during his brief periods of sanity? What was it like to be isolated inside the prison of his mind, to be overpowered by a voice that commanded him to do its bidding? How had he faced this powerlessness? Was that the reason he had tried to end his life three times, twice by jumping into the swollen well in the middle of the monsoon season, and once by trying to set fire to the clothes he was wearing? Was it to have some control over his life, his idea of a permanent healing?

Was there symbolism in Pinky's return, in the return of a childhood memory? She thought of the fear inside her belly, coiled like a cobra, its venom coursing deep in her veins since the time Amma had left her behind at Shanti Nilaya to join Daddy in Dubai. The fear that connected the major crises of her life: of being unwanted, rejected, ostracized. If she could only tackle the cobra's raised hood and darting forked tongue, to fling it afar into nothingness.

She shut her eyes. Her lips quivered. It was from the weight of wanting something more than life.

"Facing is healing," she whispered. Uncle Anand's words now made sense to her. The tears found a way out of her closed eyes. She pulled Pinky into her chest, holding her tightly, her fingers tangled in matted golden hair. She let the doll's plastic ear reverberate the beat of her full heart.

An idea came to her that night, upstairs in her childhood sanctuary, after she had spent a couple of hours sweeping, mopping, and dusting it clean. She sat on a rickety teakwood chair, peering at the rows of books. A solitary incandescent light bulb lit the room, and a lizard kept watch over her from a cracked beam on the old tiled ceiling. She was not mindful of the tiny reptile; she had overcome that fear a long time ago, when a dragon in psychosis had prowled downstairs spouting fiery doctrine.

When the idea hit her, she rushed down to get a pen from her purse, climbing two steps at a time during her return upstairs. She pulled *Anna Karenina* from the bottom shelf, a random choice, and started writing in the blank margins around its yellowing pages.

My first acts of self-determination at the age of thirty-six made me a pariah. My crime? I had walked out of a loveless, abusive marriage, she began. She wrote past midnight with the passion of an artist—shoulders hunched over the book, unaware of the stiffness in her back—even though it wasn't art she was creating. When she was done, she felt like she had rewritten her future.

In the morning, she dressed calmly in black pants and a lilac blouse, taking care to tame her hair with gel. Her purse sagged with the weight of Daddy's copy of a Russian classic. Her feet, clad in black ballerina shoes, were firm as she walked up the new asphalted road to the rickshaw stand past the Pentecostal church. She engaged a rickshaw, telling the khaki clad driver to take her to the offices of the *Morning Herald*. She had contemplated going to an Internet café instead and emailing her opinion piece to Sharat, her former colleague, but she didn't know if he still used his Hotmail, or if he still worked at the *Morning Herald,* or if he'd forward the essay to the editor for consideration.

This was far too important to leave to chance.

Chapter 29

The day before her *mehndi* ceremony, Nina arrived in a rickshaw, glowing in her dressy fuchsia and orange silk salwar suit. She came to the point as soon as she had kicked off her six-inch stilettoes and settled on the sofa. "Come to the wedding," she said, heavily mascaraed eyes dramatically earnest.

"You are sweet, Nina." Tara cupped her cousin's chin. "But you know I cannot. They don't want me there."

"I do. My fiancé, Rajeev, does."

"You told your fiancé?"

"Yes. He admires you. We both do. You had the courage to follow your heart."

"Elders think differently, Nina."

Nina flapped her hands in exasperation, the orange and fuchsia bangles jingling furiously on her wrists. Tara reached out to grasp Nina's hands, to calm their agitation. "Tell me about Rajeev. Is he strong enough to withstand pressure from his family, if it comes to that?"

Nina nodded vigorously. "Of course. He is open-minded and forward. He will stand up for what is right."

"Let me think about it, Nina."

"At least come to the mehndi. Rajeev's family won't be there."

"But the rest of the community will congregate. Word gets around quickly."

"We'll show them we don't give a shit."

Tara laughed. "I wish I'd had your spirit at your age, Nina."

She'd go, she decided. She'd face a hostile community for Nina, but mostly, she'd do it for herself. It was as if the universe was conspiring to lay out an *agnipariksha*, a trial by fire, for her to walk through. If she didn't do it now, she probably never would.

Nina threw her arms around Tara, kissing her on both cheeks, leaving dark lipstick stains on her moist skin. "Oh, and there is another reason why you must be there tomorrow." Her eyes danced with excitement. "Cyrus said he would call."

Tara's chest expanded at the mention of his name, a burst of adrenalin that forced her mouth open to breathe. "Cyrus said he'd call? Has he called before?"

"Several times. I happened to answer his call today. I told him you had holed up at Shanti Nilaya because everyone was mean to you."

"What did he say to that?"

"Cyrus seemed to be in a hurry, and frustrated. He was at a play, and the curtains were going up in a minute. I told him I'd make sure you'd be home on mehndi night, and to be sure to call on my mobile."

The play. Tara had woken up that morning feeling drained, the guilt racking her insides for abandoning Cyrus on his important day. Now, her heart swung wildly—lifting one minute because he had wanted to speak to her just before his performance, and sinking because she had made no effort to offer him her good wishes.

❦

After Nina left, as the sun turned the deep blue of dusk, she felt a desperate need to be connected to Cyrus, to be in his space. Her feet bounded eastward, to the road that began at the Hanuman shrine, and ended at Second Bridge, where the Saldanha homes lay. She came to the tall iron gates of Saldanha Villa. The driveway was lit up, and the house looked freshly painted, but thankfully, not much had changed in a quarter century by way of renovation. The lawns and flowering shrubs were in darkness, but she could tell that the house's ochre façade remained the same. She tamed her hair, pressing it back with her fingers, an old habit. She looked through the white bars, almost expecting to see them all, like old times—James, Annette, Angela, Michelle, and Cyrus. The open verandah was faintly lit but empty. She slipped down to her haunches, her curled fingers sliding down the bars. She rested her forehead against the cool iron of the gate and closed her eyes.

She smiled when his sixteen-year-old version dramatically cleared his throat, threw his head back, closed his eyes, and sang, his arms stretched like in prayer, swaying from side to side:

Star light, star bright,
The first stargoddess I see tonight;
I wish I may, I wish I might,
Have the wish I wish tonight.

She laughed. It was as if she were standing at the gates of her own heart, peering inside. A mild evening breeze cooled her face, but a stronger thought washed over her. How magical it was that they had met again half the world away as adults, their pull for each other undiminished after a quarter of a century—as if by a metaphysical hand that had led them to each other, bound them for eternity. How ungrateful she was being to the forces that had conspired for them, succumbing to little worldly insecurities and hurts.

She felt ready for the heavy lifting—to bare her soul to

Cyrus, to work through her fears, their issues. She stayed on her haunches until Saldanha Villa was only a gray silhouette in the early darkness. She felt love; it threatened to spill over as if it were an overflowing well in the monsoon season. She would return after the mehndi to visit James and his family. She would visit Dadda in the next villa and ask him to take her to see the children who called her Amma. She would embrace the world she had married into, envelop her little foster children in a river of love. She was conscious of the shift in her mood, the spiraling energy that stemmed from an impulsive act which was making its way through the editorial pipeline at the *Morning Herald*.

There was a wedding at Raj Bungalow; even the neighbor furthest down the road could tell. A bright red, yellow, and green *shamiana*, a gigantic awning, draped with valances of marigold garlands, sheltered the front yard. At the far end of the lawns, by the compound wall, was a raised platform covered in red carpet with an intricate floral backdrop. The front door had been left open, a warm invitation for guests to walk in on the auspicious days of the wedding. A string of fresh mango leaves was stretched across the top frame of the front door to stop negative energy from entering the house.

Raj Bungalow would start filling with people in the evening. Relatives and their relatives and their relatives. They had enough extended family in and around Mangalore to fill Mangala Stadium. Tara thought she had beaten the crowd by arriving mid-morning, but she was wrong. A quick, sweeping glance revealed women in silk saris and thick gold jewelry chitchatting in the living and dining space. She held her head up as she walked in, her bare feet firm on the cool marble floor; a steady, prepared walk. A sturdy hand stopped her in the hallway, taking her by surprise. She turned around to face her brother from California.

"So good to see you, Sis."

"When did you arrive, Vijay?"

"Last night, via Dubai."

She allowed Vijay to lead her by the arm to his empty room upstairs. Her brother appeared older; a tiny bit of flab around his girth showed through his Adidas T-shirt and Levi's jeans. He rested his backside delicately on the edge of the desk. She occupied the desk chair.

"How are you, Tara?"

Even though she had to look up at him, her gaze was steady. "I am fine. I know the elders don't want me here, but I am attending the mehndi. I have Nina's invitation."

"That was one bomb of an article in the *Morning Herald*."

She was unprepared for this bit of information; she had built no defenses against it. She gasped involuntarily, a sharp intake of air. "Is it published?"

"Didn't you know? It appeared in today's edition and created quite a stir in the house, as you can imagine." Her brother looked surprised, but she noticed no other expression.

"Oh! I thought it was appearing next week." She leaned forward, fist over her mouth. The bravado she had adopted walking into the house quickly left her, replaced with the tightening of her chest and the constricting of her throat. She imagined a house full of guests leering at her for her audacity, her shamelessness, her deliberate attempt to wreck Nina's marriage. It was the last bit that worried her the most. Her eyes closed involuntarily, as if to shut the door on the world.

"Chin up, Tara. Chin up," she heard Vijay say. She opened her eyes with a start, searched his face. His mellow expression surprised her.

"Don't take anybody's shit. Tell them to eff off. Your life is your business." He put a reassuring hand on her shoulder, squeezed it.

Why the change? her surprised eyes asked him.

"Sorry for being a jackass, Sis," he replied aloud. "Listen, I am off to Bajpe airport to pick up the Bombay crowd. I owe you a proper apology when I return."

This was her big day, bigger than she had imagined, walking into the house. Her agnipariksha. She closed her eyes and imagined a humongous pile of firewood being stacked outside, a fire being lit for her trial, as Uncle Anand had done, a long time ago. "Show them your purity, your virtue. A test of fire is what they seek," the voices in his head had asked of her, before she knew what *virtue* actually meant.

"I am not Sita, I am Tara," she had cried out to Uncle Anand. *I am Tara*, she whispered to the walls of Vijay's room. She took deep breaths to bring air into her constricted lungs, until the tension in her shoulders eased somewhat. Slowly, as she opened her eyes, she was reminded of the biggest truth of her present moment: she wasn't the person who had last left this room eight years earlier. She was a different Tara.

As she bumped into Aunty Nanda in the hallway, she noticed her aunt's face change color, transform from preoccupied to belligerent, reminding Tara of the bhuta kola oracle dancer of her childhood. She was mindful of greeting her wheezing aunt with a nod as she squeezed past her and made her way to her room.

She opened her closet door and settled on her knees, rifling through the shelf where she had left her silk saris behind when she moved to Atlanta. They were all there: Kanjeevarams, Benarasis, Gadhwals. Amma had individually wrapped them in protective semitransparent muslin sheets. She began to pry open each bag, looking for one with the least fancy gold-dipped silver zari work. The clink of gold bangles, the heavy breathing told her that Aunty Nanda had followed her into the room.

"Why are you doing this, Tara?"

"Nina invited me, Aunty Nanda." Tara's voice was even, a sharp contrast to her aunt's distressed tone.

"Why the article? Why advertise your adventures to the world?"

"Our society needs to change, Aunty Nanda."

"And you thought today was the right day to change the world?" The sarcasm bounced off her aunt's words. "Because you were not invited?"

"Oh, but I am invited, Aunty Nanda. Nina came to Shanti Nilaya and convinced me to come."

"Nina is a child. What does she know?"

Tara smiled. "Why are you getting a child married, Aunty Nanda? Isn't marriage for grown-ups?"

Aunty Nanda collapsed into the bed, her face close to tears. "You were such a shrinking violet before you went to America. How you have changed."

"Aunty Nanda, I was once told I am a rare purple lotus."

Aunty Nanda's face crumpled with rage and helplessness. Tara quickly turned her attention back to the saris before guilt weakened her. She felt sorry for Aunty Nanda; burdened with tradition, fearful of gossip smearing their pride, threatening the alliance she and her husband had decided was perfect for their daughter. But for once, Tara would stand her ground.

She heard a male voice call out her name; it was Aunty Nanda's husband, Uncle Satish, who had just walked into the room. He stood by his wife, but his hands were on his hips.

"This drama was quite unnecessary," he said in English, his voice too loud, too grating for his slight frame. "Word travels fast. Everybody in our community is talking about the article."

"I had no idea the article would be published today, Uncle. That was not my intention."

"But pray, what was its purpose? Are we going to forget the conventions and beliefs our forefathers have been following for hundreds of years? Over some American ideas? Westerners don't have the same values we do. Here, we consider marriage sacred; our vows are meant for seven lifetimes. If every woman puts her own desires above her family and community, that will be the death of society."

Tara pulled herself up from her kneeling position, squaring her shoulders, remembering that she was a couple of inches taller than her bank manager uncle. "A community that does not accord its women basic human rights has no future either, Uncle Satish. It is already a dead society."

She had not raised her voice for her first confrontation with an extended family member, even though Uncle Satish's face was grim, the flaring of his broad nose aggressive.

"What basic rights of yours were violated that you had to beat drums? Were you starved? Imprisoned in your house? Tortured?"

"I don't owe you or anybody else an explanation for taking charge of my life."

From her peripheral view, she saw Daddy appear in the doorway, arms crossed. For the first time in her life, she felt ready to deal with him.

"You heard me, Daddy. I don't owe anybody an explanation for taking responsibility for my happiness."

She curled her forefinger—which had momentarily pointed at Daddy—back into her palm—but he wasn't looking at her. Though his eyes flashed with anger, and his jaw was rigid, Daddy's attention was on Uncle Satish.

"Leave Tara alone." His tone was assertive. "If you cannot be nice to the daughter of this house, you are welcome to take your bridal party elsewhere."

Uncle Satish and Aunty Nanda fell silent, the conviction on their faces diminishing. The shock choked Tara, a sudden filling of her heart. She caught a vibration, a hint of change in Daddy's words. She searched his face, and this time, Daddy did not turn his face away from her probing eyes.

Another face appeared behind his—Amma, who brushed past him, a large shopping bag in her hand. Her lips were tightly pursed, as if she were trying hard to stop a tirade. She thrust the bag into Tara's hands. "I bought these for you at the silk *bhandar* on Thursday. They are the latest fashion. Try them on."

With a firm hand on Tara's elbow, Amma steered her out of the room. At the door, she turned to look at her younger sister and brother-in-law. "Nobody will bother you again, Tara. Your parents are still alive." Amma's voice had new vigor.

In the master bedroom, Amma put her focus on pulling a heavy lehenga out of the shopping bag.

"What do you mean, you bought these on Thursday? You didn't want me at the wedding celebrations." Tara frowned at the lavishly embroidered, crystal-studded, royal blue velvet bodice and hot pink flared skirt that Amma was unfolding on the bed.

"Don't be silly, Tara. I sent Nina to invite you."

"Why didn't you come?"

"Don't I know you, Tara? As hot-headed and as stubborn as your father. I knew Nina had a better chance of bringing you back home."

"Aunty Nanda was so mean to me the day I arrived, and you did nothing but cry."

"I cried thinking that you would face such talk from everyone."

"I am ready to confront loose talkers, Amma. I have Mangala Devi's trident inside me."

Amma stretched her arms out for a hug. "Me too, darling. One thing I've realized is that if I am strong, it will be easier for all of us to face people."

Tara stooped into Amma's arms, soaking in their warmth. For the first time since she was eight, she felt no anger, no hurt—only a keen awareness that her parents and brother were shifting to her side of the battle; that something had shifted inside of her too.

The lehenga fit her perfectly. She did her own makeup—foundation, compact, an extra coat of mascara, eyeliner, bright lipstick—not caring to get in the long queue of young women who waited for the hired beautician to first finish the bride's face and hair. She let her hair loose in its natural texture—curly, bouncy, unfettered—and carried a blue velvet embroidered *potli* purse, a gift from Nina, its short slings hanging from her forearm. In the purse was Nina's cell phone, which Cyrus had said he would call. Happily, for Tara, Nina had insisted that she carry it. Hearing his voice, telling him how much she loved him would complete her day. She felt bright and sparkly—like the lehenga she was wearing.

She occupied a chair up front, facing the elevated platform where the bride was seated on a flower-decked swing. Nina glowed, resplendent in a Nalli silk peacock blue-and-fuchsia Kanjeevaram sari. A henna artist sat on a red plastic chair beside Nina, decorating her hands, arms, and feet with intricate patterns. Young members of the extended Raj family took turns on the raised platform, performing dance numbers set to popular Bollywood songs. Every once in a while, a younger relative dropped by to ask Tara about college or job prospects in America. A few whispered that they had read her article and were proud of her. She couldn't tell what the older majority, the keepers of tradition, were thinking because not one person actually told her she was an outcast. She ignored groups that whispered, that turned conspicuously to look at her, the occasional snigger that reached her ears. Ultimately, her memories of the evening would be crafted from her perception of it. She felt peaceful, perhaps because she was on a mission, perhaps because her family had finally rallied a protective boundary around her, perhaps because she had discovered so much about herself in the past few days.

Amma commanded the henna artist, who had moved her station to a less conspicuous spot in the garden, to craft delicate floral motifs on Tara's hands and arms right after the bride's. As first cousin, that was the rightful order. On a whim, Tara asked the artist, a twenty-something woman with a sweet manner, to pipe *Breaking Taboos* across her right palm between floral patterns, a reminder of the importance of taking stances, of courage.

Daddy had a smiling face when he took the empty chair next to hers, when he put a reassuring arm around her.

"Our Rotary Club president called a while ago. He wants you to speak on women's empowerment at the anniversary celebrations of Mahila Sevashrama in Talpady next week. It is a center for abandoned women that our club supports."

Tara absorbed the news, the significance of it. Her article had made some positive impact. She had never addressed a crowd before, not made a speech even in front of a mirror. Yet she was filled more with an adrenaline rush than with dread, like a child waiting in line for a thrill ride at Disney. She looked at the two words drying on her right palm, blazing orange stains forming under the drying mud-green henna.

"I'll do it, Daddy," she said. She would worry later about addressing a crowd, making her voice heard, keeping her knees from buckling with fright.

"Can you believe that our local member of the state legislature, whom we invited as chief guest, suggested your name as speaker to our club president? He read your article on his flight home from Bangalore."

"Was it in the Bangalore edition, too?"

Daddy nodded. There was no mistaking the pride in his eyes when he said, "Who knew my daughter would one day be invited to give speeches on women's empowerment?"

Later, Vijay occupied the chair vacated by Daddy, raising his hand to high-five her. He had heard the news of the Rotary invite from Daddy. She held her hands up, apology on her face, to indicate that the henna was still not completely dry.

"You will now have huge expectations to live by. I am happy to be let off the hook," he joked.

Tara understood what he meant. In high school, Vijay had grumbled about the high expectations Daddy and Amma had of him, the pressure to excel in everything he did—debate, cricket, school tests, the board exams.

"Why is Tara let off so easy?" he had yelled at Daddy once, after being admonished for letting his math grades slip.

"I envied you my whole life for being the golden son; the one they were proud of," she said now. "I was left behind so I could become an engineer or doctor, and I became neither."

"That was not right, leaving you behind. At least not after Mom and Dad learned about Uncle Anand's psychosis." Vijay shook his head. "Amma and I should have stayed back at Shanti Nilaya."

"On the bright side, being isolated in a room with books made me a writer," she said, and laughed.

They watched for a while in silence, a six-year-old relative's *Bharata Natyam* dance performance on stage; an older sister hovering beside the little girl, prompting the footwork, the hand gestures, the facial expressions. The moment seemed right for Tara to reveal her innards, get a lifelong guilt off her chest. "Remember the time Daddy took us to Summer Sands resort when you visited the first time in 1979?" She told him about the sandcastle they had built by the blue waters of the Arabian Sea.

"I remember. That is probably my earliest memory of the sea," Vijay said.

"I was horrible to you that day."

"You were horrible to me?"

She nodded. "I pushed your face into the sandcastle and held it down until you gasped for breath."

"Why?"

"I was furious when you said I couldn't live with you all because I was a dragon, that I had to be locked away. I was really locked up in Daddy's room, you know, because of Uncle Anand's violent episodes. It hurt, also, because I didn't get to go to Dubai."

Vijay frowned into the grass, blinking, as if trying to recollect a faded memory.

"I am sorry Vijay. I truly am. I wish I had been a better big sister to you," she said.

"It's funny, but that is not how I remember the incident," Vijay's gaze moved back to her face. "I remember you shooing the stranger away, wiping the sand off my face, hugging me. I remember being glad that I had a big sister to protect me."

He put his arm around her, and his voice was unexpectedly mellow when he said, "I like my version of the story better."

A lump formed in her throat. She was glad that they'd had this conversation, glad her brother had allowed her a peek at his softer side. There was a tender edge to her voice when she said, "Thank you, Brother."

The dinner buffet opened. Tara and Vijay got into the long line and filled their plates up with spicy fried black pomfret, fragrant mutton biryani, chicken in golden gravy, soft *akki rotti*, and an assortment of vegetables. They found seats by the potted marigolds, away from the crowd. After tucking into a whole fish fried in coconut oil and glugging half a bottle of Kingfisher beer, his eyes a bit glazed, Vijay told Tara about his broken heart.

Uma, his live-in girlfriend of six months, had broken up with him two days prior to Tara's last call inviting him to her wedding. They had met at a bar. She was a human rights lawyer by profession and a strong-willed nonconformist. He was planning to propose to her when he had learned, through common friends, of her affair with his friend Jay. He had confronted her. She had called him a closed-minded, chauvinistic jerk, which was why she was drawn to his liberal friend. She had ended it with Vijay, leaving him to wonder why he had insisted on a quality certificate for the twenty-two-carat solitaire engagement ring he had picked up at an Indian jewelry store in Artesia.

"I was hurting and angry when you called." He cupped a hand to his mouth to calm a burp. "So, I reacted like the closed-minded, chauvinistic bugger that I was."

She told him it was all right. What was important was that he had changed. She felt special for being trusted with news that could never reach her parents' ears. A live-in girlfriend was taboo. She was surprised that he had fallen in love with a nontraditional woman, that he had broken the rules too.

"I hope you are over her?" she asked.

Vijay's nod was feeble.

"You deserve better, Vijay. She ought to have ended it with you first."

Her reaction was from the heart, from the ache she felt knowing that her brother was still hurting. She understood that it was the same for him, for Daddy, and for Amma. The need to defend her was a force of love that had finally won over their belief systems.

It was a long evening. Around ten o'clock, she rubbed the dry henna off her hands, knowing that the longer she kept her hands unwashed, the more intense the stain; the more intense the stain, the stronger her husband's love for her. That was the belief. But she couldn't risk missing Cyrus's call. She eagerly pulled Nina's cell phone from her potli purse and held it in her hand. She waited for the inanimate object to come to life. It did not.

Her earlier enthusiasm of the evening left her. She felt drained and sleepy. She walked into the living room, where Aunty Nanda's father-in-law had dozed off on the chair beside the side table where the landline sat, beside a bronze statue of the laughing Buddha. She woke him up with a gentle tap to his forearm.

"Grandfather."

He opened his eyes and smiled a benign smile, making smacking noises with his lips.

"Did you take any calls tonight?"

"The Christian chap called several times, but not tonight."

"My husband called? When?"

"When you were hiding in your grandfather's house."

"Are you sure he did not call tonight?"

"The phone did not ring at all. I've been here all evening. Nobody cares for an old man."

Tara turned to leave, disappointment rising from her chest.

"I told him the last time he called," the elderly man's voice carried clearly across the room. "It was a brilliant move, marrying a Hindu girl to increase his tribe."

Indignation welled inside her, but she let it out with a long, cleansing breath and turned around to face him.

"Have you had dinner, grandfather? Can I get you something? Or would you like to sit outside for a while?"

"Laddoos. Get me some laddoos," he said with a smile.

Chapter 30

She dozed off on the sofa from the exhaustion of the evening, and from trying Cyrus's number every thirty minutes. Each time, it was his crisp recorded voice after just a ring, telling her to leave a message. It was likely that Cyrus had turned his phone off. But why? She had tried Alyona's number and got her voicemail too. Ruth had picked up, but told her that she and Dottie were in Savannah with the church group. They would check on Cyrus when they returned the next day.

When she woke up with a start, the sun was only just rising, and in the blue-gray darkness of dawn, the living room looked like it was littered with bodies. Then she heard the peaceful snoring of the sleeping guests. They were lying on thin mattresses and covered in thin handloom blankets, the men on one side, the women adjacent to them.

She tiptoed out of the living room and locked herself in the bathroom on the main floor. She was awake enough to feel restless. She had time to think as she finished her business, as she brushed her teeth by smearing toothpaste on her finger and washed her face with bar soap and water. She was still dressed in her fancy velvet lehenga, which was better than heading across the city in pajamas. She slithered back into the kitchen, looked for the ceramic jar where Amma kept small cash to pay the vegetable and fish vendors. There was no ceramic jar; but she got lucky. The cash was hidden in a black cast-iron kettle that did not belong on the top shelf. She took out a fistful of rupees, enough to engage a rickshaw to Dadda's house.

The rickshaw puttered down the lane, the driver not fully awake. The four Saldanha homes stretched down on one side like a string of pearls, the other side just a high wall of laterite bricks and cement. The homes were all architecturally similar: large traditional Mangalorean homes with red tiled roofs and sprawling green yards from which mushroomed tall, swaying coconut palms. They had all survived the building frenzy in the town.

Tara shivered in her heavy velvet ensemble, even though it was a barely cool morning. How strange, she thought, that she had not once been to her husband's home, had never seen the room where he grew up, the bed he slept in. The vortex in her chest expanded as the rickshaw stopped at the high double iron gates of Dadda's pristine white villa.

Dadda met Tara warmly in the portico. He was an early riser, he told her. Cyrus had told him she was here for a cousin's wedding when he had called a few days ago, but he had not expected to see her in wedding clothes at six in the morning.

He seated her in the inner sitting room. The shock came to her in waves, the historic nature of the moment. She had not expected to be here without Cyrus. The room appeared untouched by modernity. Grand arched wooden windows draped in lace curtains stood majestically against ochre walls. German tiles covered the floor; the low wooden beams of the ceiling reflected preserved heritage. A grand piano sat in a corner, its top covered in lace, surrounded with polished teakwood furniture topped with dark red upholstery. Tara ran her fingers over the soft fabric of the settee. She imagined a little boy with twinkling honey eyes weaving through the furniture in the room. She pictured him running out into the passageway that led to rooms beyond, into the mystery.

"How did the fundraiser go?" Dadda asked.

She bowed her head, guilt warming her cheeks.

"I've been trying to reach Cyrus. I was hoping you had heard from him about the fundraiser." Her words were a rush of anxiety and guilt. Dadda's eyebrows furrowed behind his steel-rimmed glasses. She immediately regretted passing on her unease to him. He reached over to the black antique landline phone that rested on a polished teakwood side table. She knew from his expression that he had reached the voicemail, even before he spoke to the recorder.

"Cyrus, this is Dadda. Please call me when you get this message. Tara is here and would like to speak to you."

"Maybe he decided to spend a week at the meditation center in North Carolina," she joked, forcing a bright smile to her face. "How are the children doing? I'd like to visit them soon."

"I'll take you any time you want. They are all anxious to meet you."

Dadda told her she was welcome to stay. The villa was as much hers as it was Cyrus's. She said she would return with her luggage soon.

He showed her the house. They walked along the passage, peeked into several large rooms with antique furniture. They reached the heart of Cyrus's childhood, his bedroom. Solid evidences of his life swam into her view. A teakwood dresser stood against one wall, a cupboard and a desk against the other. Above the desk, close to the entrance to the room, hung a prayer printed in papyrus font on handmade beige paper that was shaped like a medieval scroll. It was the prayer of Saint Francis of Assisi.

She crossed her hands across her chest to stop from shivering as she walked deeper into the room, past his four-poster bed covered in a beige embroidered bedspread. She felt his presence, the years he had spent in this room; growing up, learning new things, gaining new experiences, adding layers to his personality.

Back in the sitting room, she waited with Dadda, tormented by the silence of the phone. She felt silly, doing nothing to lift the burden off her chest. A middle-aged maid in a floral knee-length dress brought in tea on a wooden tray. Tara took a few sips from the dainty china cup, then mumbled about having to run errands.

"I'll be back soon, Dadda," she promised, giving him a quick hug.

"Don't worry, my dear. Cyrus is not an irresponsible lad. He will call," Dadda reassured her.

She walked down the street that led to Morgan Hill, where Cyrus had once walked with her all those years ago. Where he had said good-bye.

She stopped at the little Hanuman shrine at the top of Morgan Hill to ring the bell. For most of her life, her mind had associated temple chimes with loss, with sorrow. Yet, her feet had instinctively led her to the shrine, and her hand had reached up to the slim brass bell that hung from a thick rope. She stood a few seconds looking at the monkey god, painted green, the symbol of strength and perseverance. She was a believer, she knew. She had always been. Even when her prayers hadn't manifested. Even when her conscious, skeptical mind told her she wasn't. Even though she hadn't put her hands together in prayer for most of her life.

The whole of the universe is inside you. To rule yourself is to rule the world. Uncle Anand had been right, as he often was. She joined her hands together now and closed her eyes. A simple acknowledgement of the higher consciousness inside her; a deep love that connected her with her universe. A simple effort to keep her hope strong—stronger than her fears.

The spare key to Shanti Nilaya, which Gangamma often used, was under a laterite brick on which sat a nondescript neem pot in the front yard. Once in, she headed to the new bathroom for a long bath, filling a large bucket with hot water from the geyser, then pouring water over herself out of a plastic mug—a calming ritual from her childhood. She had until nine before businesses would open. Her plan was to go to the currency exchange in Balmatta and get enough rupees to buy her a ticket back to Atlanta.

She brushed her teeth again, this time with her toothbrush, pulled on a pastel yellow tunic and jeans, ran a comb through her hair, and rummaged through her suitcase for the black pouch that held her passport and wallet. When she was ready, she picked Pinky from the middle of her bed and lay down, setting the doll on her belly. She needed reassurance that the lost could be found, that what was yours eventually came back to you. She waited for the grandfather clock in the old part of the house to strike nine times.

Her mind went back to the last two months of her relationship with Cyrus, of living through her deepest fear. Munmun was in love with her husband. She still believed that. Could she have handled that knowledge differently—given her own love for Cyrus its rightful place instead of letting her ego think for her? Allowed her heart to talk to Cyrus rather than her fear? Despite her best efforts to calm herself, she felt desperation rise from her belly, sharp like a serrated knife "Where are you, Cyrus?" she cried. "I need to talk to you, my love."

A little before nine, she made her way out of Shanti Nilaya, closing the new wrought iron double gate and latching it distractedly behind her. The winding asphalted road up Morgan Hill was glinting in the sun. She imagined again a sixteen-year-old boy at the top of the hill waving at her, the sunlight bouncing off his happy face. Then she saw him. She squinted to make sure he wasn't a mirage or her imagination, holding her breath so his visage wouldn't disappear. But he was there even when she finally let out a sharp breath, even after she closed her eyes for a good many seconds and opened them again. He wasn't sixteen anymore, but Cyrus was making his way down the hill. The smile on his face wasn't radiant like the sun. It was slow to spread when his eyes fell upon her, as if breaking free from anxious thoughts.

She ran up to him on deer-like feet, almost throwing him off balance when she fell into his arms, knocking away the slim suitcase he held in his hand. She stayed there a long time, feeling the relief in the long release of his breath on her neck, feeling the power of love in the way his hand cradled the back of her head, the other tightly wound around her back. His first words to her, and her first words to him were, "I'm sorry." They had both uttered those words at the same moment. For now, that was enough.

Chapter 31

She smiled at his handsome face, still deep in sleep. Her fingers were asleep too, entwined in his, over the rhythm of his peacefully heaving chest. It was morning, and they had a lot to do. But for now, she was content to simply glow in the memory of their long, hungry lovemaking in his childhood bed, to fill her heart with his proximity.

Although she had been right about Munmun, her actions had been incredibly immature. He had noticed the attention Munmun was giving him, but hadn't sensed the reasons attached to it. He was guilty of ignoring the signs that he ought to have addressed, guilty of not understanding Tara's angst. They had both learned a lesson in trust and honesty, in the power of sharing fears, discussing insecurities.

Two days before the staging of the play, Munmun had stayed back after rehearsals after the cast had left. She had helped Cyrus conjoin, with nails and hammer, two parts of an elaborate backdrop—a garden with flowering bushes, green trees, and a gurgling fountain. It was the last piece to be loaded into the U-Haul truck that Cyrus had rented. He would later drive it across the city to the venue.

She had directed their conversation to personal issues. Her husband had two adult children from his first wife and didn't want any more. She yearned for a child; she had grown up in a large extended family, and the silence at home was too much to get used to.

He had tried to gently steer the conversation back to the fundraiser. She had taken his disinterest as naivete, a man who had trouble understanding signs, so she had been blunt. Each time she closed her eyes, she told him, he appeared, a playful Krishna to her Radha. He had occupied her mind every minute since the first day of rehearsals. She had never felt a pull quite as primal before. She had put her arms around his neck, burying her face in the fabric of his kurta. He had pulled away from her lock, stepping back, but allowing his hands to rest on her shoulders.

"Munmun, I am sorry, I do hope you'll find a way to work through your issues with Dr. Das, but I cannot give you what you are looking for."

"Tara left you when you needed her."

"It's a personal matter."

"She doesn't need to know. Nobody needs to know."

He had looked her in the eye and told her firmly, "Munmun, I love my wife very much, and right now, I am terribly worried because she is unreachable. I'd really appreciate it if you would leave."

Munmun's face was a mirror as she absorbed the rejection, as it turned the crimson of her *bindi* beneath the moist of her sweat, the razor sharpness of her breath. "Your wife ought to play Anara. Find her, because I am done."

He had not attempted to stop her. Instead, he had made a list of people he would need to contact the next morning to cancel the event. The financial losses he would bear, with a personal check to the foundation.

Early the next morning, however, he had received a text message from Munmun:

"I'm sorry I overreacted. I'll reach the auditorium on time tomorrow."

During their performance, they concentrated on getting their onstage love story right, their rehearsed lines correct. He had spoken to Nina just before the play and found out that Tara was holed up in her grandparents' old home, a victim of her own relatives' archaic attitudes. His focus was on getting through the evening, hopping on the earliest flight to Mangalore, and rushing to Shanti Nilaya. To be a better husband than he had been in the past two months.

Perhaps it was this restlessness that had prompted him to tell Munmun, in the green room after the play, about the Star-Cyrus story, of a love so powerful it had led them to each other after a quarter-century. Perhaps the deep emotions he felt had embellished his narration, like the embroidery on the camel-colored sherwani he wore for the final act. When he was done, Munmun, who had watched his face keenly, almost without blinking while he spoke, rose silently from her perch on the stool, and put her hand on his shoulder.

"You are a fortunate man, Cyrus. Go, find your Star." Just as suddenly as she had come into their lives, she had vanished, the tinkling of her anklets receding into silence.

The night before, after Cyrus had narrated the happenings of the past week, he had reached for Tara's hand, pressing it to his chest, as if to reassure himself of her presence. They had left a table light on because they wanted to see each other's face while they talked in bed.

"The day you told me over the phone that you regretted marrying me, I spent three hours in meditation at the monastery off Dresden Drive. By the end of the evening, I understood who the elephant in the room was, even though you had denied she was the problem. I came home ready to talk about Munmun, convince you that I was never, for a single minute, vulnerable to her attention, that I'd do anything not to threaten our marriage. But you insisted on dealing with your issues alone, and I had to respect that, to give you space and time."

She sighed. "I let my ego think for me, not my heart."

She couldn't find any ill-feeling in her heart toward Munmun anymore. She hadn't walked in Munmun's pretty jeweled feet, never seen the emptiness in her beautiful kohl-lined eyes, never seen the yearning in her bosom.

Tara had journeyed deep enough within herself to let go of Munmun.

The Annette Saldanha Home for Children was a large traditional house with a red clay-tiled roof, a spacious portico, and an enormous front yard. It was a larger version of the Shanti Nilaya of Tara's childhood. The children were playing cricket and volleyball in the yard when Tara arrived with Cyrus. The ones who were watching the matches on the sidelines ran toward their chauffeur-driven Cadillac, encircling it, faces smiling. "Good morning," they greeted. The older ones offered to carry the canvas bags filled with goodies—individual waxed paper packets of golden laddoos, translucent *jilebis*, roasted cashews, and crispy savory *chaklis* that Tara had ordered from Zeenat.

Two young women in crisp cotton saris and bright smiles came out to greet the visitors. Cyrus introduced Tara to Jessie and Kala, the wardens of the home, who wrapped their arms around her, smiling broadly. They entered the office; a small square room attached to the verandah with a table and four chairs. On the table were stacked glossy brochures with an appeal in bold blue letters, above various group photos of the children: SPONSOR A CHILD

FOR ONLY RS. 6000 ($150) A YEAR. They were the same flyers that Tara and Cyrus had distributed from their booth at the Festival of India last August. That was when she had made it a habit to push herself beyond her comfort zone.

For a moment, the purpose of her visit sat heavy on her chest. Amma could be a Pied Piper wherever she went. Tara had not inherited that ability; children did not flock to her. She had never truly missed being a mother.

Kala appeared with four stainless steel tumblers filled with lime sherbet, and before long, they were headed to the large, bright yellow-painted central hall, where the children had gathered to meet the visitors. Cyrus introduced her to the children as their mother. They welcomed her with applause. She raised an unsteady hand to wave back at them, aware of sweat pooling into the thin fabric of her kurta under her arm. The kids quickly diverted their attention and thronged around Cyrus, telling him stories and riddles and jokes. He was without doubt their father; that bond had lit up his eyes like Diwali *diyas*, as it had theirs. With her, they maintained a polite distance.

From Cyrus, she heard the stories behind the faces. Son of a prostitute who had committed suicide; a daughter who had lost both parents to AIDS; another who was deserted for being female and brought to the home five years later by her grandmother; a son and a daughter who didn't know whom to go to when their abusive, alcoholic father turned them out of the house after he remarried. Each story uniquely tragic, yet each tragedy veiled in smiles, she thought.

The youngest among the children was four-year-old Mira, whose mother had jumped into a dry well after her father died in a road accident. Tara knew she hadn't been at the home very long. Mira sat on the floor nearby, enormous eyes on a waif-thin body following Cyrus around the room like Tara had once followed Uncle Anand. When Tara stooped down to pat her cheek, she simply said, "Amma?" It was a question, dark eyes searching Tara's face.

How did one comfort a four-year-old whose mother was never going to come back? She ought to have known, from her own experience. But Amma and Daddy had come back to claim Tara, to raise her, to love her. She didn't have to deal with the finality of death; of never seeing a parent's face, never hearing their voice, never taking their love for granted. That was the absolute reality imprinted on every face at the home. A lifelong feeling, entrenched in her gut, morphed into a question as it twisted its way up—had she taken her parents' love for granted, been needlessly merciless toward Amma and cold toward Daddy for most of her life?

When Mira tugged at her kurta, an idea came to Tara's mind. The project would take all day. It would involve going back to Shanti Nilaya, picking up Pinky from her bedroom, peeling off her clothes, washing her thoroughly with shampoo, untangling and brushing her hair until its shine was restored. It would involve going to Hampanakatta to look for fabric and a hand sewing kit to stitch a new dress quickly.

That evening, she wrapped a fully restored Pinky in shining fuchsia gift wrap paper. She and Cyrus watched fascinated, Tara on her knees, as Mira tore open the gift wrap impatiently in the portico. The evening light caught the astonishment in her enormous eyes when they fell on Pinky, whose arms and face were raised to the sky. A smile spread across her thin face as she ran her fingers over Pinky's violet open eyes, as she gently felt the velvet purple fabric. The rest of the children who had gathered around Mira broke out in cheers.

Tara couldn't help but claim Mira's smile for herself; as if she had been finally compensated for the joy that had been taken away from her thirty-two years ago. She stayed on her knees until they felt sore; until after Mira had run in with her prized possession; until, she realized with a start, that the water droplets that were creating wet patches on the cement were her own tears. They were as real as the love she felt in her heart— for Mira, for all her children, for Cyrus, for her family, for the universe, for herself.

Chapter 32

A mma and Daddy met their new son-in-law in their marble-floored sitting room. People surrounded them, like extras in a Bollywood wedding scene, present but barely in the background, curiously looking from a distance, as if at celebrities. Or circus tigers. Most walked deeper into the house, or outside to lounge under the shade of the giant shamiana. Only Vijay, who would have been an active part of the scene, was out at the caterer's with a last-minute alteration in the wedding lunch menu.

It helped that Cyrus bowed down to touch their feet—first Amma's, then Daddy's; that they first connected with their son-in-law physically, a gentle hand over his bent head as blessing, a positive exchange of energy.

She noticed her parents' rigid body language at first. Daddy overtly polite, asking about Obama's prospects in the upcoming elections; Amma focusing entirely on bringing out snacks and tea, piling Cyrus's plate with *vada* chutney, fried cashews, and plantain chips. But they warmed up quickly to Cyrus's easy manner, his ready smile. Before long, Cyrus had promised Amma a one-on-one meditation and cleansing session, a solution for her insomnia, and convinced Daddy of the benefits of *surya namaskar*, sun salutations. He had wrangled a promise from them that they would visit Atlanta during Christmas.

Daddy had questions about running a charity, an NGO as he called it, and expressed his desire to one day convert Shanti Nilaya into a shelter for the homeless mentally ill. He would call the home Anand Prakash, a place where *anand*—joy—and *prakash*—light—would converge to bring dignity to those on the fringes of sanity and of society. Cyrus said their foundation would be happy to partner in this wonderful initiative, help get it off the ground, raise funds in America. Tara had never heard Daddy express this desire before. His altruism thus far had been limited to Rotary Club meetings. It surprised her, this shift, the forming of new perspectives, new attitudes toward life.

"Let's do it, Daddy," she said, eyes shining. "It would be a wonderful way to honor Uncle Anand's life."

Cyrus was presented with an invitation to their niece's wedding, a glossy white card with gold lettering, a symbol of Lord Ganesha embossed on the top. "You must come," Amma said. "Vijay can take you shopping for a sherwani when he returns." She apologized for the absence of the bride and her parents. They were out at the venue, supervising the decoration, but of course, the invitation had come from them.

She saw the pride on Daddy's face as he brought out a copy of the *Morning Herald* from his study, reading glasses perched on his nose, the sheets folded neatly so that Tara's opinion piece was on the front. "Have you read it yet?" he asked over his glasses, gaze moving from her to Cyrus. "A women's college in Udupi has nominated Tara for their annual 'Young Changemaker Award'. You must stay back two more weeks to receive it."

Cyrus eagerly took the copy from Daddy's hands. His father had changed his subscription from the *Morning Herald* to the *Times of India*, so they hadn't been able to lay their hands on a copy, he said.

Tara overcame her sudden embarrassment, the urge to tear the sheets away from Cyrus's hands, to ask him to read the essay later when they were by themselves. After all, it was the power of her words that had changed her universe, even the universe inside her.

They read the essay together, the broadsheet spread across their laps, her parents watching them from the across the room, as if they alone mattered in a house full of wedding guests.

My first act of self-determination at the age of thirty-six made me a pariah. My crime? I walked out of an abusive, loveless marriage. Up until that point, I was only fodder for gossip. First, because I was not good enough, pretty enough, smart enough, outgoing enough to win a husband in an arranged marriage. Next, because the man who married me abandoned me for three years. No reasons were asked of him. It was my fault. I hadn't tried hard enough to be worthy of him.

Ours is a culture where a man's word is The Word. So when my ex had a change of heart and sent for me, my family only felt relief. I was packed off to the US, no questions asked. I felt relief too, to escape the torment that our society reserves for an abandoned wife.

When I landed in America, the land of dreams, I already felt like a zero, my sense of self-worth crushed by my own people. It got worse. I was ignored, neglected, denied a wife's place, and yet, the onus was on me to try harder, to make the marriage work. My ex told me the marriage was a mistake. I begged him not to send me back. If I had returned, they would have branded me an even bigger failure.

It escalated to emotional and physical violence. He was still not answerable to anyone. When he threw me out, I summoned the courage to move on. But my ex had a change of heart and was ready to accept me back. I was told I had no choice but to go back. Good wives make peace with their circumstances; they don't fight their destiny; they don't put their own happiness before their family's reputation, I was told.

Forcing people to get back together does not magically breed love. My ex and I both knew that. There was nothing to bind us together: not love, not affection, not shared interests, not shared dreams.

Initially, there were three of us in our marriage, and I was the irrelevant part. A year into our life together, my ex told me of his great love for his Helen of Troy, with whom he carried on, while I simply existed, invisible, like dust under the carpet. It hurt, because I was not dust under the carpet. Dust is inanimate; it does not have a heart that can bleed for trying and failing.

Then something magical happened to me. One day, five years into a meaningless, miserable marriage, I realized that I deserve better. When I walked out into the unknown, strangely, I wasn't dying. My spirit was only then finding rebirth. My life in the months that followed was filled with the love and kindness of friends, which was driven by my own courage. I was finally a person with dreams, desires, and many reasons to live. I had finally taken control of my life. Sadly, this basic right is denied to many of us.

To the modern-day keepers of our traditions, I ask: Why is it always the woman who is instructed to try harder to win over her husband, to adjust, to stay silent, to make peace with the injustices she faces? When things go wrong, why can't she turn to her family? If she finally decides to stand up for herself, why does her family not stand with her? Why is the victim victimized even further? Why are no questions asked of the perpetrator?

I eventually got remarried to my soulmate. If this were a Bollywood movie, that would be the expected happy climax, love triumphing over social dictates, over the baddies, the audience applauding. But Bollywood is make-believe. In real life, a woman who steps out of line blackens her family honor. She is branded an outcast. There is thrill in dragging a woman's name through the muck by repeating her story to all and sundry. In my case, not only had I dared to remarry for love, but my soulmate was born into a different faith. That was enough scandal to last three generations of my family.

My ex, meanwhile, lives without stigma. I know I will be maligned for one more reason when this essay is published—airing dirty laundry in public. A man can do it with no fear of social censure, safe in the knowledge that even his wife's own family would disown her. I fear censure, for it is but a form of rejection. I have feared rejection all my life. And yet, I had to tell my version of my story, for this is not my story alone. It is the story of countless other women like me.

A feature I did for the Morning Herald with a senior colleague in the late nineties comes to my mind. It was a heartbreaking interview with Kamala, whose alcoholic husband had set her on fire in a drunken rage. Kamala had refused to implicate her husband up until her death a week later. Afraid of retribution from her husband and his family in case she survived the burns, Kamala claimed the fire was an accident. The story quickly made national headlines. Public sympathy for Kamala grew into a massive wave, pushing the police into action. The husband was labeled a monster. The law quickly caught up with him, and as far as I know, he is still serving out his life sentence.

Not all monsters are egregious. Some stay hidden in plain sight. They wear a "normal" mask. They don't set you on fire. They crush your spirit slowly, until you die every day, from loneliness, purposelessness, worthlessness, hopelessness. The monster is not the perpetrator alone. The ones who breed him, the ones who victimize the victim—the relatives and neighbors and town people who judge unfairly—they are monsters too.

The monster is the anachronistic mindset that needs to change.

I was expected to exist for society. I chose to live. To love. I take heart in the knowledge that the monsters around me do not sully me, because the names they have for me are not the names I give myself.

Acknowledgments

It took ten long years, several drafts, and countless rejection letters from literary agents before *Purple Lotus* saw the light of day. The manuscript would have continued to languish in the slush pile of agents had my incredible publishers at She Writes Press not seen value in it.

Winning the She Writes Press and SparkPress Toward Equality in Publishing contest was one of the most important and joyful moments of my life. Thank you, Brooke Warner and Lauren Wise, for believing in this immigrant woman's story, and for championing diversity in publishing.

To the extraordinarily talented Brigid Pearson: thank you for the stunning cover that stands out on the shelves and screen. Big thanks also to my copy editor, Jennifer Caven, for your keen attention to detail.

To Crystal Patriarche and Keely Platte of BookSparks: I offer my heartfelt gratitude for all your creative publicity efforts.

I am indebted to my developmental editor, Tiffany Yates Martin, who saw potential for a resonant work of art when it was rough marble, and whose invaluable feedback helped me sculpt this novel into shape.

Dr. Ruby Lal, author and Professor of South Asian Studies at Emory University—your valuable feedback is deeply appreciated.

To my friends Navami Naik, Daryl Wilcher, Jyothsna Hegde, Denise Huddlestun, Atika Nadaf, Girija Vaidya, Reena Raghu, Vidya Waikar, Paromita Sengupta, Priti Bandi, Nirjari Dalal, Andi Plotsky, Trudie Oshman, Ramya Govindrajan, Bojana Ginn, Melanie Hollis Villard and Patti Tripathi—I love you all for being so supportive of my writing dreams. Monsoon Vaz, our brave warrior, your enthusiasm for *Purple Lotus*, and for life, will always remain close to my heart.

To Ram, who offered new insights, and stood behind this project: thank you, 333 times over.

My rock stars, Frances West and Nancy Haden—I am forever indebted to you for being the Ruth and Dottie of my life. Ma, you are missed every day.

Thank you, Amma, for your steadfast prayers for the book to be published. Brother Rajesh, sister Reena, sister-in-law Rachana, and brother-in-law Rahul—thank you for dreaming my dream with me.

And finally, to my son Aditya, who never let me give up on my dream of being a published author: thank you, my love, for being my motivator, counselor, critic, copy editor, proofreader and biggest cheerleader. High five! We did it!

About the Author

Veena Rao was born and raised in India but calls Atlanta home. A journalist by profession, she is the founding editor and publisher of *NRI Pulse*, a popular Indian-American newspaper. Although her day job involves news reports, interviews, and meeting press deadlines, she devotes her spare time to creative writing and long walks in the woods. *Purple Lotus*, her debut novel, is the winner of the She Writes Press and SparkPress Toward Equality in Publishing (STEP) contest.

Author photo © Sumi's Photography

SELECTED TITLES FROM SHE WRITES PRESS

She Writes Press is an independent publishing company founded to serve women writers everywhere. Visit us at www.shewritespress.com.

Again and Again by Ellen Bravo. $16.95, 978-1-63152-939-9. When the man who raped her roommate in college becomes a Senate candidate, women's rights leader Deborah Borenstein must make a choice—one that could determine control of the Senate, the course of a friendship, and the fate of a marriage.

Faint Promise of Rain by Anjali Mitter Duva. $16.95, 978-1-93831-497-1. Adhira, a young girl born to a family of Hindu temple dancers, is raised to be dutiful—but ultimately, as the world around her changes, it is her own bold choice that will determine the fate of her family and of their tradition.

Cleans Up Nicely by Linda Dahl. $16.95, 978-1-938314-38-4. The story of one gifted young woman's path from self-destruction to self-knowledge, set in mid-1970s Manhattan.

Appetite by Sheila Grinell. $16.95, 978-1-63152-022-8. When twenty-five-year-old Jenn Adler brings home a guru fiancé from Bangalore, her parents must come to grips with the impending marriage—and its effect on their own relationship.

Trespassers by Andrea Miles. $16.95, 978-1-63152-903-0. Sexual abuse survivor Melanie must make a choice: choose forgiveness and begin to heal from her emotional wounds, or exact revenge for the crimes committed against her—even if it destroys her family.

In a Silent Way by Mary Jo Hetzel. $16.95, 978-1-63152-135-5. When Jeanna Kendall—a young white teacher at a progressive urban school—becomes involved with a community activist group, she finds herself grappling with issues of racism, sexism, and oppression of various shades in both her professional and personal life.